LORD BENNETT, OF ASHWOOD HALL

The Caretaker

M.A. Grant

XXI

"Wake up! Wake up!" the apparition cried, and suddenly, his body had weight again. "Sir, please wake up!"

When he did finally open his eyes, he found that the lights were far too loud… how was that even possible? The sun coming in through the window was a brutal assault on all of his senses.

His vision cleared, and he did not find himself anywhere he recognised.

The stark white walls he was surrounded by did remind him of the Webbs' house, and for the smallest moment, he was overcome with rapture— that is, until he realised the ceiling was too low, and the windows were completely different. Upon closer inspection, there were more blemishes and cracks in the paint, as well. The furnishings were that of bare pine, and the curtains were plain blue. The bed he was in was narrow; his feet and shoulders nearly spilled over the sides, and he sank far into it. It was all alien to him.

Likewise, he had no recollection of the two figures looming over him.

The closer and taller of the pair was a brightly smiling young woman with coffee-brown curls tucked into a cap, and a dress that matched her tresses. Beside her was a man with closely cropped mousy hair, a neat moustache, and plain grey dress. His eyes were strikingly pale blue, almost white.

"Ah, thank the heavens!" cried the voice that shook him from his blissful slumber, belonging to the woman. "We was so afraid you'd never wake up! Thought you were frozen dead!"

"How do you feel? You've been lying there almost fourteen hours. Took a long time to thaw you out," the man reached out a hand and grasped Michael's fingers. The contact smarted.

He was too disoriented to be afraid of these two strangers that detained him, and had much ado just to draw in a breath to form his answer. The effort of doing so sent pain shooting through his left flank. Something was broken.

"I don't feel much," Michael answered, and that was true aside from his aching side, his hot head pounding with each beat of his heart, and his stomach, hands, feet, and throat smouldering.

The man knit his brow.

"Well, can you move?"

He folded his hands over his breast. The pressure burned as though he'd touched a hot stove.

"I can move indeed."

"That's wonderful, truly!" the woman clasped her own hands at her bosom. "Sir, do you have a name we could call you?"

"I am Michael Bennett," there was no need to attach his title to his name, and he had no reservations about giving it to them. It was of no significance, and if the magistrate's friends decided to pursue him and abandon the Webbs, that was all well. They could even kill him if they wanted to.

"Michael Bennett," she repeated, and the pair exchanged a curious glance before she turned to him and spoke again. "My name is Ruth Evans, and this fellow here is my brother, Peter."

"Nice to make your acquaintance, Mr. Bennett!" Peter thrust out his hand again, and Michael took great pains to grab ahold of it. "We found you out on the street last night, half froze to death and mumbling such strange things! You had a big, heavy trunk with you, I remember— don't worry, it is at the foot of the bed, we didn't touch anything in it. Look through it whenever you please."

Ruth and Peter were very kind to bring him into what he assumed to be their home: too kind. They likely saw his fine clothes and expected to solicit some reward for saving him. Well, if he could find his chequebook, he would gladly do so, but first he wanted to test their intentions for curiosity's sake.

"Ah, I'm afraid I've not one penny on my person," Michael said, and it was no lie. He'd emptied his pockets at the tavern the night before.

"No? It does not signify!" Ruth shook her head, and her hanging locks flew about her face. "You are welcome to stay here until you are back on your feet, good sir."

Michael did not detect any change in her disposition that suggested disappointment or contempt. As far as he could tell, they were genuine.

"Well, I am sure I shall not trouble you for very long," he struggled and strained to pull himself upright in bed, coughing violently as he did so. "I am indebted to you both for saving my life."

But a part of him sorely resented them for rescuing him. He wanted to cease all strife and succumb to death peacefully. It was an unnatural and perverted feeling, but it had attached itself to him fervently.

"You must be famished. Please eat a little," said Ruth, presenting him with a cake of crumbling rice bread.

Unable to restrain himself beyond a dignified gesture of thanks, he devoured it in two bites, nearly choking himself, as his mouth was parched and raw. He was given cool water, and he drank. It was bitter.

He looked himself over, and saw that he was still in the clothes he had on while vomiting and wallowing in the street. He was somewhat grateful that his senses were dulled.

"Terribly sorry we left you in your soiled clothes, sir," Mr. Evans explained. "We wanted you to know for sure that we left all of your belongings just the way they are, and we wanted to preserve your modesty. We'll gladly step out so that you can clean yourself up."

They passed out of the room and left him a basin of lukewarm water to clean his face, but they left just a sliver of the door open. The effort of sitting up nearly brought him to his knees.

Michael gently sponged at his hands and face, finding them still quite raw from the cold. Touching them reminded him of the sting of Alma's menthol cream that she insisted upon… he could smell it…

He dashed the damp rag onto the floor, as if to toss the thought away with it. After a laborious coughing fit, he dressed himself quietly and listened to what they whispered about him. He took off his boots as softly as possible, checking that all of his toes were present and accounted for, and put them back on, all the while listening intently.

"He is liable to be a madman, to be so thoroughly packed and well-dressed, but drifting through the street," said Peter.

"Maybe so, but he does not seem to be dangerous! And it's lucky too, considering his size. I think he was right flustered out of his head when we found him. He probably gambled away all of his money and went to drink himself to death over it!" his sister answered.

"The name 'Bennett' is familiar. I think they are an old family that had a degree of influence at some time before they just about faded into oblivion. They say the house has been boarded up, and the one scion became a penniless wanderer, dropped off the face of the earth."

His ears burned to hear them speak his family name in that way. There was some truth in their speculations.

"I wonder if we could contact anybody about him. Surely we should ask. How does a man that big just disappear?"

"It is possible he does not want to be found. That is his business. Either way, we should take care of him for a little while, at least until he has his strength back."

"Aye, we should! You know, aside from his strange nose, he has a pleasing face. I think once he is cleaned up, he may be quite a handsome fellow."

His ears burned with even more intensity at this praise, though it meant nothing to him.

"You are naturally drawn to strange, damaged men. That is all," her brother said in a dismissive tone. "With that in mind, I will examine him myself."

Peter slipped into the room just as Michael had finished fastening his boots and laid his tattered jacket out on the foot of his bed.

"Ah, do you feel well, Mr. Bennett?" he asked.

"Well enough to sit up," Michael coughed again, and now he was concerned.

"You've caught yourself a nice cold, I see. I wonder, though, if there is anybody you would like us to contact? Is there anybody who would claim you?"

"Nobody, sir."

Again, Abraham would have taken him, but Michael wanted to minimise the people he was a burden to. As it was, he planned to leave the Evans siblings the moment he had the strength to walk out the door. And after that… he did not know.

"Nobody? How strange, as you are so young and dressed so well," Peter commented with a distressed expression, but there was a hint of satisfaction in his tone, as if his speculations were confirmed, and this delighted him.

Dressed so well… where was his big cloak? He looked around, and did not find it.

"Mr. Evans, did you put my coat anywhere?"

"You did not have a coat when we found you."

10

If they didn't take any of his other things, they likely didn't take his grandfather's cloak, but someone clearly did. He was running out of coats.

"Well, Mr. Bennett," Evans continued. "You seem to have taken ill, and you favour leaning on your right side. I advise you to stay put for now, and I'll get you a doctor if you'd like."

"Get me nothing of the sort, but fetch my cheque book, if you please. You will find it in my trunk. Here is the key."

Mr. Evans did as he was asked, and Michael slowly and carefully scribbled and tore off a note for twenty-five pounds.

"For your trouble, Peter Evans," he presented it to the bewildered fellow.

"My, Mr. Bennett, do you really have all this to spare?" he peered at it, and tapped his fingers on the paper, as if to make sure it was real. "If you won't be needing this, I thank you, and I will make good use of it!"

"It is no trouble, and I feel it is the least I could do. My banker is Alvin Howard. Write to him, and all should run smoothly," said Michael, very pleased that somebody had accepted the money without a fuss for once.

"Well," Evans eagerly slipped the paper into his pocket. "Please rest, Mr. Bennett. Dinner will be ready soon, if you can eat."

Michael did try to eat, and allowed himself to be questioned by Ruth; she brought him food, after all. He gave his answers between coughing fits and choking down bits of rice and stewed fish. She offered him coffee, and he accepted, though not to drink it, but to hold it under his nose. The steam soothed his throat and reminded him of more pleasant times.

"Where did you live before you came here, Michael? What did you do?"

He found it strange that she addressed him so informally after having just met him, but he was a guest, so he allowed it.

"I have taken various odds and ends jobs out in the country," said he. Feeling very cautious even towards this kind young lady, he did not want to disclose the location of the Webbs.

"And did you have many friends? I'm sorry if that's too much."

"I did have a few, more dear to me than the blood in my body. A tragedy has torn me from them, and I am sure I can not return any time soon. It is my own fault."

Ruth grimaced, as if she ached for him, and scraped more stew onto his plate, even though he had only gotten through half of what he was already given.

"You must have had such a hard time coming here," she decided. "But you will be taken care of. Peter can perhaps direct you towards good work here, and you can reestablish yourself."

"Perhaps he can. Could I also ask you a question, then, Miss?"

"Absolutely, you can!"

"Why did you take a big drunken heap such as myself into your home, not knowing who or what I was?"

"Well, what else were we to do?" Ruth cried. "It'd have been too cruel to leave you out on the street to waste away, do you not think? And you happened to be so close! 'Tis a good thing that Peter saw you just as he come down to lock up the store. He needed help carrying you up the stairs because you's so heavy! It must have been fate!"

"Suppose my fate that you thwarted was to wither away in that spot, and suppose I deserved it… "

She then leaned forward into the lamp light, and he saw that her eyes were the same rich brown as her hair and clothes, and they were heavy-lidded and gentle, set deep into her round face. She looked so much like his mother.

"Sir, you needn't say such things," said she. "It is not up to man to decide who is deserving of life, certainly not up to me. All are equal in the eyes of God, and it would be a sin to leave one of His wonderful creatures to perish so horribly, and not even offer a hand or a prayer!"

So that was her answer, and by her earnest expression, she believed it herself. She was naive, but she meant well.

Ruth took away his dishes and retreated to the threshold.

"Well, get some rest, Mr. Bennett, sir. If you don't want your coffee, I'll take it."

He let her have the cup, and she departed.

Now he knew why they tried to avoid closing
the door. It sounded as if she had to pull with all
of her weight to force it shut.

There was no reason to distrust them now,
considering they had every chance to kill him
and take all of his possessions while he was
unconscious, and showed no hostility or unrest.
If anything, *he* was suspect.

He immediately tried to stand and explore. The
room was small enough that he could hold
himself up with his right arm and skirt the walls
to navigate it. It smelled musty and damp. From
the looks of it, boxes, crates, and cans had been
hastily cast off into one corner. In the opposite
corner was his cot and two very small windows,
and a dusting of cobwebs. The little table that
his wash basin rested on was crowded with
assorted papers and old-fashioned lamps. This
was likely a storage room, but Michael was
grateful that they'd found a place for him.

He looked over his belongings, and determined
that they were indeed undisturbed, so he couldn't
have been laid out on the streets for more than
an hour. Most importantly, his pistol was still in
its case, and all of the bullets remained.
Whatever soul had grabbed only the coat off of
his back obviously needed it more than he did.
The most likely explanation was that they fled
the scene when Mr. Evans approached.

Stooping over the trunk inflamed his tender left side. Michael lay himself down on the thin cot and covered himself with the wool blanket that he was fairly sure was actually a curtain, but he did not rest. He could not fight these bitter, resentful feelings towards these kind people, though he knew it was wrong of him. Yes, he was grateful, but he did not want to be. Knowing he was possibly the last of the Bennett house, he knew it was his duty to persevere, as now that was all he could do for his family name. He could only passively accept death when it came to him, and they had robbed him of that opportunity.

A new opportunity may have arisen faster than anticipated. Very soon, that very night, his cough had worsened so that every breath was a struggle, and he could not lie flat on his back without feeling he was being drowned from within. He could not eat, as anything solid was too much of an effort to swallow, and there was an awful sensation of great pressure on his chest at all times.

Every cough sent needles stabbing into his side. Many times, he spit up something foul. The cold had indeed gotten to him, and it could take him if it pleased.

At least, that was how he thought until it really came for him. He'd never really taken a serious illness before, and did not know what to expect.

Even lying down, he was not at rest. His heart had never beat so fast in his whole life, and never had he panted so desperately and still he could get no air. As the sickness seemed to descend deeper and deeper into his chest, breathing became more of a chore.

In those days, he couldn't quite sleep. He only lapsed into a half-conscious trance and grew so hot that he soaked his clothes, but he could not stop shivering. The passage of time was nothing to him. It could have been days, months, or years. Sometimes he vomited, but as no meat had touched his lips in so long, he only heaved pitiful handfuls of liquid that burned his mouth.

He didn't bring anything he could use to pass the time, nor could he summon the willpower even if he had, so all he could do was lie there and listen to the world go by around him— without him. As it was a shared building, he occasionally heard people's footsteps and muddy splashes of conversation through the walls. Sometimes, he tried to get up, but the throbbing in his side pulled him back down.

When he found himself dreaming, it was of Alma's hands, pleasantly cool on his face as she smoothed his hair, and her soft humming throughout the room. He tried to call out for her, but there came no discernable answer. Was it true that if you saw somebody in your dream, they were thinking of you? What did she think of him now? What was she doing? And what of Dr. Webb? Did he consider Michael a coward and a traitor? Did he assume that he was already dead in a ditch? Did they mourn him?

It was only Alma who visited him in his dreams. Sometimes, she sang and cut flowers, and once in a while she smothered him with a pillow or attempted to drown him. He never tried to fight her when she attacked, fearing that she would vanish. When he saw her, he felt he did not want to die, not without apologising to her. He was so cold to her when he left, and he could not leave this world after being so cruel. His actions no longer felt just and unwavering, or even like a necessary evil. As the veil between life and death grew thin, he saw himself for what he really was.

Maybe he should have never courted her at all… he should have left her be, and taken longing and uncertainty over wounding her. He never should have stoked that fire.

Undoubtedly, she could find herself a far better man, now, in any case.

He fought unconsciousness, even though his dreams were his only escape. Now, he saw them as the silken snare of a spiderweb. He tried to fight the bouts of coughing when they came, but fighting made them worse, and wracked his body with aching spasms.

Ruth and Peter Evans continuously fretted over him, though they sometimes appeared distorted and far away. He was alerted to their presence when the door could be heard grinding open and shut. His ears roared at the sound as if somebody had fired a gun over his head. They gave him spoonfuls of water or broth, and sponged away what ghastly muck he regurgitated. He grappled feebly with whatever figure hung over him and loosened his shirt collar, believing in that moment that he was being throttled. They begged him to consent to have a doctor see him, for his temperature was frightfully high, but he stubbornly refused, as he was afraid he would simply be told he had only hours to live, and ignorance was bliss… right?

He coughed into the handkerchief offered to him, and found it spotted with blood. Terror seized him, and he desperately clawed and pulled himself upright, as if lying back down would have been certain death. He did not try to bargain or plead. He was not lucid enough for that.

"Ah, sir, please be still! Don't strain yourself!" Peter grabbed him and tried to force him back down without touching his left side. Michael made a pitiful effort to wrestle with him.

"I don't want to die," he wheezed between coughs that made him feel his ribs might shatter. "I can't die. I tell you, I cannot!"

"Sir, be calm! Whatever happens next is in the hands of God! Give it to God!"

The last of his strength had left him, and he slumped back into the bedding whether he wanted to or not. Give it to God? What did that mean? He scarcely had the energy to ponder it.

Well, if he could do nothing himself, he figured he may as well resolve to be peaceful.

Do what you will, then, God, he decided. *Take me or leave me, but make up your mind.*

Alma said she would pray for him continuously. Was she doing that now? Could he trust in her prayers, and He who answered them? Was he about to get what he deserved? It was out of his hands, now, and since there was nothing he could do, he had no fear. He'd spent the last of his strength, and had no more to spare on being afraid. The pain subsided and his vision faded as

Peter Evans moved his hair away from his face
and wiped his feverish brow.

He dreamed of beating Albert Gillman as he did
on that night many weeks ago. He stopped, and
turned to look for Ida when he could not hear
her cries. When he turned back, he was holding
Alma's bloodied and battered body instead, and
he tried to scream, but he could only gurgle and
silently cough up blood. He fell upon her and
retched from the effort of trying to take just one
full breath.

"You should not have done it, Michael," Alma
murmured, turning her head towards him with a
grin spreading to her ears, displaying a mouthful
of way too many broken, bleeding teeth.

When he regained his senses, he was in the
Evans's spare room, with his face buried in the
pillow, and his flank aching still. He dislodged
himself and drew in a miraculously easy breath.
It still crackled and hissed, and he gave a dry
whistling cough at the end of it, but he had not
breathed so easily in what felt like an eternity.
Finally, he had triumphed.

Or God had spared him.

"So you've not died after all!" Peter Evans
watched him from a small armchair at the table.

How long had he been there? "You must allow us to fetch you a doctor, Mr. Bennett."

"No doctor," he insisted. "I feel better."

"Well, if you're so sure… I thought you'd really perish that time! I'd been here since dawn, waiting for you to stop breathing. You were so hot, we felt it standing at your bedside, and you slept still as stone for just about sixteen hours! I suppose you needed it, then. If you feel better, will you be inclined to eat soon? You've not had a real repast in five days, and we're quite worried you may waste away."

His clothes certainly did feel looser…

"I'll make an attempt," Michael said, as the faintest impression of an appetite was returning at the mention of food. "I will say again, that I am indebted to you and your sister."

"Nonsense, sir— we have means enough to accommodate you until you are well, especially owing to your generous gift. Think of it in this way, if you will: rest as much as you absolutely need to, and you will be ready to leave sooner rather than later."

He smiled. "You have a point, Mr. Evans. In that case, I would request a little water to wash myself. I'm afraid I'm quite filthy, nearly stuck to the linens and my clothes."

"How repulsive. I'll get you some warm water, and a little soap as well, and then I shall get back to minding the store."

Michael peeled off his old shirt and put on a clean one. While buttoning up, he found that he was still bruised and very tender. He tried to knead that sore spot and find out what was damaged, and immediately regretted it.

He had been mostly confined to that tiny chamber for days, and had little perception of the world around him aside from a view of the street out one little window (it seemed the pair lived above a shop that they ran together). Now that he could stand without feeling he was being crushed by his own weight, he cautioned venturing outside the spare room, lured out by the smell of frying fish.

The door gave a dry rasp when he pulled, and he had to brace himself against the frame to open it. A grey cat fled to a dark corner as he peered out. Miss Ruth was bent over a tiny stove, in a kitchen so narrow that nobody could have passed by Michael without pressing near to the wall. The cramped space reminded him of sleeping in the Webbs' old storehouse. His hair touched the ceiling.

"Mr. Bennett!" she chirped so gaily at seeing him out and about. "If you're on your feet, you must be recovering well! We was so worried about you, yessir."

"You need not worry about me, Miss. I scarcely worry about myself as it is," he made a very careful and calculated attempt to manoeuvre around her to the other side of the room without brushing against her. "At the very least, my cough has subsided enough that I can finish my sentences."

"Ah, very good, very good, yes!" Ruth heaped the steaming hot fish onto a platter. "I hope you don't mind company, Mister. A good friend from church, Miss Emma White, will be coming to dinner."

"Well, I surely am in no place to object. This is your house, after all."

"We simply don't want you to be troubled, lest you not recover so well."

He walked to the corner where the cat shrank down and hid. Its golden candlelight eyes flickered as it watched him.

"That's Lambert!" Miss Ruth chirped. "He don't bite."

Michael warily reached a hand out. Lambert did bite.

Miss White arrived about ten minutes after Ruth was finished with dinner. Michael did not see much of her at first, only a long blue coat and a wisp of light hair under a veiled hat. He had sheepishly retreated back into the spare room with his plate so that his cough did not disturb anyone. As he had dreaded, though, Ruth and Peter beckoned him out to meet their guest, and he felt obligated.

He saw her start a bit when he ducked his head under the doorframe and brought his bulk into the room. She was a small lady with a neat, yet understated and unassuming look, and a sprinkle of freckles on her nose.

"Good afternoon, Miss White," he offered his hand.

"Ah, good afternoon, Mr. Bennett," she said without extending her arm even a little.

"Why, Emma! Have some manners, he don't bite!" Ruth prodded her friend towards him, though Michael had learned that Ruth's warnings should not have been taken at face value.

"It is alright, Miss, I know I don't look particularly welcoming in this state. 'Tis a pleasure to meet you," Michael brought his hand to his side.

Michael joined them for tea and dessert. The remaining chair was beside Miss White, so he chose to stand, knowing she would be inclined to draw her chair away, or he would have done so himself, which may have perhaps slighted her.

Or maybe he simply needed to stop thinking so much, since everyone in that room was taking up space.

The "dessert" was a slice of bread with a lot of butter and jam, but he was glad for it. Ruth and Emma carried most of the conversation, mostly about church attendance, dyeing napkins, and what Emma's brother was doing at his new occupation, and the two gentlemen listened passively.

Ruth left after dinner, escorting her friend, and then it was remarkably quiet. Peter stayed for a while, and asked an unexpected question:

"You like my sister, Mr. Bennett?"

"Do I like her? Sure I do, she's perfectly well."

"I see you looking at her," and now Peter was looking at him, with a scrutinising eye.

"It would be rude not to, wouldn't it?"

"Hah! You beat around the bush. I think you know what I am suggesting."

Suddenly, he felt as if his fever was coming back. It's true that he often stole glances at her, sometimes without even realising it. She was very beautiful, and he was a man, after all, but that was all: she was beautiful. When he realised he was looking, he lowered his head and did not linger. Even if he wanted to court her, he wouldn't know where to begin. She was a sweet lady that he thought he could consider a friend, but he didn't find much in common with her, and he did not feel drawn to any of her traits in a stimulating way.

"She is pretty," he admitted, which was a little uncomfortable to say to her brother. "And she is a fine, virtuous lady, just as I'd consider you a virtuous gentleman, but that's where it ends."

"She will be twenty-three this spring, as will I. We are twins— she proceeds me by five hours. She was born at ten o'clock at night, and I arrived at three the next day."

"Twenty-three is a perfectly fine age, I suppose," Michael did not know how to respond.

Peter Evans nodded, with his eyes cast absently across the room.

"You think you'd ever get married?"

"I, um… I don't know. I've never pursued women very fervently," he partially lied.

Mr. Evans looked directly at him once again. Even in that brassy light, those eyes were as cool blue as the heart of a glacier, unlike his sister's warm brown, but Michael didn't find them any less welcoming. Their coolness was that of balm, or fresh ice cream.

The man finished his tea and stood up.

"Well, I'll be settling in for bed here soon. Goodnight, Mr. Bennett. Bother me if you need anything."

"Goodnight to you, sir."

He retreated, but Peter remained; he could feel his eyes on his neck.

Michael was now alone— finally. It was not that he didn't enjoy the company of these nice people, but he now had a clear head, and a moment of peace and stillness to gather his thoughts. He slammed his weight into the door to shut it behind him.

It had been just over a week since he'd left the Webbs, but it felt like a past life. He found himself always wondering how the household fared. Were they being harassed still? Were repairs being made? Would Alma be going to London as soon as she recovered from her injuries? Was it too soon to send letters? Too late? Was that even the right thing to do?

Ashwood Hall's desolate remains had burned their imprint into his vision. The image was bitter and poignant. He considered it an emblem of his past. His feelings were yet too raw and passionate to safely dwell upon without aching as if he would bleed inwardly again. He was not well enough to weep. These dormant emotions may have exacerbated his illness, and he imagined his ailment may subside as they passed through him.

Where was he going? What would he do next? He would make the answer for himself tomorrow. For now, getting up and walking around for a bit had depleted his energy reserves faster than anticipated, and he already needed to lie back down.

He dreamed of cats: fat and lazy cats walked on him in his bed, nosing at his face, and kneading his side where it was sore. They scattered when he tried to touch them. One stayed and laid itself heavily upon his neck, and then when he grabbed it, it was a massive python. The creature was endless. Every time he picked up a coil of scaled flesh and moved it, another took its place, and the head was nowhere to be seen. He tried to stand up and follow its length, but the weight of its body riveted him to his bed. It was no longer amusing. Now he just wanted to get up.

And get up, he did. He shot upright in bed, and a familiar throbbing ache in his side pulled him back down. Needless to say, there were no animals.

After his very first restful sleep since leaving the Webbs, he was finally able to climb out of bed without taking half an hour to prepare himself in advance. He'd missed that feeling. Nothing was more confining to him than not having his strength. It may not fully return for many months, if ever… it was all that he had.

Now that he could think clearly, Michael knew he had to face the truth that had been so intolerable before, yet would have saved him so much grief: it was time to start over. He was pretty sure he still had several thousand pounds stored away. That was a substantial nest egg to establish himself comfortably and find his own way.

That was the what, but now he needed to know the why and how. Why bother starting over? What precise reason did he have to continue?

He would go out and look for one.

He shaved, then put on clean clothes, and realised he did not fill them out the way he used to. His collar was very loose, and his trousers could not stay up on their own. Without a coat, he put on many shirts in order to brave the frigid wind.

For now, he left his belongings with the Evans. He had no reason not to trust them.

"Mr. Bennett!" Ruth called as he passed her in the kitchen, where she was sipping on coffee and heating a pot of soup. "Where are you going in such a hurry? You haven't had any breakfast and you still have a cough— you shouldn't be out in the cold with no coat! Your lips still have no colour!"

"Oh, my lips never had any colour," he waved away her words. "I'm no pretty, rosy thing like you. Anyway, I'm just going to consult somebody about… ah, property and assets. Don't wait for me, Miss."

That was the easiest way to explain what he was thinking. Thankfully, she did not question him further.

This was probably the longest stretch of time that he had ever been indoors, and he was beginning to feel suffocated. It seemed they lived in only four little rooms, including the spare chamber his cot was set up in. He descended the rickety cast iron stair outside and looked inside the store as he passed. It had a higher ceiling. Dry goods, sewing supplies, and cheap kitchenware were sold, along with jars of colourful sweets. It was a quaint, well-kept little storefront.

The sky was a deep and beautiful bluish purple. Hopefully, he was not setting out too early. Though it was probably not the best thing for him, the cold air was a pleasant balm on his throat.

First, he pawned one of his good knives to have enough pocket money to get around. Its loss would be worth it if he could just have some answers.

Strangely, he felt compelled to go to the old solicitor's office. Perhaps he could learn about what had been done to Ashwood Hall and gain some closure— if he would even have that information. There was only one way to find out.

It was a thirty minute trip, so the sun was out by then. As he'd stumbled in with no appointment made, the solicitor was already impatient with him before he'd even begun asking him any questions.

"Sir, you may not recognise me, but I am… *Lord* Michael Bennett. Nearly a year ago, I signed off Ashwood Hall and all of the property connected to it to some Americans, quite a rash decision on my part."

"Well, I'd say it's too late to change your mind, *Lord Bennett.*"

"Of course, of course. Though I went to have a look at the manor, and it had been desecrated and left to ruin. Do you know what they have done, or plan to do with it?"

"Sir, that is their business, and theirs only, as the property rightfully belongs to them— well, from what I've gathered, the remains of Ashwood will be torn down, and the land portioned off for industry. It need not concern you what is done with it, unless you are looking to buy a portion."

Buy? It was up for sale again?

"They are selling some of it? What is on the market?"

"I do know they are selling an old dower house tucked in the woods somewhere. I suppose they didn't think it was worth scrapping, so they're selling it for cheap."

"How cheap?"

"Roughly two thousand pounds, sir."

"How much? Repeat that, please."

"Two… thou-sand… pounds," the man recited the syllables in a dead monotone.

Michael thought his heart might burst, and his brain would boil. He couldn't believe what he was hearing. He began to feel faint again, so he sought the chair nearest to him and let himself drop into it— plunging the edge into his left flank as he landed, sending him into the throes of another convulsing coughing fit.

"Lord Bennett, are you alright?" the solicitor asked, not sounding concerned at all.

"Oh, I'm… I'm alright," he croaked, with his knees to his chin. "I'm recovering from an illness, and my lungs were not prepared for this shock."

The solicitor was not moved in the slightest. Not that Michael expected him to be.

The old dower house… he'd not been there since before he was in breeches, visiting Grandmother Berthe, and didn't even recall what it looked like, nor did he know what state of disrepair it was bound to be in. It had been mostly abandoned for years. He hadn't even considered it when he signed off the properties. It was not ideal, but at that point, it was far more than he could have hoped for.

Through his delirious rapture, though, he could not help but curse himself when he thought of the trouble he might have saved himself from if he'd planned ahead. Well, it was too late now.

"Sir, thank you for this information," he lunged over the solicitor's desk without thinking and grasped his hands, much to his dismay. "Could you tell me how I might contact them?"

"Only if you never touch me again!" he pulled his hands free and took up a pen. "I will write to them this afternoon and see if an arrangement can be made."

"Thank you!" Michael cried, shaking the air in front of him since he could not embrace the man. "Thank you for your service, I shall never forget this!"

"Nor shall I… no matter how hard I try."

Michael sprang out of the solicitor's office with a new vigour like no other, only to immediately double over in yet another bout of coughing. His body was just not ready. A letter was not a guarantee, but it was a lead.

He was not sure how he would explain this to the Evans siblings, as they probably wouldn't have understood any of what he was saying.

"Miss Ruth! Mr. Evans!" he knocked on the outside door at the top of the stairs.

Peter Evans came to the door.

"Mr. Bennett! I was wondering where you'd gone so early. I thought you surely would not have vanished forever without taking any of your belongings!"

"I'm afraid I can't explain right now, but it will not bring any harm or unwanted attention to you

or your sister, I guarantee it," it was refreshing to
be able to say that with absolute certainty.

"Oh? Well in that case, I shall take your word for
it, and respect your privacy," Peter moved to one
side so that Michael could enter. "Come in, then.
I say, you are still not well enough to be out in
the elements. It won't do to have you keel over
so soon after you'd gotten back on your feet."

The Misses Emma and Ruth were seated at the
kitchen table, with their heads bent towards each
other in quiet congress, and a solemn air about
them.

"Morning, ladies," he bowed his head as he
passed, then apologised profusely when he'd
accidentally stepped on a corner of Miss Emma's
dress.

"That is alright, sir. No damage has been done,"
she replied ever so softly, without turning her
head towards him.

So she was shy and seemingly rather lenient, if a
bit curt… just like his Alma… like Miss Alma
Webb. Was she equally as warm and passionate?

"And good morning, Mr. Evans," Miss White
held her hand out to Peter, who gave a very
slight, shuddering start at first, then sheepishly
shook her little fingers with a light rosy glow in

his countenance. He smiled and bowed his head, but did not speak.

That was certainly an interesting sight. She clearly had some preference for him, and he was timid around her.

"Well, it is good to see you in high spirits after you'd been so sick and miserable," he noted.

"It is good indeed, and I thank you once again," now that Michael felt well and able, he had to examine that door, and knelt to inspect the frame. The issue was glaringly apparent now that he actually had a look and saw half of the door intimately touching one side of the frame, and the other half near to the opposite side. The paint worn away at these stress points was also an eyesore. "My, this door is quite out of plumb. If you have the tools, it would be easy for me to fix. I've worked on barns before."

"We don't have you here for maintenance, Mr. Bennett," Mr. Evans replied, then cast a quick glance over his shoulder and added in a low voice: "though I doubt it would mean much to us soon, anyway."

"What do you mean by that?" Michael asked, and Peter discreetly took his arm to pull him into the next room.

He kicked the door shut, and Michael winced, knowing he was hearing the doorframe being ground into splinters, and the hinges being bent.

"We are leasing this place," Peter explained very quietly, standing to the far end of the room. "And though business had been going well enough until now, we are losing profits rapidly, as people gravitate towards larger stores with a bulk of factory goods. As it is, we may not have this building for much longer, even though we've been taking extra work here and there."

Another good thing was being lost to industrialisation. Michael acknowledged and appreciated the necessity of mass production, but he still scorned some of its side effects: the near destruction of smaller livelihoods, the abandonment of rural communities, and pungent, polluted air.

"That's terrible. Does Miss Ruth know about it?"

"She knows money is scarce, but I hold the contract, and I've not told her the extent of the situation."

"Do you not think she has the right to know?"

"I wouldn't like to trouble her with it. Women are not disposed to handling financial strain very well."

"The same cannot be said of all women. If my memory serves me well—which, mind you, it rarely does— it was my mother who kept the Bennetts out of complete financial ruin before her passing. My parents largely lived off of her dowry until my father gained the estate, and she managed it well."

And Alma was always so sedulous about saving and planning almost to a miserly extreme, he added inwardly.

"Hmm," was all Peter had to say to that. "Well, we have had to do without many luxuries to keep the business running, but aside from the lease and taxes, we benefit from being our own employers. Working at a larger establishment would pay better, but we'd be losing a measure of freedom, and would have to move from this street we've pretty well lived on all of our lives."

"And you have no relatives?"

"None but a few cousins in Yorkshire, quite a distance away."

Admittedly, Michael did not know what to do about that at all, and did not trust himself to offer any real advice. He did not wish the agony of abruptly uprooting oneself upon anybody, and he thought it was rather unfair for Peter to hide it from family.

But what he could do was give.

"Mr. Evans," Michael scribbled yet another cheque, for two hundred this time. "I don't know what you will do with this, but put it to good use."

Peter raised his hand, practically ready to snatch the paper, but he hesitated.

"Mr. Bennett, you've given us enough already."

"On the contrary, I don't feel this will ever cover my debt to you. I used to think my life was not worth a farthing, but what you and your sister have given me is invaluable: a second chance. My life has impetus and purpose once again, and I'd have never found it without your hospitality. I am more grateful to you than I can say," he thrust the cheque towards his preserver. "But maybe this will realise a fraction of my words."

Peter did not speak for a few seconds' pause, so Michael continued his impassioned speech.

"They say that money cannot buy happiness, and that the love of money is the root of all evil, but I do not believe it is wrong to seek security in it and appreciate its importance in the material world. Besides, I am sure you will be happy to have stability for a little longer. Take it, and do not be ashamed."

In a sense, Michael *was* buying happiness in that moment. He was expressing his gratitude with the only resource currently at his disposal, and the transaction made him feel so warm.

"Then I must ask… where did you even get all of this money to give freely, if you seem to be a drifter yourself?" Peter's hand still loomed over the cheque.

"Not by fraudulent or immoral means, I assure you. It is true that I am of Ashwood Hall—"

"Ah! You are gentry after all!" Peter interrupted.

"Yes, quite correct— or, I was once before— and it is shut up because I sold all that I owned of the estate to cancel my father's debts, and left it at the mercy of its new owners. I lived a comparatively meagre lifestyle and saved all that I had out of sheer stubbornness, with a foolish dream of buying it back in its entirety before I died. I've made some very idiotic decisions, to say the least— but I digress. Take the money, Mr. Evans. It would please me."

Finally, he closed his fingers over the note.

"Well, I thank you, Mr. Bennett. I'd say you've helped us much more than we've helped you. May God reward you for your kindness."

"I have my reward!" Michael insisted, and tugged Peter Evans into a cautious embrace, which he surprisingly accepted.

Michael did not know whether or not Peter had told Ruth the whole truth, but she must have heard quite a bit for her to crash into his chamber after dinner and throw herself upon him.

"Mr. Bennett!" she cried and clung to him like a snake winding up a tree trunk. "Thank you so much! Peter told me what you did! You are an angel, I say! We's so grateful! Thank you!"

She then began kissing all over his face. It drew a burning hot blush to his cheeks, and nearly took the breath out of his lungs.

"Ah, Miss Ruth! Miss Ruth!" he embraced her but pried her away from his face so that she could peck at him no more. "You are very welcome, I was happy to do it. And… you are truly very sweet and lovely, but I'm sorry, I do not fancy you in that way."

She froze, and all expression dropped from her features. He expected tears or anger, but instead, she released him and threw her head back in a bout of hearty laughter— she laughed until her whole face was red, and then he was confused.

"Oh, Mr. Bennett! Nor do I! Have you had no sisters to kiss you? I'm just so grateful for what you've done for us, I couldn't contain myself!"

"Oh… " Michael's face burned even more than it did initially, and now he felt like a dunce, and wanted to retreat into his shirt to hide himself as a turtle might have done.

"My mistake… I appreciate the gesture, but… do you really think of me as a brother, to kiss me like that?"

"Indeed I do!" Ruth chirped. "All men and women are my brothers and sisters, as we are all God's children!" she added before his ego could get too big.

Still, he could not deny that he enjoyed the caresses. Even if the sentiment was not specially for him, it tickled him in a bittersweet sort of way, and made him wonder if this was what it felt like to have a sister, love her, and be loved by her. He'd never had the chance to grow up with his, nor was he close friends with many young girls.

"Then I shall think of you as a sister," he placed a kiss on her curly head and released her. "And God willing, I will care for you just the same."

Everything began to move at lightning speed. In those next few weeks, Michael had many letters to write, and documents to sign. He attended several meetings with the solicitor, and hired an accountant to assist him. He hadn't written so much since grammar school, and thought his hand might seize up. His penmanship began to suffer. When he was a small boy, he'd had his hands lashed many times if he wrote poorly.

In the meantime, he did indeed help fix and paint that offending door, and at his own insistence, he was put to work in the store. This aided in restoring his strength and keeping his mind sharp, as he had to lift many things, take inventory, and count quickly. This also freed up Ruth to attend appointments of some sort with Emma White, but he did not know what they were for, and did not ask.

Ashwood Hall was being torn down on the twenty-second day of February, and he stood and watched from his father's grave. He wept as he saw the past dismantled in front of him, but these tears were not a shameful burden. Strange as it was, he wished Abraham was standing there with him.

Abraham!

He needed to write the old man, and see about him. What was one more letter? He no longer felt shame and disgust when he tried to write to old acquaintances. It was a lot to explain, and he was unsure of how to begin, and did not want to give him a terrible start, but he wrote very plainly that he had left the Webbs, and was making a new life for himself.

Michael had not prayed in several months, because he began to feel his prayers were a script of unfeeling words he recited since childhood because he was told that's what he was supposed to do. Now, when he was alone, he knelt and gave thanks to God. His words were not pretty and neatly strung together, but they were his most genuine feelings, and he let them flow unimpeded.

His twentieth birthday came and went, and the dower house became his.

It was finished in 1752, and named Brownwall: not very imaginative, but an apt description. He took a ride into the wild, overgrown woods to see it, and he took Ruth and Peter Evans with him. Ruth hummed and buzzed in anticipation, as they'd never gone far into the country before. The property was near an old family chapel, and one of the burial plots. On the other side of it, there was a sprawl of wilderness. Past the twisting branches and briar, and iron gate, he could see it in its entirety: a three-storey structure of brown brick, in a tall Gothic arrangement, set superbly against the trees, and surrounded by a gravel walkway. The modest courtyard had been nearly overtaken by the woods. A solitary covered well sat in a clearing. Much of the stonework was partially eroded and painted with ivy and lichen. There was an old stable that likely couldn't be saved.

The wooden steps were green and rotting, and groaned in agony under Michael's weight. The interior was barely lit by the sun, and all was dusty. The curtains were faded, and some crumbled when he touched them. There were spiders in every corner, much to Ruth's horror, Peter's indifference, and Michael's delight. Now it was time to assess the damage. He scoured every room, taking time to marvel at the abandoned relics of the past.

He may have never even been to the old dower house again, had it not been for Ashwood being torn down. It truly felt as though he'd stepped into the past, and made him feel intimately connected with his family's history, to see how the departed ladies lived in the absence of their husbands. There were photos he'd never seen before, and scraps of personal memorabilia that may have been lost to the sands of time; he gathered those up and put them in a chest for safe keeping.

The parlour was lined with beautiful ivory and rose wallpaper, and the mahogany furniture miraculously still shone as if newly polished. Mercilessly bright pink drapes jumped out at him against the soothingly feminine, almost maternal furnishings. The side that faced the sun had faded to ivory. Thankfully, there was a piano.

Michael's vitals were put to the test when his foot went through one of the stairs in the hall. Peter barely caught him before he could fall back and take everyone down with him.

Nonetheless, many treasures awaited them at the top. The largest bedroom had blonde lace curtains around the bed, and a toilette table stood opposite of the windows, with more drawers than he would ever need. This was most definitely a woman's room, but he claimed it for its big and tall bed. On the wall was a portrait depicting the elder Berthe Bennett in her youth, and she was just as Abraham described her.

In one wooden trunk at the corner of an unfurnished third storey room, he found a collection of old toys, including some sweet little porcelain dolls that looked older than his father, wrapped in shattering silk. The painted lips and eyes were rubbed away. They were probably well-loved by whomever had owned them before, so he wrapped them back up and tucked them back into their place.

Abraham was absolutely elated to hear from him, and learn of his new friends and what he had been doing. He promised that he would come to see Michael himself once he had taken care of some affairs in Liverpool. Michael expected a harsh scolding when he reunited with his old friend.

Early in the spring, when his side had finally healed enough to allow him to exert himself, he hired Peter and Ruth to help him with repairs and renovations; Peter had to guide him through

some of the more intricate work. The well was
also made serviceable. It took many weeks,
starting with the first storey, of course. They
occupied those finished rooms and worked their
way to the rest of the house, little by little, and
had to have supplies carted in from town.
Fortunately, the house was sealed well, so there
was not much moisture damage, but the
wallpaper in half of the rooms needed to be
disposed of. Dry-rotted rugs and woodwork
were burned. At night, they gathered by the
warmth of the kitchen stove and shared hot tea
and a cold meal on freshly washed dishes,
discussing their plans for the next day.
Sometimes, they abused the old piano in the
parlour. It desperately needed to be tuned, but
Michael got a good laugh from playing a melody
by memory and hearing how distorted it had
become.

This feeling of fellowship renewed him, but
there was a bitter taste of melancholy in his last
sip of tea as he listened to Ruth say a prayer over
their sleep before they retired. Sometimes it
lingered late into the night, and pulled him out
of bed to listlessly wander through the woods.

As the brush became lush and green, Michael
sifted through the flora in the yard to determine
what he wanted to keep, what would be trimmed
back, and what would be removed. The
blackberry briar was attractive for winemaking.

Stinging nettles, on the other hand, did not appeal to him.

In place of his sister's current grave marker, he had 'Little Berthe Bennett' engraved on a stone plate, with his one picture of her framed in glass above her name. He wouldn't have been at peace until that was taken care of.

He was counting the days until Abraham's letter stating he would be coming soon. It finally came in late April, and just in time. Michael and his friends had +made most of the house liveable, and a room was prepared for him, as promised. He did offer a space to the Evans siblings, but they declined. He did not press, but went with them to gather the rest of his belongings.

"It has been so wonderful to have you with us," Ruth kissed him all over one cheek, and he let her do it. "You have to write or come see us often!"

"Of course I will! I owe you my life, after all," Michael laughed at stroked her head.

"You have been a blessing in disguise, Mr. Bennett," Peter firmly shook his hand, and Michael offered a jovial thanks, pretending he had not just been insulted.

He left them, taking the remainder of his possessions, and was now settled into Brownwall.

That solved the issue of his living arrangements. He thought he would feel complete, now that he'd reclaimed a reserve of his ancestral property, but now that he was there… what did he do next? He had to occupy himself and start making money fast. The repairs had eaten up almost as much money as the price of the house, and though it was habitable, there was more to be done.

For the time being, he took up work at the docks in the next town.

He started on a Wednesday in early May. It had taken months for him to fully get his strength back after his illness, and being useful again was thrilling.

Most of his dockmates were of Irish background. The majority were hard-working people, but some of them seemed to only be toiling at the docks because no other profession would take them. They did their work recklessly and drank after every shift. Sometimes, he was invited. As it turned out, this was only so that they could boast their superior "manhood." They were loud and drank to excess, and their attitude towards women and even young girls was profoundly distasteful. The congregation was so mortifying, he had to apologise to the women who'd been slighted, and then elected to never be graced by their company outside of obligation ever again.

The prodding continued. They questioned his "experience" with women. He had none that he would tell them about, and no, he was not interested in "learning" any time soon. Before long, there were whispers that he was "one of *them.*"

From then on, he was the "pretty fellow" that they whistled at when he came to the docks (if he was indeed the fairest of them all, one can imagine how rough these creatures looked), meanwhile he ignored them unless it involved cargo.

But they persisted. Usually, it rolled right off of him, as he had no desire to quarrel with them. One day, however, he had his back turned to one of the older gentlemen, who approached close behind him.

"Say there, you pretty little darling, don't be so uppity," he cooed at him, as if he was one of those women that he preyed upon, and then Michael felt a leathery hand reach under his collar and scrape the back of his neck.

It was as though Michael had only blinked, and that mosquito of a man had been launched like a cannonball into a stack of barrels. The other workers stood agape.

"Oh! So sorry!" Michael stammered. "I'd not realised I moved so roughly!"

But the men were not angry at all, nor did they intend to have him punished. In fact, they admired how easily he had delivered the offending blow, and applauded him for finally "acting like a man."

The teasing ended, but from then on, they were pestering him to enter underground boxing fights… which they could then place bets on. He knew they were still using him for their own amusement, but he consented, because after all, he missed the sport. He partook roughly once a week after his shift.

After work, he came home pleasantly sore late in the evening, and set aside time to practise on the piano. There was no shortage of sheet music; somebody really had an appetite for Mozart. This house had wonderful acoustics. He fancied himself a concert pianist; of course, his only audience was the spiders in the attic. When he finished playing, he went into the attic to pick up the spiders and let them crawl on him.

There wasn't much to read in the house, but there was a Bible. Perhaps he should have picked it up, but it conjured up bittersweet memories that he wasn't ready for. He reached for it every once in a while, but left it where it was, and went to sleep.

The soreness was only pleasant when it did not persist into the next day of work. Then, it was entirely unwelcome, but he pushed through it anyway. On those days, he came home aching, trembling, and sick with fatigue. When his muscles were wrought to their limit, he was considered a danger to work with and banished to taking inventory until he had recovered. They rotated men this way in order to keep them in peak condition. As he continued, though, he built up endurance and was able to be out on the docks for longer stretches, even considered an asset for his youth.

When he went onto the decks of larger vessels, he reminisced about travelling with his father, and had just a bit of a craving for that kind of adventure again. Perhaps when he finally settled on a path for his studies, it would provide him with more opportunities.

His meals were rough and barely appealing. He hunted wild birds, and roasted potatoes whole and dry, as if over a fire. At least he could make toast without ruining it.

After he'd only been working on the docks for a few weeks, a new batch of workers arrived: Arab men. They were wholly different from the Irish ruffians, not just in their manner of speech and dress, but how they rose to the task. They worked to the best of their abilities, and then asked to be given more to do, eager to please their employers.

Michael got on better with most of them, as well. They did not condemn his abstinence from alcohol and chasing women, and once in a while, he visited their dwellings. Many of these fellows were there to make money to send back to their families, or stake out a better home for them. A Turkish fellow was appalled that Michael had lived for as long as he did without ever learning to cook anything… and pitied his inability to grow a full beard. He went out of his own way to teach Michael to cook a palatable stew on the stove. He was glad to learn, though he had burned the roux an embarrassing number of times before he improved. It was not identical, but it was very similar to the Indian curries his mother made, and the aroma quelled up many long-buried memories. It smelled like youth… like peace.

At Brownwall, he made it only once or twice a week, as the spices were hard to find. It made even his sad potatoes quite appetising, and helped make his house the home that he yearned for.

Since he saw no need to deviate from a formula that worked so well, it was the only good thing that he cooked. Michael was most certainly a glutton of spice.

There was also a handful of Scandinavians at the docks before long. They were just fine, though Michael found them wholly uninteresting, and the feeling was likely mutual. They understood English, but when he tried to start a conversation with them, they nodded and slowly wandered away, and after work was finished, they were nowhere to be seen.

While in town one day, he picked up a newspaper for the first time in years, and his blood curdled when he read about a series of dreadful, heinous murders of several women in London— not just slain, but butchered, and the monster had not been found! His heart nearly stopped each time he dared to check the names of the victims. When he recognised none of them, he could breathe easily, though he was still shaken and sickened by what he'd read.

XXIV

The woods around the property needed to be explored. Time outdoors was always treasured, especially when it rained the night before. The weather the next day was bright but damp. He merrily tramped into the bush, off of the lightly beaten path in the tall grass, until the trees became thick and the forest floor was a carpet where very little light reached. The woods made him feel less lonely. There was something peculiarly comforting about being so small. The walls of the house imprisoned him, but the trees embraced him.

He reached a tiny, slow-flowing shallow stream that fed into the pond near the house, and possibly the well. There was not a lot of wind, but the foliage seemed to move out the corner of his eye. He lunged upon the leaves — carefully— and produced a newt. It wriggled and writhed in his fingers, obviously not pleased with having been caught. Anything would have been upset about a giant hairless ape plucking them off of the ground.

"Hang on! I only want to look at you, that's all! Just let me look at you," he gently cupped the little thing into his hands. It had a beautifully mottled greenish brown body. He may have never seen it if it didn't move; it became less frantic as he held still. He knew he could not handle them much, as their skin was so thin and delicate.

"Well, alright, I'll put you right back where I found you. You are fascinating."

He didn't understand how people could be afraid of them or find them repulsive. They were lovely creatures, and posed no significant threat, unless one were to perhaps kiss it, but everybody knew by now that an amphibian wouldn't turn into a prince.

He had mentally noted that they were not a threat when handled properly, but shortly after releasing it, he foolishly rubbed one of his eyes with his unwashed hands, and the burn was like no other, worse than any bee sting. When the pain became disorienting, he decided to walk back. By the time he returned to the house, his left eye was quite swollen, streaming with tears.

The encounter conjured up pleasant memories of handling similar creatures in that family acquaintance's garden. Was he still living in the same place, and did he still own all of those animals?

After dinner, he began looking through old letters and documents, trying to find the address of that man with the animal collection. All he had from memory was a name… Kelley? Andrew Kelley? Allan? He'd not been at his residence in years, but remembered he was near to the west coast. He was a middle aged fellow, maybe fifteen years older than Michael's father.

Adam Kelley, from Bristol! That was very close! What was the likelihood that he was in the same place? The man loved to travel, and held many charity events; that was where Nathaniel Bennett had the idea to set up Samuel and Mary. All he had to do was write a letter and see for himself. Would he even remember Michael?

He received a reply within two weeks:

'Dear Lord Michael Ashley Bennett,

It is a pleasure to get word from you. I was so sorry to hear of Samuel Bennett's passing. He was a generous patron. Thank you for putting the rumours to rest. It pleases me to know that the Bennett family has not gone to complete ruin. I am glad that you are doing well for yourself. Last I saw you, you were a young lad without even any hair on your face, and yet I hear you are a man now!

Thank you, also, for enquiring about my animals and myself. I am getting on well enough for my age, though I do not travel at all anymore. My

*garden is still open and encourages donations.
Do come and visit any time— and say hello.
Perhaps we may discuss all that has happened
these past few years.*

Adam Gregory Allen Kelley'

How exciting! He prepared to leave by the end
of the month.

Ruth and Peter Evans had not visited him yet,
nor had Michael visited them, but they wrote
each other every other week. As it turned out,
Ruth had gotten engaged to Emma White's
brother, a train guard of about thirty, and a
"decent enough, hard-working fellow." Miss
White herself arranged the match, and Ruth
entreated Michael to attend their wedding.

He agreed to come no matter what, also
hoping—though not saying it— that this union
would bring financial stability. Furthermore, he
wrote that he hoped Mr. White would stay a
decent enough fellow, or Michael may have to
knock out some of his teeth. This was said in
jest... mostly.

By the middle of June, he set out for Bristo: to
Mr. Kelley and his creatures. It was a short trip,
and he arrived half past noon.

Mr. Kelley's house was at the end of a long avenue tucked within walking distance of the city streets, and the fenced plot adjacent to it was where he kept his plants and creatures.

"Why! Michael Ashley Bennett, as I live and breathe!" Mr. Kelley and his mane of wispy silver hair and whiskers intercepted him at the door. The wide eyes and feathery brows were exactly as he remembered.

"And thank God for that! You look fantastic, better than me!" Michael grasped one of his gnarled hands; the man had been scratched and/or bitten by everything that moved.

"You're almost a head taller than last I saw you!" the old fellow chuckled and grinned broadly, revealing all of his chipped teeth. "I say, there's few people I enjoy anymore, but you're one of the tolerable ones!"

"And since it's been so long, perhaps you'd be kind enough to give me a tour, yes?"

"Oh, right this way, right this way!" Mr. Kelley descended the steps.

He walked with a shiny cane that he didn't need; he used it for dramatic effect, or occasionally to discourage an animal from striking at him. He led Michael down a winding path, past several gates.

Michael sorely missed this garden. It was more enriching than anything he'd gotten from educational books. When he spent his summers there as a young lad, he learned how to handle snakes and lizards from Mr. Kelley, who could naturally charm just about all crawling things. He likened snakes to women: beautiful things that were difficult to get ahold of, but unable to resist a gentle approach.

Mr. Kelley was a life-long bachelor, and Michael had never even seen him stand near a woman. Furthermore, he warned Michael to be very cautious about voicing that analogy.

"I know I said so once before, but 'tis a pleasure to see you again, boy," he stood to one side and overlooked his domain. "I knew you couldn't stay away from this place."

"I couldn't possibly. Even aside from being one of the last reserves of my youth, it is a little paradise of its own. Seems you've expanded it quite a bit," Michael walked ahead of him and marvelled at the new structures and creatures.

"Oh, it is nothing much, really… it pales in comparison to corners of the Earth where you could find these fellows in their own habitat."

"Do you ever regret displacing them?"

"Indeed I do, though some of them have been injured and may never be able to be released again. I think of it as a public service, though, as it provides a safe and controlled environment for creatures that would otherwise have no chance."

Mr. Kelley spoke his piece all in one breath, and then he began a new one.

"It is nice, though, having my creatures so close, now that I can no longer travel. I built this garden up with my own hands. I'm up at dawn and tend to it into the night. It is my life! I want to die here. I want to be buried here! Don't waste any time making up a pretty casket for my old bones, just stick what's left of me straight in the ground and let me become *one with the soil!*"

He shook his fists in Michael's face as he said this, and his eyes had the wild spark of a bird that had its wings clipped and could not soar.

"I sensed it when you first came here, Michael Bennett," he continued still, when he did not receive a response. "You are a creature of action and adventure like your father, and his father before, and like me. Stillness does not become you. You know… I never could marry for that reason. It is best that lads like us never marry. We are too restless, not meant to be grounded."

That may have been true for Mr. Kelley, but not for him. He knew what and whom he thought of, but he forced it back down.

"There is so much that I want to share with a wife," was all that he said.

"And I have much to share as well; I built this little sanctuary to be an escape from the encroaching urban corruption, and its polluting air."

"There is necessity to it, no matter how unsavoury some of its attributes are, as the population is growing so very quickly."

"Completely unnatural, and incompatible with a hygienic way of living!"

"I'd say this place is unnatural as well, as I'm sure these enclosures and walls did not spring from the ground, and many of these plants and animals do not belong on English soil. That said, I understand your argument."

This discussion reminded him of his taste for learning that he had lost some time ago, and it appealed to his passions.

"You have inspired me, though, Mr. Kelley, sir. You have enlightened me! I believe I have some of the answers I've been seeking now."

"Ah? And what might you be seeking?"

"Well, I have a favour to ask of you, a very big favour!" Michael's enthusiasm nearly matched Mr. Kelley's, now. "I feel I've found my purpose; would you be my mentor, and allow me to learn here? I imagine you need an extra hand, getting up in years and all."

He ran his weathered fingers through his whiskers.

"I admit, my strength is beginning to fail. You love this garden nearly as much as I do, and as I have no heir of any kind, I can't think of a better helping hand in my old age."

"That's the spirit! I'll be of good use, I promise! Then you will have me, yes?"

"Absolutely!" Mr. Kelley offered his hand.

Michael felt like kissing the old man, but he settled for a hearty handshake, as he never did enjoy physical contact; this was the best he would get.

"Oh, I'm indebted to you, I really am!" he laughed, unable to contain his excitement. "I will even draw in more people if you'd like. Surely you must be lonely, not getting out and about much anymore."

One corner of his smile dropped, and a bit of the gleam faded from his eyes.

"I wish I could cut ties with all of humanity and live out the rest of my days unmolested, deep in the mountains… but the guests garner sponsors, and maybe some bright young minds who come here will go on to do good in the world, if it can indeed be salvaged."

He wanted to ask what made the old man spurn humanity. Who had injured him so severely that he declared himself unable to marry, and suggested the same of Michael? The best he could do about it was prove him wrong in his own way.

"Well, no promises there, but I will certainly try to make the best of my time."

Unfortunately, he could not stay for long. While he was there, Michael gleefully wore some of the snakes like fine satin scarves. He'd missed it. There were likely more reptiles in this garden than in all of England.

"Goodbye, Mr. Kelley!" he waved his hat over his head as he departed. "I look forward to working for you!"

"No, no, no!" Mr. Kelley replied, much to Michael's initial surprise. "You will work *with* me, for these animals. This establishment is theirs!"

Technicalities, technicalities… he was no less excited about his future profession.

He stayed in a hotel for the night, but couldn't sleep. Mr. Kelley had told him that men such as themselves were unfit for marriage. If that was true, then why did he feel sick with the desire? He wanted to be married, but only under specific circumstances… circumstances that were looking more and more detached from reality each day.

Michael started work in July, one of the most active months of the year. He would stay in Bristol, with room and board provided by Mr. Kelley, and would be home three days in a week. It was quite a bit of travel back and forth compared to what he was accustomed to.

He aided the old man with maintenance and construction, and tended to his animals under close supervision (being paid fairly handsomely for it, as well). Most often, he worked in his old hunting garb, for ease of movement without shedding too many layers, and for the many large pockets.

Some of the work that should have been easier was hindered by a lack of modern machinery; for example, water was drawn from a well or stream, and sometimes hauled several miles, even though they could have easily afforded piped water. Mr. Kelley desired to "stray from the natural way of things as little as possible."

"Then I suppose we should also remove all of our clothes, and do away with the roof," Michael noted.

"As little as possible without being arrested," Mr. Kelley clarified.

Of course, he did not expect to enjoy every aspect of his work, but since leaving something half-finished was intolerable to him, he still did the tedious tasks very well, and only complained a little.

Michael awoke at four o'clock each morning, and was praised for his punctuality. Mr. Kelley always prepared his meals: fish, cabbage, and bread, for every meal, every single day, without even any salt. Having already eaten, Kelley sat and watched Michael eat, so that he could give him his tasks at once. He worked twelve hours in a day, and went to sleep at nine o'clock, if he could manage it, but often had trouble nodding off until close to eleven.

He tried to have an hour of leisure time before he settled in, but Mr. Kelley had no instruments, no cards, and very few books, so Michael often wandered the grounds at night until he could sleep. It was much larger than he initially thought.

His garden was mostly reptiles, but there were amphibians as well, and a few mammals. He showed off an assortment of salamanders that Michael wanted to watch for hours. Most of them fed on insects, mice, and eggs, but the more voracious eaters consumed whole chickens. Per written instructions, he precisely measured every morsel of food so that nothing was wasted. Every scrap was reused or repurposed. He ruined the compost heap a few times, not knowing how to manage it, thinking it was too simple to ask for help, and not wanting to look like a dunce; thus, he made himself out to be even more of a dunce. Such was his entire existence.

It was a lot to remember, and a lot more running around, but it was easier labour than being on the docks. Michael was also an asset in that he didn't loathe talking to people. He could greet and speak to visitors freely, and Mr. Kelley could hermit himself away and be happily apart from humanity at large. It was even enjoyable to meet new people and answer as many of their questions as he could (though there was an instance in which he was cleaning an empty enclosure, and a jeering visitor asked if they now had gorillas on display. Admittedly, he had a good laugh himself).

That made him wonder why the old man hadn't hired any staff before, but he explained that he wouldn't trust another living soul to tend to the animals; he was only an exception because he grew up visiting each summer, and Mr. Kelley knew Michael's parents before that. He always wondered how exactly Mr. Kelley acquired an affection for such creatures, and he got his answer one day while watching him deposit some sizeable lizards into a brand new enclosure.

"You know, this reminds me," Mr. Kelley mused aloud, and probably would have done so whether Michael was listening or not. "These fellows remind me of my very first trip to Africa. I wouldn't have been much older than you, and I was with a group of other men, subsisting on quinine and hard bread, and hunting Nile crocodiles. I was meant to shoot one."

His speaking slowed, and his eyes lost focus.

"I mean… how could I? They were the most fascinating creatures I'd ever seen. There are sights that stick to a man for the rest of his life. All of nature interacting together was a heavenly symphony. I was in love. Nothing since then has ever come close to that rapture. And what were we shooting them for… trophies? Leather we didn't need? Before I knew it, I grew older, watching as entire communities were destroyed even here, all around us. I never wanted to cause that much destruction. I vowed I never would."

That sentiment was surprisingly touching, and it seemed that Michael finally had some insight into that peculiar character. It still didn't explain his complete aversion to marriage, but it was a start.

"Well, Mr. Kelley, I must say— in your own way, you are beautiful."

"Hah! I sure used to be," he chuckled and ran a hand through his feathery white hair. "But beauty is only good for breeding and advertising."

According to his father, Mr. Kelley was indeed a very attractive man at some point, even quite sought-after by young ladies— but that was not his sentiment.

"I do think that human beings are just as much a part of nature as any other beast. You've done a great service by offering an opportunity to see nature the way you do."

He left it at that. Michael didn't bother trying to convince him to enjoy human beings a little more. At roughly sixty years old, he was likely set in his ways, and he feared surfacing some dark recollections in the old man.

He of course wrote to Abraham about it right away. He was wary of Michael's new profession, but accepted it, as he was pleased with it and received both physical and mental exercise from the position.

The set date for Ruth's wedding was in late August, so he did his best to plan his leisure days around that, and packed his fine morning suit. He never was good at selecting gifts, but he thought a nice collection of cast iron cookware and perfumes would be a good contribution.

"Mr. Bennett!" Ruth greeted him with a kiss when he came to the door. Emma White stood behind her.

"It certainly has been a while!" Michael took off his coat and hat. "You look well, Miss Ruth, as do you, Miss White. And how is Peter?"

"He's been quite busy, as have I, but no worse
for wear! He'll be home soon, and tomorrow
you'll meet Mr. White."

"Mr. White! How wonderful! Then I shall judge
whether or not he is suitable."

Ruth tittered as she ambled about and took his
coat. "Well, you know where our spare room is,
so you can make yourself at home."

"I do, indeed," he moved his belongings into the
little cupboard where he'd been rescued from his
brush with death many months ago.

Tea was served in the kitchen, as always. At
first, he thought he would be pressured to speak,
but the two women carried on a conversation
just fine without him. Most of it involved
wedding plans, which he knew nothing about.
They all played a few games of cards after they
put the dishes away.

Ruth asked for help with a worried seam on her
dress, and they disappeared into her chamber.
Michael was left alone to finish his lukewarm
tea. After an interval, Peter Evans arrived.

"Evans!" Michael rose and held out his arms,
and strangely enough, Peter kissed him but did
not embrace him.

"Bennett," he replied coolly. "Are you well?"

"I couldn't be better, my friend!" he pulled up the only chair that didn't have an empty cup beside it, and sat down across from it. "Your sister seems quite fond of her groom, and is already set on loving him."

"She is set on loving most living things, yes," Peter sat.

"Eh? What do you mean by that?"

"Love, for women, is more superficial than it is for men. They love so easily and prolifically because it means less to them. They may have more friends, yes, but men take quality over quantity; consider the profound friendship of David and Jonathan."

"That— ah— hmm—"

Michael bit his tongue, swallowed his words, and started his sentence over.

"And what will happen once she is married? Will she stay here?"

"No. She will live closer to the train station, with Mr. White and his sister, and I will continue to live here and run the shop until the lease is terminated."

"I hope I don't sound flippant in suggesting it," Michael began his thought carefully. "Mind you, my parents were arranged to marry for money first and foremost, and matched very well, so I do not intend to slight dear Ruth and Mr. White in saying this… but this union means financial stability, yes?"

"That is so," Peter poured himself some tea without heating it and solemnly gazed into the trembling liquid. "It is an advantageous pairing, and she has accepted him gladly. She will be taken good care of."

"But what of you?"

"Once the lease is terminated at the end of this year— I've not renewed it— I will shut up this place and seek a life in a monastery on the continent."

Michael could not believe what he was hearing.

"You will walk away from your home? Even after you told me your worries about leaving it behind only last winter?"

"To tell you the truth, I stayed here only for Ruth. But now that I know she is secure and will not be required to move far from here, I can seek

freedom in simplicity and routine, away from
the temptations of the world."

That didn't sound like much of a life to him… it
sounded like resignation, or even like he was
trying to flee from his own family. Still, Michael
resolved to be glad for Peter and his decision.

"Will that really make you happy? Is that what
you want?"

"You sound taken aback," he sipped his tea at
last. "As if happiness is all that matters in life!
Well, what is it that you want?"

Here he was, casting judgement on Mr. Evans,
when he couldn't even make up his own mind.
As it was, he still felt his life had no purpose.
Well, not everybody had to be extraordinary, and
simplicity on its own did not sound so bad. After
the initial shock had passed through him,
Michael saw Peter's resolution from a new light.
Why should he be tied down by a place that did
not serve him?

"I want to work hard and be content," he
decided.

"A fair wish," Peter replied.

Ruth's gown was a blushing rosy pink, and she
wore yellow blossoms in her hair. The pale hues

made her eyes really shine. He knew the wedding apparel was her first new addition to her wardrobe in years, so it was sweet to see her so enamoured with it.

As for Mr. White, he crossed paths with the fellow at the church. He seemed a plain and unassuming man, but he had a firm handshake, a luxurious red beard, and a large set of teeth. He spoke very softly, like his sister, Emma.

The ceremony was quiet and quick, as the priest was busy that day. Attending strangers bore witness to the ordeal. There was a breakfast held at the Whites' house, about an hour away. They were fairly well-to-do from the looks of it. Miss White was sober and silent, on what should have been a time of merriment. In truth, he felt a stinging throb of bitterness, himself (maybe not for the same reasons, whatever they were), but he made an effort to repress it. They shared an understanding look across the table. He did not know why.

The Whites were gracious hosts and seemingly decent people, and he felt at ease knowing that Ruth was in good hands. Even Peter seemed serene.

"Well, Mr. Evans," Michael met with Peter at the door as the party dispersed. "I suppose I'll never see you again."

"Possibly not," he confirmed.

Needless to say, Michael's heart sank. Less than a year ago, this man saved his life.

"Does… Ruth know about this?" he lowered his voice.

"She will… after she leaves for her honeymoon, I will leave as well. I will write to her when I arrive at my destination."

"Why haven't you told her? Why can't you tell her now?"

"She is not ready to receive that type of shock."

This confirmed for him that Peter was trying to wash his hands of her.

But when he realised this was where they would be parting ways, his anger quickly cooled into sullen brooding.

"Write at least, will you?"

"Yes, whenever possible."

"And what will happen to old Lambert?" he couldn't help but ask.

Peter released a strange little scoff.

"How typical of you! Mister and Mistress White will be taking him with them. He will be all well."

"So this is goodbye, then," Michael held out his arms once more.

Peter Evans only stared at him for a minute with a peculiar look that was not unlike the ones he sometimes received from Alma. He advanced and accepted the embrace, and kissed his cheek.

"It is goodbye, indeed. Farewell, Mr. Bennett."

After that, Michael found it difficult to talk to Ruth. Though he was more attached to her than he was to her brother, he believed once more that to conceal such things from her was unfair. Luckily for him, she did enough talking for everybody. He waved her off when she departed with her new husband, feeling like a traitor.

XXV

In autumn, many of the animals were put away
for hibernation, and guests stopped turning up.
Now, his primary focus was on maintenance.
Mr. Kelley took great pride in how diligently he
looked after his garden all year long, from dawn
to dusk.

Finally, Michael convinced Mr. Kelley to hire a
secretary, as he was running a business, after all,
and his bookkeeping was abysmal. He took on
Dolores Gaye, a twenty year-old records keeper
from a library in town. She was a timid wee
thing who wore bifocals and kept her dark hair
in braids; she had no contact with the animals.

She arrived on a Thursday morning, and Mr.
Kelley gave her a theatrical speech about their
role in preserving nature. She was not visibly
moved. Michael bowed and reached out to pick
up her bags to take them to her office.

"Do not touch my things. Your hands are filthy,"
was all that she said.

Michael looked down at his hands in confusion.
They were not visibly besmirched, but he had
been handling a large toad not long ago.

"Oh! Alright, sorry, madam," he replied, as he'd had a thought to explain to her that toads were not a threat, but his voice froze in his teeth at her tone. He elected to simply direct her to her destination and take his leave, so that Mr. Kelley could deal with her.

"You are off schedule by nearly ten minutes, Michael Ashley Bennett!" Mr. Kelley scolded him as he passed. "She can find her own way around. You do your own work and stop chasing skirts!"

"Sorry," he said once more, and continued on his way, though he was bruised by the skirt-chasing accusation.

Michael tried to become familiar with Miss Gaye on a few occasions, but had no luck. She was intimidated by Mr. Kelley (no surprises there), and didn't seem to like Michael all that much— she did her job well, but interacted with them both as little as possible. One day, he had a legitimate excuse to approach her while on duty, but when he came into the office for some documents, she nearly riveted herself to the opposite wall upon seeing him. He was perplexed until he remembered the lizard perched on his shoulder.

"Sorry," he sheepishly bowed under her glare and pawed through the drawers. "He's harmless, I promise. This is Quincy!"

"Do any women work here?" she asked, to his surprise.

"Well, I know one does for sure. You can usually find her in this office."

She didn't laugh.

"Ah, no, ma'am. Not yet."

"How old are you?"

"About twenty. Why do you ask?"

"You ought to act your age," she declared, with a cool and unchanging expression.

"Act my age?" he'd intended to come and go, but now his interest was piqued. "Well, since you're the expert, how might a fellow my age act?"

"You could stand to be a touch more dignified in how you carry yourself and speak to women, instead of acting like a little boy."

He was then more vexed than curious. She had a lot of nerve to look down upon him and his manner when she spoke to nobody and made no effort to befriend anyone.

"Put on airs, you mean? Act miserable? I tried that, once, Miss. I made a fool of myself. Better to know I'm a fool than go through life pretending otherwise, I'd say. Well, thank you. I have what I need."

Michael looked back at her on his way out, and froze; she looked mournful, and had her eyes fixed with a wistful glisten.

He waited while her face grew red as she stared into oblivion, and she finally spoke up:

"I didn't mean to say that."

"Then what did you mean to say?"

She huffed and rubbed at her eyes behind her glasses.

"How can you speak to people so freely, without a care?"

So… she envied him? That was new!

"Hah! I suppose I make it look easier than it is," he admitted, and stepped back towards the door. "Truly, it helps if you don't think too hard. You can't care about things you don't think about!"

She smiled, at last. It was only a small tug at the corners of her pale lips, but it was a start to getting past that icy facade. Her moods sure changed rapidly.

"There we are! All better," Michael held out a hand. "I must write something down. Could I have a pen?"

She handed him one of the pens stuck in her hair, and he made sure his little friend was secure, then wrote standing at her desk.

"You write so beautifully," she commented, leaning over his writing.

"I used to get hit if I didn't."

She looked up with a mortified expression. He laughed, and again, she smiled sheepishly.

"Thank you, Madam," he actually left that time.

From then on, Miss Gaye was easier to talk to: that is to say, she was gay— at least more so than in their previous encounters. They didn't always cross paths when they had free time, but she was a degree warmer, and more willing to have a conversation. Maybe she was not quite a friend, and maybe she'd never grow to like him, but she was one more new person in his little corner of the world.

And soon, he would be welcoming in an old friend, as well. At long last, he received news that Abraham would be coming shortly! He was due to arrive in early November, and Michael went over his quarters once again to make sure that they were prepared well.

Now, on a wet and overcast morning, Michael waited at the train station for Abraham to step down.

"Ah! My lovely boy! Master Bennett!" Abraham dropped his belongings and raised his shaking arms. Michael kissed him and took his luggage.

"Abraham, I tell you, you do not need to call me that!" he walked right behind the old man. "I am not your master."

"And I tell you I will always serve the Bennetts, even if only in spirit!" was his reply.

"Today, I shall serve you," Michael went ahead of him and carried his belongings, and they arrived at their destination before the day was over.

Abraham was all the more elated to arrive at the house. He vividly remembered Brownwall, and happily described the days he had spent there on occasion. The details of his recounting were fine and precise, though he often had trouble placing them in chronological order.

"You know, Lady Berthe never lost her taste for extravagant parties, even as she advanced in age. Ah, you might not have been old enough to remember. She brought her tradition of festivities with her here to Brownwall, and continued them up until her death. Yes, she was dressed in all her finery even on her dying bed, and buried with half of it."

Michael was, indeed, not old enough to remember, because Lady Berthe had died shortly before he was born.

"I'm glad you have such fond attachments to this place, Abraham," Michael set his friend's luggage down in the hall. "Soon, we will be fetching all that you want from your old residence in Liverpool, and moving it here. I've made up a nice, plain and pristine little room on the first storey for you. This is your home now, Abraham."

"Master Bennett!" he sighed, as if he may faint, and his eyes welled up as he removed his hat. "You needn't accommodate me. I don't want to be a burden to you—"

"You! A burden!" Michael couldn't even grasp what he'd just heard. "You, who faithfully took care of my family for multiple generations? A burden to me? Abandon that ludicrous idea. Besides, we are dear friends, just about as close as two men can be. You would be doing me a great service by living here, yes, you would."

"If that is the case, I should like to be useful to you, at the very least. You know, it is not my habit to stop working, after all these years."

"You need not be *useful* to me, my friend, but if it would please you, I can find something to occupy you with, for example, taking care of my paperwork, straightening the cutlery I didn't put in precisely the right place, or swatting my hands when I pluck at a loose thread from my waistcoat."

"Those, I'm sure I would do regardless."

"I don't doubt it."

Michael had managed to learn the secrets of the old stove in the kitchen (special thanks to Miss Ruth for cleaning it properly) and put on water for their tea. Because he was certain that Abraham would not tolerate hot curries very well, dinner would be unevenly sliced bread and cold butter. Abraham no longer had the coordination or eyesight to correct his use of the knife.

They ate by the light of a single candle in the parlour.

"Master Bennett, my boy, I've been thinking that there's much you do not know about your family, particularly on your mother's side. I feel I should tell you all I know."

"Was she not an orphan found by her uncle as a young woman?"

"Oh, indeed she is, that is true. However, there is far more to it."

"Well, I would like to hear it," Michael entreated him, though he half dreaded that he would learn of some unsavoury family secret.

"Let's see… your grandparents— your mother's parents— came from Australia many years ago, when your mother was only a little baby. And your grandmother is thought to be the daughter of an unnamed native woman."

Abraham paused to let him absorb this information, as if it may have been some great shock to him. It was certainly a little surprising, but not troubling or awe-inspiring: definitely a family secret, but a fairly benign one. That said, he had never seen any pictures of his maternal grandparents, and did not know what his grandmother looked like.

"The woman was not married to your great grandfather, but she was a servant in his house, and his wife took the child and raised her for herself, driving the young mother away."

So, that was the unsavoury part.

"This was, of course, omitted from any official documents concerning your mother after they came here, and the purpose was for her to have a more promising future," Abraham finished, and now it was Michael's turn to speak.

"So, how did you find this out, Abraham?"

"Mmm… the late Lord Bennett mentioned it to me, based on some letters in your mother's possession, written by her parents before they died. Her uncle concealed these details when arranging for her to be married, of course, but Samuel Bennett never was bothered by it."

"And what would I do with this information?"

"Ah, well… whatever you'd like, I suppose. Your grandparents loved to travel, and your grandmother was particularly fond of Russia as well! That makes sense, though, as I'm told it's where her father was born. She had a ring made there, with a gem she'd had since she was a young girl."

"That would certainly explain the opal in that ring—" Michael's words caught in his throat as he remembered it. What did Alma do with the ring? Had she pawned it already, along with the other jewellery he'd left behind? Had she made use of her wedding dress?

He did not yet have the fortitude to message the Webbs. Maybe he never would. No matter what, he hoped she was well.

In bed, he was kept awake into the early morning, weighed down by all of this new information, and the painful chord that it struck from his shattered heart strings.

Michael had not forgotten Alma. She was always tickling at the back of his head, and she was ever-present in his dreams, often floating in sunshine on the horizon, always visible but just out of his reach. When he awoke, his bed felt cold, and he pined for the sun's warmth. The sensation was akin to a wound that never fully heals as one continues to pick at it and wear away the protective layers. It was not a fresh and searing pain… until it was. He still wept early in the morning, when the dream was fresh. Remorse was heavy on his chest upon rising.

Abraham was cooking breakfast when Michael came out of his chamber. He never told him to do that, but there was no stopping him, as he did what he wanted, and would continue to do so until he no longer had the facilities. A kettle was heating on the stove, and Michael reached for the tea. There was coffee next to it. He did not remember buying it, and of course, he wouldn't drink it, but he was tempted to brew it just for the scent…

"Will you have some coffee, Abraham?" he asked.

"No, sir, it doesn't sit right with me these days. It rattles these old bones."

Michael dejectedly put the coffee away.

"Master Bennett, I do hope you have considered what job you would like to do for the rest of your life," he brought a platter of toast and fried ham to the table. "Can you really handle lizards and spiders forever?"

"Surely I can. I'm getting paid to do one of my favourite things."

"Hmm, I imagine that would suit you well. Do you think you will take up any study?"

"I do a great deal of studying as it is now! There are many scientific books that I read in my leisure time, and it is not all about creatures. I must also do maintenance, and that requires woodworking. Should I ever have to leave Mr. Kelley's employment for any reason, I am still honing other marketable skills."

"Well… I will support you, whatever path you choose."

"Unless I take to some illicit activities, that is."

"Ah, nonsense, that goes without saying. I know you will do the right thing, always."

Michael was not so sure of that. Maybe his actions were not largely immoral, but certainly had a tendency to be irrational. He had not told Abraham the whole truth about why he had left the Webbs, only because he had not asked him. Maybe it was just his nerves, but Abraham's comment had a peculiar tone to it, as though he knew more than he was letting on.

Abraham was writing letters as well, though Michael did not know to whom they were addressed. Was he still corresponding with Dr. Webb? If so, did he mention Michael?

He kept his own chamber spotless and occasionally ventured upstairs to dust and tidy

up Michael's room without his prompting.
Actually, Abraham had very little in his room,
and nothing of his was in the rest of the house.

Michael spent Christmas in Bristol, and enjoyed
Abraham's company in the new year of 1889.
He'd given the old man a set of fine pens, only to
be told that he was waiting to send for his pens
he left in Liverpool, but the new year arrived,
and he heard nothing of it.

XXVI

Finally, in March, Michael had to ask:

"Abraham, when will we go to Liverpool and fetch the rest of your things? Do you simply not want them? Did you pawn it all off months ago?"

"Ah, yes! Forgive me, Master Bennett, little things slip my mind often at this age. Currently, there is somebody taking care of my residence until I terminate my lease, and I will write that person a letter announcing your arrival in advance; yes, I have to ask you to go alone, sir. I'm afraid I've not been feeling up for travel and lifting, as of late."

Was he really asking Michael to do something for him, and saying he was not up to a task?

"Why, Abraham, do you feel alright?" Michael made a show of placing his hand on the old man's wrinkled forehead. "Have you come down with something terrible, that you're spouting such outlandish things?"

"Nonsense, my boy… I've just finally begun to come to terms with my advancing age, I suppose. It is getting more difficult to even climb up to the second storey."

It concerned him a bit to see Abraham losing his vigour, but he knew he would have to accept it, and was happy that he was allowing himself to rely on Michael.

"Just say the word, and I will go straight to Liverpool, and be back before you know it!"

The order to march came on the fourteenth of April. Michael was to retrieve some clothes, linens, photos, and various little collections. Most of the furniture would be sold, as there was plenty at Brownwall.

Abraham insisted that he catch a later train so that he could put on his best travelling suit and get a proper haircut before he left.

"Oh, Abraham, I'm not aiming to impress anyone, this is not a social visit," he asserted. "I'll toss your associate a sovereign, and he'll forget he lay his eyes on me."

Michael wanted to have it taken care of as soon as possible, so he departed immediately after breakfast, arriving in Liverpool at midday. It was warm enough, but pouring rain when he left the station. Despite being the middle of the day, the sky was dark and hazy as soot. He did not bring an umbrella, and though he generally did not mind being rained on, it was uncouth to present oneself completely soaked. His hair was a bit long, too, and readily took on water, even wearing a proper hat for once. In a very strange and desperate situation, he bought an older woman's umbrella from her for two shillings. She gave him a sideways look, but did not object.

Luckily, he remembered the address, and Abraham only needed to remind him three times before he left. For all his talk about forgetfulness and decline, his mind still seemed much sharper than Michael's.

He rapped at the door, and tried to shake the water out of his hair while he waited.

"Hillo!" Michael called. "This is Bennett, come to pick up Mr. Abraham Reed's belongings!"

There was no answer after maybe half a minute. He tried the knob, and found it was unlocked, so he let himself in, whatever the consequences would be.

"Anybody here?" he asked into the still, unlit hall. There were light footsteps above him, and they sent a sort of shudder through his frame. If somebody was here, why had they not answered? He scaled the staircase very carefully, trying to prepare himself for anybody or anything. Why was he so nervous? He knew exactly why he was here, and he was surely expected.

The whole apartment was empty. That must have been it. He'd never seen it this way before, and that was surely the reason for his unease.

Still, the only sounds were soft footsteps, and the pouring rain, and now that he was inside, his damp clothes gave him a chill.

"Hello, anyone?" he called once more, and waited. There was no answer.

He came up the stairs and saw the door to Abraham's bed chamber was ajar. There was a solitary dim lamp burning at one end of the room, and on the other end, he saw a small silhouette, a woman, bent over a table, and a flickering shadow thrown over the curtains. The image was uncanny and somewhat ethereal in this light. Some unknown terror seized him. He felt he was in the presence of a supernatural being.

"You there! Are you here to take care of the house?"

"Yes, I am, among other things," the figure turned its head, and Michael gave an involuntary gasp as the voice made every hair on his body stand up.

The shape and size were exactly as he remembered, but the amber tartan dress, and small eyeglasses were new, and the hair was done up in a high and tidy coiffure, with a fringe of little ringlets framing the face— the beautiful face. The countenance was as inquisitive and mystifying as ever.

Michael was composed, not faint or giddy, though he thought he should have been.

"Alma," he slowly and reflexively removed his hat.

"Yes?"

He felt helpless and unable to breathe, just as he had been when he was sick and thought he might die. They were both there to carry out an assigned task, but… what was he supposed to say to her?

And why her? Why had Abraham dispatched Alma Webb to take care of his affairs? How long had he been in contact with her?

"Sir, speak up if you have something to say," she prompted him in such a familiar tone.

Suddenly, he could move again.

"Yes, I'm here to retrieve Mr. Reed's belongings, as I'm sure he has told you."

"Indeed he has."

Michael advanced, with his hand out to take one of the trunks she had just fastened, but as he got closer, his heart beat so fast it might have torn itself to pieces.

She was just looking up at him, not doing or saying anything, but torturing him. Was he really going to just grab these bags and leave? He had to speak to her for just a little bit or he might not live.

He took great pains to swallow down his nerves before he opened his mouth again.

"Alma, might we sit down and talk a little? It's been so long."

She produced a little brass watch from her bodice and checked the time.

"Alright."

Michael pulled out a chair for her from the writing desk, and he leaned himself against the adjacent wall. She seated herself. There were so many conflicting thoughts and feelings clamouring at once. He was a degree calmer now, but he couldn't for the life of him think of where to start. Maybe he should just let her speak.

He knew that he looked terrible. He was wearing a mixture of clothes from several decades, and his hair was sloppily shorn at his eyes and shoulders. He wished he'd heeded Abraham's warning.

"You look so… put-together," he tried. "Much more so than I, that is certain. Have you been to London? You are a professional woman now, yes?"

"I graduated from training months ago. I am a nurse."

"You are! I'm sure you are one of the best. Have you taken root in London with your mother?"

"I stay with three other women while I'm there," Alma removed her gloves, and Michael stole glances at her pretty little hands, looking for any rings. He found none.

"A busy lady, you are! What possessed you to take charge of Mr. Abraham Reed's house? My old butler, of all people?"

"It is something of a long story…"

"Well, I'd be glad to hear it," he replied sharply at the very end of her sentence, almost desperately, as would a beggar asking for her last crust of bread. "Do tell, if you have the time."

Her eyes darted every which way, sometimes fixing on him, and coming to rest on the desk.

"When you left, I looked for any clue that could tell me where you might have gone— not that I expected I could go looking for you, just for peace of mind. In Papa's old mail, I found letters from an Abraham Reed, and Papa told me of his relation to you. I decided to write to him myself. Not even he knew where you went, and he was devastated to learn you had vanished! I made up my mind to visit him myself, and he was beside himself with worry. I kept myself composed for his sake. He loves you so much, Michael."

He sank his bulk against the wall, hoping he could bleed through it and disappear. Shame and remorse weighed him down again.

"He still writes me letters about you. He has told
me all that you've been doing."

*He had? Was she pleased with it? Why did it
really matter?*

"Then you know… I have a permanent residence
now, and decent means, as I had wanted, and…
as I promised to prepare."

"Indeed, you have done well for yourself."

"Nothing compared to your accomplishments,
I'm sure. I certainly never saved anyone's life…
possibly ruined a few. Well, how is everything in
your little corner of the world? How is everyone
getting on?"

"Papa is well enough, in his study or at work
much of the day as he's always been. The barn
has been rebuilt with the help of neighbours. Ida
is in school, and almost as tall as me now. James
has taken up my position at the pharmacy, but he
has not changed much."

"Do you know of John Briggs, the innkeeper? Is
his business doing better?"

"Yes, it has been rebuilt, and he tells me you
gave him the money for it, but that you did not
want him to tell anyone."

"Fair enough. You are not just anyone, after all. And… has anything notable happened in town?"

She clasped her hands and drew in a sharp breath, apparently preparing to tell a very peculiar tale.

"The old magistrate has died unexpectedly. He had an apoplectic attack in his bed and slowly faded away through the night. And his nephew… when people searched the magistrate's house after his passing to overlook his possessions, they found… *something* belonging to Albert Gillman, and whatever it was, it was enough for them to have him sent to an insane asylum far north without a second thought— almost as though they'd been waiting to do so all this time. I don't know what has happened to him since then, but the community was in a state of shock for many weeks after the magistrate's passing. But of course, a new one was appointed quickly, and life went on…."

"The magistrate is dead… " Michael had to take a moment to digest this information. This was a turn of events he certainly did not expect. He just died, and his nephew was locked away, just like that? "Then have things been peaceful in your home?"

"Yes… Michael, you were foolish for doing all that you did."

"I know that. But what was the right or wrong thing to do? I'm always trying to figure that out."

"We all are, I suppose."

"Is that all you have to say about it?"

"It is all that I think I should say."

Undoubtedly, she had much harsher words, and could have really bruised him if she felt inclined, even crushed him between her thumb and forefinger. He waited for her to snarl at him, but she never did.

Michael didn't come here for a tête-à-tête. He came to do a favour for Abraham, or so he'd thought. But once he had packed everything, he knew he was supposed to leave. Now he didn't want to.

While he was watching the rain out the window, Alma's little fingers encased his clenched fist. The sensation almost broke him down.

"Alma, I did come here with a task to take care of punctually… but could I see you again?"

"You could."

He relaxed his hand and took hold of hers.

"You know, spring becomes you. Yellow and green are lovely colours, and they make your hair so rich."

It was delightful to bring a blush to her face again, and the shades of yellow, blue, and green in her dress made her cheeks shine. Her lips grew taut, and he could not determine what emotion she was making an effort to conceal.

"How long will you be in Liverpool?" Michael continued when she did not reply. "Where are you going later?"

"I am leaving on the next train to London. It departs in two hours."

"Then I won't keep you any longer," he loosened his grip. "You can leave now if you want, and I'll finish up all that must be done here."

She braced herself to rise from the chair, but then she froze.

"Will you need help carrying all of these things?"

"Alma, if I can't carry something, you most certainly couldn't carry it either," he chuckled and walked back to the table. He found what he guessed to be her hat, purse, and umbrella, and presented them to her.

She put her gloves back on, tied the straw hat down under her chin, fastened the purse to her hip, and then took the umbrella.

"Goodbye, then, Michael," she slowly backed towards the door.

"Oh, wait just a moment, Alma!" he called her back, despite his previous declaration. He wasn't ready to see her leave, but he probably never would be. "I forgot to ask… how are Sophie and her little ones?"

"Ah! Well… they're not so little anymore. An old lady from church took the two boys, and Ida has the little grey girl kitty. She named her Ruby. I sat down with her and told her all she needed to do to care for her, and made sure she knew how to do it, then I walked home with her and made sure Aunt Elisabeth was alright with having a cat. The rest are still at home with Sophie. They're great at catching mice. We're trying to keep them separated from the feral cats so that we don't have more babies running around…"

She stopped herself when she realised she had been talking for so long. Not that he minded. He knew she loved talking about her cats.

"I must be going," she insisted, and retreated to the hallway.

"Alma!" Michael called once more. "Oh, um… might we see each other again?"

"Come back to Papa's house, but write first. I will be home in the beginning of June, so you should write in May."

"Alright, I will do so… take care, Alma."

"Yes. Goodbye again, Michael."

"Would you want an escort to the station?" he asked. It seemed his enquiries grew increasingly more audacious every time he opened his mouth.

"I made it here on my own. I can find my way back on my own."

"Right… Good—" he checked his words when he felt his voice failing him. "Goodbye, Alma."

"Goodbye."

She stood and watched him for maybe a minute, then she departed. He had much ado to avoid chasing her down the hall and snatching her up, but he ran to the window to watch her disappear down the street.

"Well, I'd better take all of this downstairs,"
Michael spoke into the empty room.
Thankfully, nobody answered.

He had seen Alma again. He should have been
ecstatic, but he only felt hollow and desperate,
as he was given just a sip to drink from a
fountain of bliss. A romantic poet of the olden
days would have told him that just a few minutes
with her should have filled his heart for life, and
he wanted to feel that way, but it simply wasn't
reality. He found himself disowning his grief,
and nursing hopes that he had no right to rear:
that she had abstained from marriage, and still
wanted to be his. Why should she want to? She
likely felt abandoned and discarded, and was
simply too timid and too sweet to upbraid him.

Upon arriving home late in the evening, he had
to put the luggage down and wipe away his tears
so that Abraham wouldn't see them.

"Abraham Reed, you damned, conspiring
snake!" Michael snarled as he unloaded the old
man's belongings in front of his chamber door,
but there was no genuine anger in his tone. "You
knew everything and never told me! You sent
me to Liverpool alone, knowing Alma would be
there, and planned for it!"

"Sir, please, it is too late for you to be shouting,"
Abraham emerged from his room with an
unassuming little smile. "I am sorry for the
concealment, but Miss Webb— she is a dear
little lady— told me how erratic you'd been, and
I knew I had to tread lightly. You are stubborn,
just like your father, and when stressed, you are
unpredictable. But just like him, you are
unflinchingly true and tender, indeed, a true
man. You must hold onto a woman like that,
whether you marry or not! I would not allow you
to cut ties with her. She is good for you, and
maybe you could be good for her."

With that, Abraham reached just his arm out of
the door and pulled his things into his room.

"Thank you very much, Master Bennett."

"Anything for you. Try something like that
again, and I'll pull out your eyelashes."

XXVII

For the next two weeks or so, Michael was like a spoiled brat impatiently brooding during the last days before Christmas. At work, he nearly amputated his toes in his distraction when he dropped a barrel he was hauling. Mr. Kelley scolded him countless times, reminding him that the only reason his position was secure was because of his father's patronage.

While he was sitting idly at home, he told himself ridiculous things, such as, "In three hours and sixteen minutes, there will be only eight hours left in the day, and then it will be tomorrow. Then there will be only six days left until May."

Even then, he resolved not to write his letter on the first of the month. He did not want to seem too eager, nor did he want to give a short notice.

He tried to draw Alma, knowing that it would be a fruitless attempt and a waste of his time— that was the plan: to waste time. Her likeness was perfectly vivid in his mind's eye, but when he finished his charcoal sketch, the end result was a distorted, unsightly mess. Along with all of his previous artistic endeavours, it went into the fire. If only he had a portrait of her, he could perhaps make something human, but then he wouldn't have to try to draw her in the first place. Perhaps he could get her to draw a self portrait…

But at last, he was able to put his paper to practical use, and prepared to write a letter to the Webbs. All was well, until he actually sat down to write.

Now he truly struggled. What did he say to his former employer, whom he abandoned in his time of need? What would he say when he saw him in person? Would he even be able to face him? He'd already discarded three drafts. After over an hour of staring at a blank page, he penned his fourth and final attempt, trying to keep it brief:

'To Dr. Webb,

I hope you have not forgotten me. I've not forgotten you. I know I left unannounced and under suspicious circumstances, and it was wrong, regardless of my intentions; I should have confided in you. I will gladly explain all of it soon.

If it is alright, I wish to return and reconcile. I await hearing from you.

Michael A. Bennett.'

He did not like it, but it would just have to do, or
he would never have a letter finished. He mailed
it on May 3, and then he had five more days to
suffer.

Michael pounced on the mail when he saw the
name *Henry T. Webb* on an envelope. As soon as
he opened it, he dreaded reading; he was deathly
afraid of being declined. Then what would he
do?

'Michael Bennett,

*Alma has explained everything to me. I will
spare you the trouble. You are welcome here at
any time; only pick up some tobacco for me on
the way over, and all will be forgiven.*

Henry Webb.'

Well, those instructions were simple enough. An
incredible feeling of relief rushed over him as he
continuously read the words over and over to
make sure they were right. It was a peaceable
invitation, and yet, there was a terrible
foreboding over him when the rapture subsided.

Still, Michael worked six weeks straight with no
days of rest so that he could have the remainder
of June, and then he packed up all that he
thought he would need, and reserved a seat on
the very first train down south. He announced to

Abraham that he would be leaving, and he invited him to come along, but he declined, insisting that this was a private matter. Giddiness made him feel faint, but he was also restless and unable to hold still. He was in a trance.

It had been many months, more than a year, even. Michael wondered if anybody in town would recognise him. Whether they would have or not, he would have to handle that later. For now, he hurried to the Webb residence. There was a new and mysterious air about the whole place, though very little had visibly changed. It was eerie, and made him feel he did not belong. Little children that he'd seen before were nearly a head taller, and some had new school clothes, but the buildings were the same.

The Webbs' rebuilt barn shone bright and golden with new wood. Nothing else had really changed.

He froze with his fist floating in front of the door, not knowing how he would be received when it was opened for him.

The angry shriek of a chicken somewhere nearly rent his soul from his body. He took a second to collect himself and knocked at last. It unlatched and creaked open very slowly. James stood before him at the threshold.

"Ah, Mr. Webb!" Michael tipped his hat. "How have you bee—"

In the time it took him to blink, Michael was struck across the face and dashed onto the porch. He lay sprawled out in a daze, not remembering the last five seconds for a while. He tasted blood and realised just then what had happened, and saw that he landed mere inches away from tumbling down the steps and breaking his neck.

"My, that was a good one!" Michael chuckled and tried to take the attack with grace. His first primal instinct was to spring to his feet and start swinging as soon as his head stopped spinning, but he restrained himself. "How long have you been planning for that?"

"Since I first laid my eyes on you," James spat, glowering down at him as he retrieved his hat. "Why did you come back?"

"I was invited to come here, by Miss and Dr. Webb," he dusted off his hat and put it back on. "Glad you got it out of your system, then."

James only huffed and continued to obstruct the doorway.

"The fact that you won't fight back just vexes me even more. I thought you boxed."

"I have no quarrel with you, so unless you'd like to formally challenge me, I won't raise a hand at you. This blow was deserved, and I will take it," he wiped the blood from his nose and mouth.

"Gillman never formally challenged you. Didn't even defend himself."

"… I know, James. May I come in?"

James stood rooted to his place for a minute, then finally grumbled under his breath and moved to one side.

Just like the town outside, nothing in the house had really changed. He had to remind himself that he'd been gone less than two years. It felt like twenty.

He first checked the parlour, lured by the familiar perfume of the doctor's pipe, and then he saw the man himself, in his favourite chair.

"Dr. Webb," he stood and bowed in the doorway, then set his luggage down and used the hand that wasn't pressing a handkerchief to his nose to present the tin of tobacco he brought.

He looked up with such a cool and serene mein, as if completely undisturbed by the commotion from just a minute ago.

"Michael. Sit down," he pointed his pipe at the seat nearest to his own.

"Yes sir," Michael did as he was told and handed him the tin as he sat.

"What happened to your face?" Dr. Webb took the tobacco and set it on a side table.

"James, sir."

He nodded.

"As I have said, Alma told me everything. Still, I've decided I would like to hear from you, anyway. Explain yourself, son."

Since he had ample time to ponder his words, Michael did so, confidently:

"I would not ask you to excuse me or take pity on me, sir, but I thank you for hearing me. The fact of the matter is, I responded out of fear. It is as simple as that. I am generally too quick to jump to conclusions, and too proud to admit when things are beyond my control. But I am not too proud to admit that I am in error, at least, though the damage has already been done."

It seemed Dr. Webb had also been thinking of this exchange for quite some time, as he replied readily.

"You really should have confided in me, Michael. As your master, did you not trust me to be able to aid you? Instead, you left in the dead of night, without a word. And worst of all, you made Alma lie to me. Do you know why lying is one of the worst sins, Michael? I knew nothing of the danger she was in. Had Mr. Briggs not stepped in, that lie could have gotten her and James killed."

Worded in that way, it cut deeply into his heart. He'd come prepared to boldly take ownership of his mistakes without even knowing the extent of the damage they had caused. Michael never meant to hurt anyone, and now he charged himself with attempted murder. *He* almost killed Alma, by making her his accomplice and causing her to stumble.

"And now, I must clean my own rifles and shine my own shoes!" Dr. Webb added in the silence.

It drew a smile out of him, but Michael did not have it in him to produce a hearty laugh at the moment.

"Did you ever learn anything about those attacks?" he asked. "Were they even the work of the magistrate's men, or was my departure needless— more needless than it already was?"

"I sent that hair to a laboratory in London, and they confirmed it was human head hair. I then pressed the higher authorities with great pains over several months, but their findings were inconclusive. That is, if they searched at all."

"And if it was his doing… he just passes in his sleep and goes unpunished."

"Michael, vengeance is for the Lord. If he has done wrong, he is in the hands of God now. I know— it is difficult to accept, when all that you know is what you can see and hear."

"Will you also tell me it was wrong to thrash Gillman?"

It was a redundant thing to ask, but he desperately needed an answer, from *somebody*.

"That, I truly cannot say. We often find ourselves in such difficult situations. I cannot judge you for what you did in that moment: only for your subsequent conduct."

Dr. Webb took one of those long, dramatic draughts of his pipe until it was finished, and set it down to finish his verdict.

"But I will not repeat myself. You know how I feel, and what you have done wrong. As promised, all is forgiven now. You are back—

and I'm told you are an independent man now,
owning your own property?"

"Really, the latter was not an achievement on my
part. I only bought a small reserve of the Bennett
estate with the money from selling the rest of it."

"But in either case, you have your own means
now. Many young men of your station break into
two extremes: either they become miserly to the
point of counting every drop of oil in a lamp, or
they simply cannot hold onto their money and
take to spending far more than they can afford.
Initially I half expected you to turn to the
former, but I err. I imagine, though, that you
have good credit, and spend very wisely."

"I hired an advisor before making the purchase. I
struggle to do many things on my own, as I have
no servants. I have been cooking the very
simplest of meals, ruining cast iron kitchenware,
and venturing into town to get my clothes and
linens laundered."

"Really? It sounds as though you should have a
wife," he chuckled with a strange resonance.
"I'm sure that even with your irregular features,
there are many women eyeing you."

"No, sir. I tend not to be out and about enough
for women to even take notice of me to begin
with."

"No? A fellow your age should be socialising, so you don't end up a pitiful recluse like me," Dr. Webb stood up, and to Michael's surprise, he reached out his hand. "Well, it has been a pleasure to catch up with you a little. I shall be going up to the study for a while, as I still have work to do."

Michael wanted to talk to the doctor a little more, but did not pursue, as he sensed he was only making an excuse to take leave. Why he would do that, he did not know. Perhaps he was mentally fatigued by current events.

At any rate, he decided to rise from his seat and amble about the house. Soon, he found Sophie and a pair of grown kittens almost as big as she was.

"Sophie! Mama!" Michael knelt and held out his hands for the cats to smell. He cooed and stroked them, now understanding Alma's delighted squeals as they brought their spongy wet noses up to his cheek as if kissing him (or investigating the scent of blood). "So you do recognise me! I missed all of you while I was gone! Sorry I don't have any little treats for you."

He started when a door creaked open in the hallway. He knew exactly which door it was, and sprang to his feet. The cats howled in protest and rubbed their heads against his legs.

Alma was standing in the doorway of her chamber, in her plain grey wrapper.

"Alma, hello," Michael fought the urge to gather her to his breast and simply offered his hand. That was probably a safe gesture.

She took his hand but did not return the greeting, only stepped aside to allow him into her room. That shocked him, to say the least.

"Oh, you— I, um— alright, thank you," he stepped inside.

Her tables and shelves were neater than they had been when he was last there. The books and papers were stacked, and nothing was spilling onto the floor.

"What happened to your face?" Alma reached towards his bruised nose and lip, but did not touch.

"James."

She drew in a sharp breath and parted her lips as if to yell.

"No, no, it's alright, really," he stopped her. "I've gotten my face banged up so many times, it didn't even hurt."

"Sit down, then," she perched demurely on the edge of the bed.

Again, he took the safest option, and pulled out the chair at her desk, though it was a bit small, and he probably looked stupid with his knees tucked up to his sternum.

"And what have you been up to?" Michael asked.

"Working… walking around… drawing pictures."

"Drawing pictures? May I see them?"

She pointed to the books and papers behind him on the table.

"Oh, yes," he picked up a little book and flipped through its pages. It was mostly depictions of nature: insects, plants, and birds, captured in slightly messy and smudged but very detailed pencilled lines. They all had clearly been worked on with love and care.

"These are quite nice. Actually, they're lovely."

He grabbed a larger book, but instead of drawings, he found feathers, and pressed leaves and flowers, and all were labelled, with dates as old as four years ago and as recent as last week. They were preserved so artfully, and so well.

"You like nature, yes?"

"Yes, sir. You knew that."

"I did, indeed— I knew you enjoyed walks outside, but never knew you were inclined to document it. I wish you'd shown me these earlier. This is wonderful!"

"They are alright, I suppose."

"They are more than alright! They are lovely! Say it with your own mouth."

"They—" Alma quivered and grew red. "They are lovely… they are from nature, after all!" she added quickly at the end.

"Hmph! Perhaps you would like to come and see the woods around Brownwall? Take little walks there?"

"I think Brownwall is a silly name."

"It is, yes. But you didn't answer my question, Alma!"

"I would like to."

"Ah… with me?"

"Yes, with you."

That answer delighted him, but it led him to
other questions that he was initially afraid to ask.

"Then we are friends still, yes?"

"Yes," she answered with a reassuring firmness.

Friends, and what else? Before he questioned
her further, he realised he should have started
with how he'd felt; it had been eating him alive.

"Alma, I feel terrible," Michael began. "But I
imagine it doesn't come close to how you feel—
or have felt. I never meant to injure you. I've
never regretted anything more in my entire life,
and I can't begin to tell you how sorry I am," his
trembling voice warned him to keep the
sentiment brief. If he fell apart and wept, he
might have looked like a grovelling, desperate
rake. "I owe you an apology a thousand times
over, for many things, and I can't even think of
how I could make up for it, either. But I am
sorry, Alma."

"I know that."

"I don't expect things to go back to exactly the way they were. But do you forgive me, Alma?"

She blinked.

"It is quite alright if you don't!" he added quickly.

"Michael, I forgave you as soon as I saw you again."

He could not properly articulate his gratitude, so he only bowed his head low in reverence. He somewhat expected her to forgive him eventually, simply because that is what she would do, but that did not make him feel any less overwhelmed and grateful. He certainly wouldn't have forgiven himself.

She placed her hands on his head and stroked his hair.

"Things will not go back to the way they were. They will be better."

And then, as he closed his eyes, she slapped his face. Hard.

"Goodness! Everybody having a go at me today," he chuckled. "Have any more, do you?"

"No. I am satiated."

Michael seized her by her sleeves and pulled her close. She embraced him with no hesitation. The smell of her hair was exactly as he remembered it. Studying her closely, though, he saw that her nose, which had always been straight and sharp, now deviated ever so slightly.

"Oh, your nose!" he traced a finger down the new line it formed. "So it *is* crooked! Not nearly as much as mine, though. I didn't even notice until you got close."

She smiled and pressed it against his. Even after all of this time, touch was so easy and natural. He moved some of the soft fringe away from her forehead and saw a pallid, feathery mark where she had struck her head.

"And you have a scar here as well."

"I don't have one on my brow, yet," she reached up and touched the notch in his left eyebrow, where hair no longer grew. "Where did that come from?"

"A chicken."

She let out a sort of gasping little titter.

"A chicken?"

"Yes. I was maybe fourteen. I'd never gotten to handle the chickens before, and wanted to try it, so I followed a maid out into the yard. A rooster leapt right at my face. The noise it made was like a banshee! I probably didn't sound much different."

"You sure made a funny sound that first summer when you dropped a chicken egg."

"You saw that!" Michael did blush knowing this, but he wasn't really ashamed.

"Yes, and I told Papa that you just didn't get along with the chickens, so he needed to put you to work doing other things."

"Well… fowl have never been my friends, and neither have cats, until recently— it depends on the cat, I suppose. I'd refuse to fish or swim if there was a goose near the water. I could never even get a falcon my father had raised as a hatchling to like me."

Michael nearly panicked when Alma released him and began to lift up her skirt. She pulled the hem to just above her right knee and showed him a scar that made a clean, long streak like a pen stroke.

"What is that?" he moved to touch it, then
realised he probably shouldn't.

"I dropped a pair of big shears I was trying to
use when I was eight years old. I was trying to
cut up a length of ribbon. Mama was furious
with me for getting into her sewing box without
asking, but she considered the cut to be a
suitable punishment on its own."

"Did you cry?"

"I did. Not because of the cut— it didn't hurt. I
cried when Mama shouted at me."

"Shouted a lot, did she?"

"She did. It really frightened me when I was
little, but I know she didn't mean anything by it.
She had a lot to deal with by herself."

She said that, but he heard a quiver at the end of
her sentence, and saw her face was turning red.
Shouting still frightened her, and that revelation
only cut him even more. He drew her close to
him again and laid her head upon his shoulder.

"Will you be staying here long?" Alma asked
him. "If so, take your trunk into your room."

His room. It was his room, even now.

"I think I will stay for a day or two, unless you would have me here longer."

"It is up to you."

He stood and went to take his things into the old guest bedroom. It was in even better condition than it had been left in. The night he departed, he had left everything he did not pack scattered on the bed, table, and floor. All was put away… or thrown away?

"Everything is there," Alma confirmed, standing behind him. "I made it all neat after I searched your room… I still believed you would come back."

"The jewellery as well?" Michael reached for a key he'd tucked underneath a drawer in the wardrobe, and stooped down to unlock his treasure box. Sure enough, it still contained the carefully wrapped ornaments.

"Did you think I would steal it?"

"No, no! Frankly, though, I figured Dr. Webb would have pawned all of my belongings that I did not come back for, and rightfully so. But on that note… what happened to the ring?"

She reached into her bodice and produced a leather cord on her neck. The ring was at the end of it, and perfectly concealed when not displaced.

"You know, pearls last longer if they are tended to often," she commented. "They love to be touched. I know what people say about them, but I think that makes them quite charming for an engagement ring."

If she still kept it on her person, then surely that meant she would still consider herself his betrothed. Though it was a Christmas present first… he wanted to find out, but he could not muster the resolve to ask straightforwardly.

"You have claim to all of this, you know," he gestured at the collection. "It is properly for the Bennett ladies, but…"

His voice trailed off, but what he wanted to say was that he could not see himself marrying if Alma was not his. That had not changed. What purpose would he have to get married if not to her? Family obligations? He was his only family, save for some distant relatives scattered throughout the world. The Bennett house had already faded into oblivion, and if he couldn't marry her— his equal, his better likeness— he would be content if the name died with him, and Brownwall was torn down.

"Mother encouraged me to continue contact with
the suitors she set up," Alma said, as if knowing
his thoughts. "I told her I did not wish to marry. I
suppose that was only partially correct."

"Then you will marry me?" Michael rose from
his haunches and crossed the floor as lightly as
though preparing to fly.

"Yes, Michael."

She had taken the ring off of its cord and
presented it to him. He took it from her and put
it on her hand, where it belonged, and kissed her
fingers, then he kissed the bridge of her nose,
and smoothed away some of the hair on her
forehead once more and kissed that, too.

"Things will indeed be better than before, I
promise you that."

XXVIII

Perhaps the best part of his visit was sitting down to dinner just as he had before. Unfortunately, James took his plate into his room to avoid even looking at Michael. Dr. Webb gladly spoke to him (and didn't hit him), and was pleased to hear about the acquaintances he made. He said he was not concerned about Alma corresponding and visiting with Abraham, as he himself had already met him many times, and considered himself an excellent judge of character. Michael missed Alma's cooking more than just about anything in the world.

"So… if you wouldn't mind telling me, are the two of you still betrothed?" Dr. Webb lit his pipe after the meal as Alma cleared the table.

"Yes, sir. If it is alright, I would like to take Alma to Brownwall tomorrow. I think she should see the house… maybe think about all the bric-a-brac she'd like to put up that she can't have here. I'll be finally moving all of my rubbish out of your house, as well."

"She may go if she consents."

"I have plenty of time," she responded as she took Michael's empty plate. "I will go with you."

"That settles that, then," the doctor blew rings of smoke towards one of the cats (a calico like her mother, but with shorter hair) that had come into the kitchen. She tried to catch one, then wrinkled her little face at the odour.

"Have you named these two?" Michael offered his hand to beckon her towards him.

"That one is Flora; Alma named her. The red one is Fauna. James thought it would be funny. Before we gave away the black and white one, he wanted to name it Fungi."

Michael laughed, both because of the absurdity of the idea, and because Flora was strangely rubbing her teeth against his nails.

They gave scraps to the cats, and then they relocated to the parlour. Though it was summer, the doctor always liked a good fire in the evening. It was one of his few impracticalities, and a habit Michael took with him. He told Alma plenty about his work and what he'd been doing, but he omitted the details of his illness. He thought it might trouble her to hear about it, and it was all behind him now.

Alma described her work as a nurse. Most of it, she considered mundane and insignificant, such as giving medicine and sustenance, changing bandages, and writing down that she did so.

"That is invaluable support, Alma," Michael insisted. "It may not be difficult work, but anything would be tiresome after many hours, and it is more important than you can imagine, even just to know somebody is looking after you. That feeling alone can give somebody the resolve to live and recover."

"You say that as if you've felt that way."

"Yes, I've been sick as a young boy before. My mother appointed herself as my nurse. And you enjoyed your much-needed repose while infirmed, I remember... I only wish I was there to continue tending to you, but... well, it is what it is."

"Indeed," Alma pressed her face against him as a cat would, and then rose up to extinguish one of the lamps. "But since I will be travelling tomorrow, I think I should turn in early, and begin packing. You should as well."

"I will. Could I have a kiss before I retire, though?"

"You can," she kissed his chin, and ran a hand through his hair, taking a lock and stretching it out. "You most definitely need your hair cut, though. It is down to your shoulders."

"Not enjoying the untamed barbarian mane to match the untamed wilderness of Brownwall?"

She pursed her lips.

"Well, closely cropped hair does not fit your idiom, but I think it is as long as it needs to be," she smiled. "Besides, your hair is so lovely, I might just become envious if you allowed it to get any longer."

"It is quite coarse, though, not silken like yours, and it does not shine quite so nicely in this lamplight without the aid of rich oils."

"Perhaps. I am fond of the smell of those oils, but I really must go to bed."

"Your own bed?" Michael stood up and put out the other lamp.

"Yes, my own bed, and you to yours."

"Very well!" he huffed in feigned indignation. "Then I will see you in the morning, my flower," he kissed that beautiful hair and retired to his chamber.

Of course, before he lay in bed, he packed up everything that he had not taken with him before, including the jewellery and his rifle. It was difficult to fall asleep, as anticipation kept him agitated. He hoped Alma would like the house, and he was so excited to bring her to Abraham, though it just so happened that they had already met. Most of all, he wanted to take those walks they'd discussed.

In the morning, he washed and dressed himself in the dark, and they left the house as soon as it was light out. Alma's luggage was lighter than his, even though they were going to *his* home. His whole life, he was led to believe women packed far more than men. Now he wanted to know what she was taking with her, and how long she planned on staying.

"Alma! You're leaving? You just came back!" Ida came speeding towards them like a bullet just as they reached the street, carrying a confused and unfortunate Ruby with a red ribbon tied around her neck.

"Ida, I told you not to put such things on her neck! She could get hurt!" Alma seized the ribbon and carefully untied it.

"Where are you going, Alma? Where is he taking you? Is he going to disappear again and take you with him?" she ignored what her cousin said and continued to interrogate her, desperately shaking and squeezing the irate cat as she did so.

"I'm not going anywhere I don't want to, Ida! I am only visiting him for a little while, and seeing his new house! I'll come back."

"Could I come with you?"

Michael absolutely did not want Ida coming with them, but Alma made her silent request with a hopeful glance. He shook his head, and she only stared more intensely.

He sighed.

"Thirty minutes!" Michael barked at Ida. "You have thirty minutes to pack and meet us in town!"

Ida darted off as fast as she could without another word.

"Make sure your mother feeds Rub— oh, just give her to Uncle Henry!" Alma called after her.

They walked through many minutes of an unusually uncomfortable silence before Michael could muster up the courage to ask:

"Why must she come with us, Alma?"

"She is not accustomed to the idea of me being gone for so long."

"You are in London quite often, are you not?"

"I am, but this is different. I come back frequently, and would not do so when I am married. Maybe if she comes with us and sees me in your house, she will have an easier time accepting it when we are gone a long time. I will make her understand, I promise!"

"She is twelve, and you speak of her as though she were two! I don't understand the process myself, but I will trust you and hold you to your word," he relented.

It was just one trip, after all. He disliked the idea of Ida consuming all of her attention, but Alma did not belong solely to him. Besides, after the proper arrangements were made, Alma would live in his house.

"We will wait for her at the inn, because I'd been meaning to say hello to Mr. Briggs," he continued as he stopped in front of the establishment in question. As soon as he approached, the man himself emerged.

"Is that Mr. Bennett I see? Michael Bennett!" John Briggs leapt right over the steps in a single bound and crushed all of the wind out of him. "Ho, Mr. Bennett, 'ow 'ave you been, old boy?"

"All is well, Briggs!" Michael rasped with his last bit of breath and tried to return the embrace. "Sorry to have vanished for so long! I've planted roots up north, and Miss Webb is accompanying me… as well as her wonderful little cousin."

"'Ow nice, 'ow nice! And this is the future Mrs. Bennett!" Briggs released Michael and pat Alma's head a little too hard. She blushed and shrank away from the gesture. "My, last I see much of you, you were all bruised up! Nice to see you 'ealed up so well! What a handsome young lady, truly! All the best to you both!"

"Yes, to you as well," Michael answered him. "I'm glad you've gotten the inn repaired."

"All thanks to thee! Please, Bennett, tell me though: you will not be gone permanently this time? Will you come see a lonely old man once in a while?"

"Of course, Briggs! I couldn't stay away if I tried! However, we must be going, in order to catch the next trai—"

"WAIT!" Ida screeched, waving a worn leather bag.

"There she is!" Michael waved back, half hoping she wouldn't have arrived in time. "Well, come on then, Ida! And good day to you, Mr. Briggs," he briefly turned his attention back to the innkeeper before they went away with a breathless Ida at their heels.

Ida had never been on a train before, and she kept shouting with glee and telling Alma exactly what was out the windows. That wasn't the part that Michael took issue with: it was that she needed to look out of *everyone's* window, and she did not care whom she had to climb on for that view.

"Ida, sit down!" he entreated and placed her in a seat next to him. "Save your energy for the woods at Brownwall. Wouldn't you like to go exploring?"

"Exploring?" she was still at once, leaning forward expectantly.

"Yes! You and Alma both could frolic through the forest like little fairies and pick berries all day long until you grow sick of it!"

That got her to be stationary for the remainder of the train ride, at least. When they left the train, she was enamoured with her new surroundings. Strangely, she was not at all impressed when she reached the iron gate and beheld Brownwall standing proudly among the trees.

"Is that really your house? It's so ugly!"

"It is the dower house of the Bennett women, Miss Ida," Michael opened the gate and ushered the women in ahead of him.

"Dour house is more like it."

Michael thought it was funny, and surprisingly clever, but Alma apparently disagreed.

"Ida! You are a guest here, be polite!" she took her cousin's bag and hurried up the walkway as naturally as though she was already a resident.

"Miss Webb, my dear!" Abraham was ready to receive them at the door. "I did not expect you! And who is this charming young lady you have with you? Is this little Miss Ida herself?"

"I'm not little! I'm almost as tall as Alma!" Ida protested immediately. Michael would have to watch her closely and make sure she did not give Abraham too much trouble.

"Ah? Well, it is a pleasure to meet you, Miss," the old man bowed and took Ida's bag from Alma. "Come with me, and I'll show you to the room where you *and Miss Webb* will be sleeping," and he eyed Michael as he said this.

"Oh, *really!*" he hissed in response. Alma was not affected.

In the meantime, Michael brought the remainder
of his things into his own apartment. Ida's
chatter could be heard echoing through the
gallery. It seemed that she was more impressed
with the house, now that she realised its size.
Abraham was undoubtedly humouring her as
best as he could.

After an interval, Abraham and Alma began
politely bickering over who would be making
dinner. Though the exchange of words from both
parties was sweet and gentle, there was a
dangerous tension, as an unstoppable force and
an immovable object were competing for a space
that neither enjoyed sharing. It was decided that
Alma would do the fine work with a knife, as
her hands were still nimble. Abraham would do
the rest.

Ida, on the other hand, was restless, and vexed
that nobody was going out to explore with her,
as it would be too dark by the time dinner was
over.

Well, Michael was the only adult with nothing
productive to do that evening…

"I'll go out with you, Ida," he offered.

"With you?" she recoiled as if he was some
monstrous thing.

"Absolutely! I'm quite familiar with these woods, and I think I should be your guide."

She huffed and scoffed, pulling at her braids.

"If you would prefer Alma, you will just have to wait until she isn't busy. It may be dark by then."

"Fine!" Ida thrust her bonnet down onto her head and stomped towards the back door.

Though Michael did not eagerly anticipate an intimate evening with Ida, it was preferable to one or both ladies wandering into the woods on their own, not knowing what was out there, or how to get around. Even to somebody familiar with the trees, their shadows could be disorienting as it grew dark, and Ida was too careless to be trusted with a lantern.

The back garden was glorious, even when untamed. Lavender was abundant, and the climbing briar was heavy with ripe berries. The various shades of purple were brilliant against lush green foliage. A rainbow of wildflowers skirted the stone walkways. Winding, twisted bushes spilled onto the walk and bore clusters of small roses. Ida stopped to smell and pick to her heart's content.

It was damp and a little overcast after the mid morning's light shower. This was ideal for finding crawling creatures.

"Are there any wolves out here?" Ida asked behind him, taking a handful of berries to munch on, and standing at the garden's edge.

"Wolves? I highly doubt it."

"What about bats?" she inched back towards the house, away from the high grass, as if they would be crawling around on the ground.

"Oh, most definitely. Loads of bats."

He saw her fear and chuckled a bit.

"Bats will not bother you. They're little different from mice; they're mice with wings, Ida. Better than mice, actually. They eat mosquitos and don't tear open sacks of grain. I imagine most are sleeping at this hour, anyway."

Finally, she advanced into the grass.

"Truly, your biggest concern out here is ticks," he warned her. "Have Alma thoroughly check you when you go back inside. Actually, keep some of that lavender in your pocket. It repels them."

Michael saw that she had stuck sprigs of the flowers in her hair. Just as well. He continued walking along his usual path. If he didn't have Ida with him, he'd have probably sought a new, untouched stretch, at a much more reckless pace.

"Now, watch your feet," he pointed at the ground as they went deep into the trees, where the detritus was thick and the light was dim. "You might step on a little friend."

Just as he said that, she let out a terrible scream and rustled some greenery behind him. Birds went flying and bugs grew silent.

He turned at once and went to look for her. Of course, she had strayed from the trail; he found her crouched by a collection of rocks. Opposite of her, a snake was winding its way through a crevice in the crag.

"You found one!" Michael came close and stooped down next to it. "Excellent work!"

"Fool! It could have killed me!"

"Pish! It's just a grass snake!" he reached out and caught hold of it as it was making a hasty retreat, and presented it to her. "Couldn't hurt you even if it wanted to!"

"Don't snakes make venom?"

"Not all of them do. In fact, most don't, especially here."

"Why didn't it bite you?"

"I didn't squeeze him, and I didn't sneak up on him. You know, they're very shy, actually."

Ida was less frantic now that she saw it was right next to her face and wasn't trying to bite it off. Now, she looked curious.

"Could I touch it?"

"Yes! Be very gentle, though," he nudged its face away from Ida's, just in case it got anxious enough to strike. "I imagine it's quite nervous."

She reached out a trembling hand, and stroked its scales. It surprised him that she was suddenly so intrigued. He imagined that teaching her anything would be about as easy as carrying water in a burlap sack.

"It's not slimy," she declared.

"No, this is a reptile. Amphibians are slimy— like newts. We have more of those than snakes."

"You like them?"

"Yes, very much so."

"How did you learn about them?"

"Oh, I was terrified of them at about your age, as you were a minute ago. I heard many terrible stories of India's deadly cobras. One day, I come face to face with a humble grass snake outside, and realised it wanted nothing to do with me. So then, I set to researching them. My father's friend had a garden full of all kinds of creatures, and he paid a lot to maintain it. That is where I started to be truly fascinated, and now I work in that garden!"

"Really? Could I see it?"

"Ho— maybe. I'd have to see if Alma would consent, and when's a good time— oh, I should put this lad down. He's getting upset," Michael set the snake on the ground and watched it dart off into an unlit stretch. "We should walk back now. I imagine they'll be finished with dinner by the time we get inside."

Ida now followed close at hand, asking a plethora of questions about snakes that he did his best to answer. Obviously, he did not know everything there was to know, but he told her that many of her questions would be answered at a zoological garden, as its owner would have told her all that he knew, whether she asked him or not. Additionally, Michael had to promise that he would take her there, and she had to promise she would be on her best behaviour— of course, that didn't mean much for her.

He searched for other animals, but her stomping and shouting likely scared them into hiding.

After dinner, everyone herded into the parlour to listen to Michael practise the piano. Ida climbed into Alma's lap, but she was promptly asked to get off; she was too big. Once displaced, she gushed to Alma about snakes and handed her some of the lavender that was in her hair. Abraham tried to tell stories, but he sometimes got the events in the wrong order, and started the entire tale over again.

At one point, Michael was the only person left. Abraham retired to bed early, and then Alma took Ida to bed, not taking no for an answer. He carried his improvised tune to a warbling loop that he was not sure how to bring to a satisfying conclusion. The activity was no longer cathartic, but now he couldn't finish. It continued for maybe six frustrating minutes before breath on his ear made him stop abruptly, on a terrible note.

"Oh. Will you play with me?" Michael asked Alma, as she had come in silently and seated herself beside him on the stool.

"I don't think I could."

"I could teach you," he took one of her hands and placed it on the keys. "Have you read music?"

"I learned by ear in the church choir. I don't think that signifies."

"Ah! Then I will play if you sing for me," he flipped through the selection of music to find a hymn she might have been familiar with.

"I don't sing well. My voice was masked by the crowd."

"Your voice is the sweetest music. I cannot leave the piano until I finish a tune. Guide me so that I might accompany you, please."

She picked the song that she wanted: *Come Thou Fount,* cited as a favourite of her father's.

Michael was unfamiliar with it, but it seemed a very simple arrangement. Alma hummed and played with the notes on the piano until she found what she wanted; he chose a key based on where she stopped. He played, and Alma straightened up and threw back her shoulders, ready to sing and put effort into it.

Her voice was soft and wavering, and sometimes
flat, but clear. It increased in intensity as the
verses progressed, resonating through the
spacious parlour and likely reaching the rest of
the house. It wavered more when he looked her
in the eye, and his gaze drew a blushing smile
from her, making the tone brighter and less
solemn.

Even for the little shortcomings, her singing was
more mesmerising than the reading. Now, he had
to figure out how to get her to do this often. This
melody was what he needed to finish playing; he
came to a sound resolution just as the final verse
drew to a close.

"Prone to wander, Lord I feel it
Prone to leave the God I love
Here's my heart, oh take and seal it
Seal it for Thy courts above"

He put up the music.

"Thank you, Alma!" Michael pulled her face
close to his and kissed her trembling lips. "You
complement my playing flawlessly. I'd even say
we could make a career of it."

"I don't think I would do well with a large
audience in a music hall," she lowered her head
and folded her hands in her lap.

"Nor a small audience of aristocrats in a pretty drawing room? Well, I like it between just the two of us, anyway. It's special. Would you be inclined to learn some contemporary pieces? I would teach you if you'd like."

"Perhaps. I have much to focus on as of now, though."

"I suppose that's true, especially with Ida in tow! Well, what do you think of the house? Too spacious for you?"

"No, it is suitable," she looked around the parlour, which was maybe a third of the size of the Webbs' first storey. "I think it would give me more freedom to decorate as I please."

It delighted him and set him at ease to know that she was already considering making the house her own. Now that he thought of it, the feminine furnishings of his chamber would probably be appropriate for her. As for him, he did not have any opinion either way as long as there was a bed and a roof.

"What do you think you would do first?"

"I like this wallpaper," she decided. "But the drapes are too intense. Pink by itself is not very relaxing. I imagine I would make them ivory or a soft, light brown that would still match the rest of the parlour."

"If I remember correctly, my grandmother was an intense lady. But so are you, just in a different way."

"I am intense?"

"Yes, in the best of ways!" Michael drew her to his side. "You are passionate and strong-willed, yet so gentle. That is where your power lies: you influence people passively, and master them with words."

"But… I am given to weeping, as you know."

"Because you *feel,* Alma. You feel things more strongly than most, and it makes you tender and sensitive."

Her brow knit together and she gazed out the window, as if she had great difficulty in making sense of what he'd said.

"My mother did not think so. She thinks it is a weakness needing to be overcome."

"Well… everyone has their own manner of thoughts and feelings, and maybe she should be mindful of that. And though it is a bit late, I should apologise for how I handled your feelings. I'm sorry I was cold towards them for so long. You are not *predictable,* Alma. You are more surprising and more stimulating than anybody I've met."

She turned her face towards the light, and he saw that she was quite florid, and her eyes were wet. She smiled broadly and leaned into his side.

"That is everything I needed to hear my whole life!" Alma sobbed, but the tone was of relief and gratitude. "I love you!"

"I love you, Alma," he cooed and gathered her to him so that she was completely flush with him. "I would do anything to make you as happy as you make me."

"Don't leave me again," she begged him.

"I promise, I won't! I couldn't possibly. If I tried, I don't think I'd live!"

She stood quite suddenly, almost knocking him off of the stool as she did so.

"Well, I can't leave you, but you can leave me?" he huffed and seized her waist.

"I am going to have some water and then go to bed, I think," she picked up the candle on the piano.

She walked towards the kitchen, and he followed, with his hands on her shoulders.

"What are you doing?" Alma looked back at him as she filled a glass.

"I'm not leaving you for even one second."

She sipped from the glass, then handed it to him half-full.

"I will be going to bed when you finish that water."

"Which bed?" Michael freed one hand to take the glass, and let the water just touch his lips.

"The little bed I share with Ida upstairs."

"And leave me to perish, will you? I promised I would not leave you, and would die if I made an attempt."

"Then do so, and I will retrieve your corpse in the morning."

"But Alma," he swallowed the contents of the glass and set it on the kitchen table, then twined his arm around her and led her towards the staircase. "Will you have a look at the apartment I inhabit? You will bed there when we are married, so I'd say you should examine it and tell me what you think."

"I will, if you insist," she let herself be escorted to the upstairs gallery, and he opened the door, making a grand gesture at its lavish interior. She held out the candle and peered inside.

"I like the curtains on the bed," she decided.

"Is that all? Look at all of this space! You could frame your drawings and little feather collections. Line the walls with them. Fill the whole house with them."

She stepped into the bedchamber, and brought the light up to the large vanity table.

"Drawers for all the jewels and powders and lace you could ever want," he observed.

"I doubt I'll use even half of these drawers."

"And the bed?" Michael beckoned her towards it. "There is plenty of room."

She bent over it and inspected the bedding.

"These are good linens."

"They are! They are worn soft as down, but very sturdy," he climbed into bed and moved to make a space for her. "Try them."

Alma giggled incredulously.

"Michael, I have to go to sleep."

"Correct," he plumped up a pillow for her.

She shifted her weight a few times and set the candle down. Its flame illuminated her burning red face.

"I only want to lie down beside you, that is all!" Michael insisted. "I missed it more than I can explain. This room is nice, but it's lonely."

"I did leave Ida in there by herself…"

"You need not be constantly attached to Ida's side just because she is here," said he. "She is not a little baby. She should get more used to not having ownership of you, and you don't need to be responsible for her at all times… do whatever you'd like."

Alma looked at the door, at Michael, and at her feet.

"What do you want?"

He leaned forward, waiting for her decision. After a stretch, she removed just her brooch and stockings, and climbed into bed beside him almost fully dressed, with her hair in plaits. She extinguished the candle, and then he could only smell her and hear her breath.

"The door is open," she noted.

"It's alright," he murmured, and nestled close to her, as he did not have the willpower to stand up. He could not run his fingers through her hair, so he grasped one of the braids and wrapped it around his hand. Drifting off to sleep with Alma beside him was much different from dropping off from exhaustion after hours of labour. Either way, he fell asleep almost as soon as he shut his eyes.

XXIX

Michael awoke at some time early in the morning, and reached for Alma's warmth. In the sun's first rays slicing through the curtains, he could hardly see. Something was very wrong. He pawed at the body next to him; the neck, shoulder, hand, and clothes were not familiar. Even the breathing was different.

"Ida!" wide awake in an instant, he tore the linens off as she squirmed and rubbed her eyes. "What are you doing in my bed?"

"The door was open!" she whined in a sleepy drawl.

"Where is Alma?"

"She left just now to go make breakfast."

"Did she not wake you up?"

"She did, and I told her I would be up in a few minutes."

"Your few minutes have passed. Go get dressed, and let me do the same."

She groaned and rolled off the edge of the bed, tumbling to her knees and then springing up like a weed to bolt out of the room.

"This room is pretty," she added as she stuck her head in one last time.

"Away with you!" Michael waved her out and shut the door behind her so that he could change his clothes and cleanse himself of the sensation of having touched Ida.

After he shaved and washed in the cold water, he made his way downstairs, lured out by the smell of frying ham.

Ida was at the stove with Alma, as she was trying to teach her the fundamentals of cooking. Reportedly, Alma had begun when she was eight, and thought Ida was at an appropriate age to learn. She watched and listened intently: likely because Alma was teaching her.

"Let me make coffee," Michael volunteered, as he saw none had been made.

"I did not know there was any!" Alma admitted. "You drink coffee now?"

"No, nor does Abraham, but… I've been saving it. You can rummage through the cupboards all you wish."

Abraham was the last to wake up. That was no surprise. As much as he liked to work, he loved to sleep, and if he had no work to do, he would gladly take advantage of the spare time.

Ida wanted to explore the third storey, and Michael accompanied her so that she didn't destroy anything. There was a large, empty room at the back end of the house that he had not paid much attention to. It would probably make a great office, study, or laboratory— whichever he eventually needed.

She found the trunk full of porcelain dolls, and was immediately taken with them.

"How pretty!" Ida recklessly dislodged them from the tattered silk. "I've never had nice dolls before! Alma made me some with clothes pegs, and then I got one made of cloth."

"You can have one," Michael offered. "Nobody here is using them."

That was true, but then there was no reason for her to not have all of them. He had no desire to sell them, and strangely enough, he felt inclined to save them. Ida chose a doll with black hair and delicate red and white robes. She did not object to only being able to have one, surprisingly.

"Take two. She should have a friend," he considered it a reward for not being greedy.

"Really!" Ida's eyes brightened. "Which can I take?"

"Doesn't matter to me. Whatever you want."

She took a second doll in a blue dress, and then ran downstairs, presumably to show Alma.

When he went and found Ida, she had turned a wooden trunk into a house for her dolls to share, and folded a sheet into a little bed for them. Alma made a napkin into a very crude shape of a dog. A handkerchief wrapped around a peg was a baby.

"They're married," she declared.

"Married? They're women," Michael knelt and tapped on the two dolls.

"Well there weren't any man dolls, so they have to be married."

"Why are you so preoccupied with marriage?"

"Why are you?"

"I'm an adult with somebody to marry. You're a child with plenty of time."

"So you're getting married because you're out of time?"

"No!" he rubbed his eyes and stood up. "Time is not the issue here. What I mean is that you need not be concerned about it now… well, it's your playtime. Do as you please."

"Alma won't be a good wife, by the way."

He turned around on his way out, even though he knew it was foolish to dignify her antics.

"What makes you say that?"

"She's quiet and nice, but she won't do what you tell her to."

"Well, that doesn't signify. I don't expect her to," he left her alone.

Abraham played cards by himself in the parlour with a glass of rum. He offered some to Michael, but he declined, as he was not on good terms with alcohol for the time being. It made him nauseous just thinking of how sick he was that one winter…

Instead, he took Alma on a walk around noon, as he'd wanted to all this time. She took a book lined with loose papers to press flowers that interested her. It seemed she loved the outdoors much more than the interior. She stopped in the garden first, and he could see she was making mental notes of what she wanted to plant, and maybe what she wanted to do with the ripening berries. It greatly pleased him to see her planning to carve out her own place in his world, and cultivate his garden.

She stepped very lightly behind him, and generally did not touch anything except to pick up a snail and admire it, or collect fallen feathers. Not only did she mark and preserve them, but she used them in various decorations, especially for hats. It shocked him to see her picking up snails, but it pleased him, too.

As for him, he was seeking bigger prey: newts and toads.

"So, you like furry and feathered friends, yes?" he asked. "Then you would surely not shy away from other crawling things. Only real difference is the exterior."

"I don't mind other animals, but I've never really gotten close. What are you trying to suggest, though?" Alma came up to his shoulder as he stalked along the edge of a shallow pool. He agitated the surrounding grass with his boot toe.

"I'm suggesting," he plucked a toad that reared its head. "That you broaden your horizons and make new friends."

He presented it to her, and she shrank away, but with a look of surprise, not fear or disgust.

"Don't those carry diseases?"

"All creatures carry diseases. Humans carry diseases. It's no more infectious than the cats you play with, or your patients, for that matter," he held it plumb to her face. "It's just a little slimy. Take it."

She stared at him for quite a while, as if he'd completely lost his mind. Maybe he had, but the toad was unrelated. Slowly, she set her book down and cupped the creature in her hands.

"See? It's not so bad, is it?" he freed his fingers.

The poor toad writhed and struggled in her weak grasp, lunging towards her face, as that was where it was pointed. She gave a little yelp and let go, letting it drop into the grass where it made its escape.

"Oh— I'm sorry, I didn't think it would frighten you!" Michael bit down hard on his lip to stifle his laughter. "When you brought it close to your face, I imagine it thought you'd devour it."

"Did I hurt it?" Alma stepped back and looked around on the ground as she retrieved her book.

"I doubt it. Probably scared it to death, though," they continued walking. "Well, I'd like you to get used to them. Would you be opposed to possibly accompanying me to an animal exhibition in Bristol? I promised I would take Ida. I wouldn't bring you anywhere dangerous."

"I suppose I wouldn't mind."

"Wonderful! Before we go back, I'd like to show you my favourite clearing just beyond this set of trees," he pointed southeast and ducked beneath a low branch that Alma passed under with ease.

They came to a well-lit stretch that was divided by a fallen tree. He seated himself upon it and placed Alma on his knee.

"Is this not a fantastic view?" Michael asked. "The garden is at the back of the house, and you can see the road from the front, but there is nothing man-made in sight out here. It's as though we were the only two people in the world: just Michael and Alma Bennett."

She frowned.

"Alma Bennett is so strange. I am not used to hearing it."

"You'd better get used to it. That will be your name very soon."

"How soon?"

"I'd hurry you to the Bennett family chapel and marry you before the sun sets on this day if you wanted. I guess, though, that you want a formal reception: a small one."

"I would, sir. I have friends and family who would wish to attend, and I need to make it known to them."

"Right, yes. In that case… I'm looking at a month? Maybe two?"

"Some time next year, I imagine."

"Next year! Do you mean to delay it as long as possible? Do you have second thoughts already?"

"No!" Alma shook her head and drew closer to him. "I simply have things I would like to arrange by myself before I get married. And since I want things to be formal, it would require a great deal of planning as well."

"Hmm," he pondered this and relaxed a bit. Michael did not have much family himself, but he wanted to meet hers. Luckily, he doubted she would pressure him for an extravagant wedding that demanded a year of preparation. She was not the sort; in fact, she discussed marriage itself far more than the wedding, the dress, or anything else. She hadn't spoken of her dress ever since finishing it, and he still wanted to know what she had done with that lace he bought.

"And do you worry that I would take you from your profession?" Michael asked finally.

"No."

"Good, I was only making sure. I would wait as long as you want me to, if I only have your promise of marrying me," he decided. "Jacob toiled for fourteen years, after all."

Alma raised an eyebrow. His biblical analogy seemed to please her.

"Don't you have any affairs you would like to have in order?" she asked.

In truth, he'd not considered that question until he was asked just now. Now that he had the home and the means, he'd only thought of making her his wife. However, he often wasn't at home for days or even weeks at a time, and how compatible would that have been with her desires? Would she come with him? More than that, he wanted to travel… and Alma likely still wanted to travel as well.

"I have made my nest, and it is ready, though I see the benefit of waiting," was all he said. "I'd not seen you in so long, though, it simultaneously feels as if we'd been separated for an eternity, and also that no time has passed at all. Don't you think so?"

"That makes sense, though I suppose it's easy to look back and say that when you are no longer living in those days."

"Were you pining for me endlessly?"

"I could not. I mourned you, but I had work to do, and my feelings could not get in the way of that."

Right. Her work ethic was unrivalled, and while she laboured away to better herself and do what she wanted, he moped in an empty house and talked to the spiders on the walls; admittedly, he made a handful of great friends that weren't spiders.

"If you would like to do some of that planning now, we can walk back to the house," Michael offered.

"No. I can handle it after dinner. I want to be out here a little longer."

"That is perfectly well with me," he took her hands and twined them around his neck.

The sky became overcast, and the air seemed to thicken. There was a single strong breeze in the stillness: the kind that subtly warns of inclement weather. It would probably rain again. Michael did not mind the rain, so he would move if she did. His only mistake was closing his eyes and relaxing a little too much.

When he opened them, he was spilling over the edge of the tree trunk, and it was too late to catch himself.

"Oh, no," he murmured as he went down, ready to accept his fate.

Alma squealed as she fell upon him, grasping at his coat as if it would stop his fall. He hit a patch of soft, damp moss and leaves.

"Ah, sorry. Are you alright?" he struggled to sit up.

She giggled, and he did too, because the fall gave him a sort of rush.

"Let's go back, then," he stood up, wanting to walk off the soreness.

Alma and Ida went back home four days later, and while Michael was escorting them to the train, he had to promise numerous times that he would bring them to Bristol with him by autumn.

Mr. Kelley didn't mind Michael bringing Alma and Ida, and though he had been so averse to the institution of marriage, he expressed approval at the woman Michael described Alma to be.

He asked Abraham to come along, but he declined, saying he no longer enjoyed travelling, and was content to stay home and keep house.

"Not even to see Mr. Kelley's fantastic creatures and familiar face?" Michael folded up the letter and put it back in its envelope.

"The truth is," he sighed and pulled on some fingers. "I never did get on well with Mr. Kelley. He was haughty, and a bit brash. Not a bad man by any means, he lived and breathed for his animals— married to his work, as I'd used to fancy myself— but a very abrasive fellow."

Michael remembered very little of his old mannerisms, so he could neither confirm nor deny such a claim, as he couldn't make a proper comparison.

"It has been a few years. He no longer travels. Maybe he has mellowed out."

"Maybe. I'd still prefer to stay put, if that's alright with you."

"Of course, do as you please! Do take care of yourself, though."

"Always. You don't live this long by letting yourself rot."

Some days, Michael felt that his body was already ruined in his early twenties. His knees sometimes ground and cracked when he bent them to lift something heavy or even just scale the stairs. Normally, he could ignore it.

Sometimes, he still boxed at the docks. It was easy money, as well as an outlet for the energy he had to spare. They were most enthusiastic about having him fight the largest man on the dock, a real behemoth almost a head taller than

Michael. Truly, he was a giant, with arms thick as tree trunks, and a barrel for a chest.

The fight proved to be an utter disappointment. For all their boasts, he was inexperienced. Where he had the advantage of being bigger and seemingly stronger, he knew it too well, and wore himself out in the first minute. Michael only needed to evade him until his strikes slowed, and then the fight was his.

Still, Michael took a hard blow to the right side of his face before he brought his opponent down. There was a sort of snapping sensation in his mouth, and a sharp pain that shot into his eye, but he ignored it until the match was brought to an end.

He was met with approval and even applause once he had triumphed. Now that he wasn't fighting, the pain was a dull throb that spread through his jaw. Probing with his tongue revealed a loose bottom tooth, and the faint taste of blood.

"Good match, old boy," Michael spoke through the corner of his mouth and tried in vain to steady himself. He fought hard to keep from vomiting.

He went straight home and didn't tell Abraham, because he would have ordered him to visit a dentist, and the mere thought made him nauseous and sent a rush of prickly cold down his spine.

Of course, the old man caught him tying a silk thread around his teeth and swabbing them with whiskey. Sticking his fingers in his mouth made him keck.

"Michael, you lunatic!" Abraham scolded him. "Even if that tooth stays, it'll be all crooked! You simply must see a dentist."

"My teeth are already crooked. And crooked as they may be, I've got a good, full set of them that I take care of."

"You also have an ancestral predisposition to pretending bad things aren't happening."

"I don't need a dentist."

"Promise me you'll go if it becomes inflamed. You know, an aunt of mine left a bad tooth untreated for weeks, and one day, she just had an apoplectic attack and dropped dead in the kitchen."

If it became inflamed, he could yank it out himself.

"It won't kill me, Abraham."

The tooth didn't kill him, but it didn't stay. It slipped out painlessly.

Alma continued to send him letters. She detailed her work (some cases were even comical, such as one instance involving a bottle removed from the body, and a large quantity of opium) and what she did with her savings. Her living quarters were also described in great detail: four women shared two rooms with one window and no privacy, and London was even more repulsive than he imagined. He wanted to move her away from that foul air as soon as possible. Of course, rampant poverty lacerated her tender heart.

And what did Michael do with his time? He worked for Mr. Kelley, and then he came home and tapped on the piano until he couldn't keep his eyes open. He often lamented over supper that in his current state, he simply wasn't adequate enough to lead a household and support a wife.

"Master Bennett, I realise this is none of my business, eternal bachelor that I am," Abraham mused as he poured a glass of bourbon for Michael. "And I know I'm essentially trying to control the weather. But Alma has been doing just fine without you, has she not?"

"… indeed she has," he didn't touch the glass.

"She can lead herself. Worry about yourself for now. You aren't married yet."

"In that case, what does she need me for?"

"She doesn't. But she does like you. Is that enough?"

"It is," Michael swallowed the bourbon and told himself it was enough over and over until he believed it.

XXX

Some time in early autumn, Ruth dropped in for a visit by herself, because she heard Alma would be there at the same time (without Ida), and she desperately wanted to meet her.

"Mr. Bennett!" Ruth gave him a kiss at the door. "And Miss Alma!" she kissed her as well, much to her bewilderment.

"Hello, *Mrs. White!*" he took her bags as she came in. "And how is the old mister?"

"He's well!" she chirped. "And he has a young son from his first wife, and he keeps me quite busy!"

"Oh! Tell me about that, and we'll have some tea!"

Michael brought it into the parlour himself, and Abraham showed her to her room, which she'd share with Alma.

Up until tea was served, Alma had been mostly silent, nodding and smiling dutifully when acknowledged, and replying with only one word; meanwhile, Ruth chattered away, about anything and everything, and Michael struggled to keep up. He knew Alma was very shy, so her silence did not signify to him, at least until he registered that Ruth had been clasping his hand the entire time they spoke.

"Ah, pardon," Alma finally spoke up, with a slight blush illuminating her cheeks, and she held up the paper she'd kept at her side. "Miss, you are so lovely… would you let me draw you?"

Ruth blushed an even deeper red.

"Why, ain't you sweet!" she stood up and smoothed her hair. "You really think so?"

"Oh, yes, you are one of the prettiest ladies I've ever seen. I'd love to draw your picture."

"My! Then I should do something nice with my hair, I suppose."

"Oh, please, take it down!" Alma pleaded, taking Ruth's hand and leading her away from the table. "Natural curls are so rich and elegant. They should be free! We must go out into the sun!"

The two ran outside, and Michael was not allowed to watch, so he played cards with Abraham.

Alma would not let him even see the drawing of Ruth. She considered it a secret between two women, but she did confide in him late at night.

She came straight into his room, and he was not ready. Even though she could not have seen much, he started and threw on a robe when she opened the door.

"Miss Ruth is truly lovely, one of the prettiest ladies I've ever seen," she spoke into the darkness from the armchair by the bedside table.

"She is a pretty lady, yes," he sat up in the bed and fumbled anxiously in the dark to light a candle. "What of it?"

"To tell you the truth," her voice now wavered. "I was quite envious of her."

"Envious? What for?" Michael peered at her lovely face as it waxed and flickered in the dim light.

"Her beauty, of course. I'd even say it somewhat intimidated me. So I made her my muse as a way to make peace with these feelings. An artist appreciates natural beauty, and to see her with an artist's eye— to exalt how the Good Lord had blessed her— would free me of that wickedness."

He used to envy the more slender and streamlined of his peers, and any man with smooth skin and an unbroken nose. He didn't really have the time to be self-conscious in recent days, but even now, he thought he and his future bride were a bit unmatched in their looks.

"Well, Alma," he cast an appreciative gesture over her. "Ruth is beautiful in a different way, and I'm sure her husband likes her perfectly well. As for you: you are a beauty crafted exactly to my liking."

Her lips parted, but he stopped her.

"Don't deny it. You *are* beautiful, and to say otherwise would be calling me a liar."

She only laughed, and fled from the room.

That morning, he and Alma rose at dawn to send Ruth off. This time, she returned Ruth's embraces.

He was hoping to never mention it, but curiosity got the better of him.

"Did you ever get word from Peter?" he asked as he carried her bags to the train.

She stopped.

"No," she admitted. "I can't write to him, because I was never told where he went. I was meaning to ask you…"

"I've not heard from him, either. Perhaps his letter got lost in transit. He's all the way in Europe, after all."

"Yes, yes! I'm still waiting for him!" Ruth answered gaily, though despite her cheerful tone, he sensed a degree of hopelessness.

As for Michael, he tried hard not to assume the worst. One way or another, he knew inwardly that he had lost a friend. He decided, for once, not to pay mind to things beyond his control, and to focus on the near future.

He interrogated Alma on their walk that day, since marriage was fresh on his mind.

"Well, Alma, it has been a month since we last discussed the wedding in detail. Do you have a date set now?"

"December will do nicely," she answered firmly.

"December of this year? Now we're getting somewhere!" Michael was elated now that he actually had a month to plan around, even if she hadn't yet selected a specific day. "I'd ask why you didn't choose to wait until spring and be a blushing June bride, but perhaps I shouldn't push while I'm ahead."

"I can blush in any month of the year. I like winter, anyway."

"What do you need to do in the meantime?"

Her face brightened, as it always did when her ambition was allowed to shine.

"You know, I feel a bit silly, turning a blind eye to the needs of my countrymen because I was so enticed by foreign soil. I don't need to travel abroad to do God's work—"

"So you no longer wish to travel?"

"No— yes— I didn't say that. I'm saying that nothing is holding me back but my own willpower, and it was the lack of experience and stimulation that made me feel more frustrated and defeated than I'd realised."

"Certainly makes sense. I imagine my blockheaded remarks didn't help your resolve."

A wicked little smile pulled at her lips.

"They did. I wasn't about to let this rich fool who couldn't iron his own trousers tell me what's what."

"I'll have you know, Miss," Michael patted down a stray lock of her hair that hung above her eye.

"I can indeed iron my trousers, and I happen to think scorch marks are very fashionable. The reason I haven't made this fashion statement public yet is because the world simply isn't ready for such ingenuity. But continue. I derailed you."

"Thank you," the smile turned sweet, and she put the hair back where it was, just to anger him. "You know I've spoken in great lengths about the horrendous conditions of London. It's deplorable, and a crime against all living things. You fret over a murdering lunatic tearing through Whitechapel, but I'm sure filth would more likely be my end."

"And this is meant to make me enjoy you living there?"

"No. It's meant to make you hate it, that's my point. Officials have put measures into place to improve the quality of life, but I don't feel they're moving fast enough. I need help, though."

"What would you have me do?"

"I would have you aid me with strength, and with your influence as a man of rank."

"In case you haven't noticed, my dear, my rank is empty."

"The title is enticing to associate with, and your singular position would make you more attractive to the common folk: instead of gambling away what little you had left and marrying into easy money or falling into poverty, you kept yourself afloat and integrated into the labouring class."

"I barely succeeded. I stubbornly refused to better myself, ran away from my benefactors, and almost died."

"But you succeeded. And I am aware of your wishful thinking in those days. You were misguided and ignorant, but for better or worse, you believe in things more strongly than most would dare to. I recognised that early on, and that fascinated me."

"Well, I recognised right away that you were a creature forged in the flames of my deepest passions, and I loved you and had to make you mine."

"You did not."

Little sprite! He knew his pathos had an effect on her, and she was just too stubborn to accept it.

"I am telling you I loved you the moment I saw you! Are you calling me a liar, when I already asked you not to?" Michael pinched her ear as he interrogated her.

"No, sir. I do believe you think that, but your memories are clouded by your feelings. You could not have known at that time."

"Really! Well, who's coarse and unsentimental now?" he pulled her face close. "Are you telling me you felt nothing?"

"I didn't say that," she withdrew, but her lips were taut, her face was completely flushed, and he could feel the heat coming off of her skin.

"And what did you feel?"

"Perplexed by this large creature in my kitchen."

"Alright," he released her. "Keep your secrets."

"Then will you assist me?"

"Nothing would make me happier. All of my resources are at your disposal, but I should warn you: you must start small."

"I'm aware, and thank you. I did like you, by the way."

"You did!" Michael lunged towards her as she stepped out.

"Indeed, I always have," she spun around on her heels and ran up the walkway before he'd even processed the end of her sentence, and the crunched, swirling leaves were the only evidence of her existence.

She went back to London the following Tuesday, and already, she sent him letters about her plans. He mulled over her ideas and intentions many times, as they intrigued him; he would have been glad to assist in any way that he could, as the cause was worthy, and, of course, he felt it was the least he could do.

He took Alma and Ida to Bristol with him in late September, before the animals would be put away for the year. Ida would not be content until she saw the snakes. She was rattling around the train during the entire trip, and it took a great deal of effort to temper her by the time they arrived; he only managed that by telling her most reptiles are easily frightened. They had their belongings checked into the hotel before they set out.

"There you are!" Mr. Kelley waved them down at the entrance. "Good to see you, as always! And who are these beautiful wee biddies you've brought? Which is your betrothed? The spirited one looks rather young, not even thirteen…" he narrowed his eyes. "I say, you aren't one of *them,* are you?"

"Ah, *this lady* is Miss Alma Webb, my betrothed," he gestured to her, and she curtseyed. "And the small one is Ida Clarke, her dear, precious cousin."

Ida did not share Alma's meekness, and skipped right up to Mr. Kelley.

"I was told you have snakes from Asia and Africa," she certainly didn't beat around the bush. "Could I see them?"

Alma was visibly disturbed by her lack of manners, but didn't say anything. Mr. Kelley, however, did not care.

"Ho, ho! I like this one already! Well, right this way," he turned without waiting for them, and Ida followed at his heels, asking any question that tickled her brain. She even asked him about bats, and he admitted that mammals were not his area of expertise.

"He is excitable, isn't he?" Alma noted, lingering at the rear of the group.

"Indeed he is," Michael replied, taking the liberty of wearing a small python on his neck.

"He may be the only person able to match Ida's energy."

"I wonder how long this fixation of hers will last."

"Is that what you think it is? Well, Ida reminds me a bit of myself when I was a child. I was a brat, never able to sit still, never where I was supposed to be, and never did well in my grammar classes— reading was no issue; it was writing that I hated."

"You write me letters all the time."

"One must give to receive. Writing for school was dull, but it is never a chore to tell you about my day, and nobody grades my letters."

"Should I?"

"Only if you never want me to write you again. But I digress: animals— nature in general— it always had my attention. So did music, to a lesser extent. I'm a competent pianist, but I wouldn't make a career out of it."

Ida dragged Alma away to show her whatever creatures caught her attention. Surprisingly, she was quite bold in approaching them, and Alma was fearful, but somewhat at ease knowing they were in secure enclosures. She kept Ida from sticking her hands inside.

"Miss Webb, is it?" Mr. Kelley called to Alma. "I don't believe we've spoken yet. How do you like this garden?"

"Oh, it's nothing you'd find out in the countryside," she replied breathlessly. "But I'm impressed, to say the least. How long have you been constructing it?"

"Nearly thirty-five years, now. Well, this young lad here has told me before that you have a keen fondness for God's green earth. Would you say so?"

"I suppose it is so. I've never seen any animals quite like these before, though."

"Nor have I!" Ida chirped. "I'd like to take one home!"

"Certainly not! Your cat would eat it or be eaten herself, assuming you didn't let it escape," Michael stopped her in her tracks.

Mr. Kelley agreed: "Aye, he's right, little one. This is where they belong."

"How did you find yourself bound to such a timid woman?" Mr. Kelley interrogated him off to the side. "You told me what a fiery and determined spirit she has, and so far, she has not delivered. I'd say your judgement is altered by her beauty, but she's a fairly plain one. Good, strong shoulders, though, from the looks of her. Nice hips."

"You must be patient with her," he said as he nudged the python's little head away from his eye. "This is all new to her, after all, and unlike Miss Ida, she was raised to be cautious."

"I surely hope you're right, or I daresay you'll never be pleased with her."

Is that how such events went for him?

Unfortunately, it was soon time to depart so that he could deposit the ladies back home.

"Good luck to you, Michael Bennett. I look forward to seeing you come back to work," Mr. Kelley smacked him on the back, which was a highly affectionate gesture for him. "Say— where will you take your bride, if— *when* you marry her?"

"She's never been to the continent, but I considered taking her southwest to see those beautiful mountains," Michael decided.

The old man scoffed.

"Those foothills? Take her to India, or far, *far* west across the pond. That's where the real mountains are, untamed by man."

"I will take that into consideration. Thank you very much, and good day to you," he hastily choked out a definite goodbye, because as inspiring as Mr. Kelley's impassioned speeches about nature were, there was just no time.

When they were settled into their apartment at the hotel, Ida commented:

"I didn't like that queer old man, but I want to see the snakes again."

Michael laughed even though he felt she should have been scolded. She kept flicking her tongue in and out of her mouth for the rest of the day, and as she'd never been in a hotel before, she had to be warned many times that she could not wander off wherever she pleased.

XXXI

After Ida had gone to sleep, Michael went to Alma to make a few propositions as she read her bible by the candlelight. He brought forth the idea of her spending time in Bristol with him, as he would be gone for days at a time, and it would be a splendid opportunity for her to draw some enchanting creatures. After he promised her that she would be perfectly safe (safer than in London, at least), she warmed up to the proposal. That was easy.

"And what would you think of visiting the United States?" he asked.

"When?"

"This December, soon after we are married; it's about a three weeks' passage, but think of the possibilities if we properly prepared. We could go to New York City, and you can further study the urban sprawl. And you will be travelling as well— with me! We could go out into the countryside. Imagine the sights to behold…"

He trailed off and finished his ramble, waiting for her verdict.

"Or, we could just go to Ireland," he offered, sensing her hesitancy.

"I think that New York is a fine idea," she declared. "Can we afford it?"

"We can indeed! And on that thought… how would you like Ida to go to a nice boarding school?"

She shut her bible and looked directly at him, over her glasses.

"Oh? What for?"

"You often worry about her lacking structure and béing a bit delayed, and I know you and Dr. Webb cannot tend to her at all times, especially so when we are married. If she has some stability and can interact with more girls her age, I think it should do her some good."

"You are saying I spend too much time with her, and not enough with you?" Alma raised an eyebrow.

Michael clenched his teeth. That was not his main concern.

"You think I merely want to be rid of her? You have already done more for her than anybody would— or *should* ask of you. You've sacrificed half of your childhood for her, and you yourself said that you should work towards making her more independent. Listen, I'll pay her tuition, that is no problem, and if she does not adjust within half a year, we'll take her out."

Her eyes wandered and fixed on the candle.

"My mother sponsored one of the girls' schools up north. I'm sure they'd love to have her if I write a letter of recommendation. Alma, think about it, please."

"I will. I need to ask her what she thinks first, but for now, I'm going to bed," she stood up and kissed his brow.

"Ah, then… good night."

The next day, they departed for Dr. Webb's house. Michael was tickled by the idea of planning a wedding until he actually had to do it, but at least it was an excuse to visit the Webbs. Alma told him that her mother would be stopping by to meet him, and in the meantime, they had to set an exact day around all of the letters she'd received from relatives. At Michael's insistence (thrusting a finger into her side and casting his eyes at Ida) Alma asked Ida what she thought of going to boarding school to be a "proper lady." The proposal had her bouncing all over the train car, and bounding gleefully all the way home.

Michael deposited Alma at her house, and they sat in the kitchen and discussed while Dr. Webb passively listened and smoked. Michael's guest list was not nearly as extensive as Alma's: Abraham, Ruth, Mr. White, and Miss Emma White. He only wished Peter had waited until after December to flee to the continent.

Mr. Kelley hated churches and solemn ceremonies. None of his former colleagues from the dock would attend, either, not even the Arabs, who loved their weddings. They were fun to catch a drink with once in a while, but they probably didn't consider him a friend. He knew he had an Aunt Hannah, his father's younger sister, but he'd never seen her, and even if he knew where to find her, he wasn't sure she'd want to attend. Was she even real? What else had been concealed from him for so many years?

They could, at least, go through Alma's eligible relatives, before he could become too morose.

"Well, Aunt Alice can't come, but Aunt Erinn and Uncle Frederick will be there without the cousins, and Aunt Eliana will be here in the morning to help me get ready… " she stopped and drew in a long breath and continued sifting through her letters. "Even Aunt Elisabeth is coming, and of course Ida is. Aunt Sophia and Uncle Dan as well, with Allan and Claire.

There's Laura— that's one of the ladies from London— she agreed to attend, but some of them don't approve of me getting married. We can also invite Mr. Briggs; I feel we should. Miss Bell from church will be devastated if she isn't invited. So I think we'll have a total of eighteen, maybe twenty people to feed."

It was decided: December 18, 1889, at eight o'clock. Michael found this more amusing than he was probably supposed to.

"Four eights, and eight added to four is twelve! You couldn't possibly forget it," Alma observed.

"You're implying that I would?"

"You'd forgotten your own birthday."

"I don't care much for my birthday. So I made it all the way around the sun once again, what a ride! Because of my insolence, I missed *yours*. It was in June, yes?"

"Yes, the ninth."

"I will certainly remember it! Anyway, I look forward to meeting some of your relatives. Sorry, I don't really have much of a family."

"Yes you do," Alma replied warmly.

"That is to say, I am the last of the Bennetts."

"For now."

Dr. Webb stood up and walked out.

"On that note— sort of— I think—" Michael cleared his throat. "I'll arrange our passage to New York City as soon as possible. You should think about what you'll pack, and how you'd like to prepare yourself."

"Oh, alright. I'll see to it later. For now," Alma rose from her seat and gathered the letters to one side. "Come with me, so I can cut your hair before my mother sees you."

"Have you cut hair before?

"I cut my fringe, and sometimes I cut Ida's hair. That besides, I can't make it look any worse than it already is!"

"Is it truly that bad?"

"It's awful. Between your hair, whiskers, and jagged teeth, you're well on your way to resembling a lion. I'll get the scissors. Come into the sewing room," she departed with the letters.

Getting his hair cut was a pleasant feeling. His last trim was six months ago. It was the one thing he'd asked Abraham for, but he no longer had the coordination, and Michael could never be bothered to visit a barber.

"Alma, you say your mother is coming today?"

"Oh, yes. She wants to meet you!"

"And… Dr. Webb will be here in the house as well, yes?"

"Yes. What of it?"

"Is that such a fine idea?"

"My parents have made peace. You've not been led into a trap."

"I will be on my best behaviour."

"Oh, not to worry. I've told my mother about your eccentricities."

"What does that mean?" Michael turned around in his seat, and felt his hair being tugged by the comb.

"Stop moving, unless you *want* me to cut your ear off. I only mean that she knows not to expect a typical nobleman."

"Is that a slight or a compliment?"

"Whichever you please."

"Hmph… earlier, when I noted I am the last of the Bennett line, you said 'for now.' Do you want children, Alma?"

"Perhaps."

"This is a serious question. Please don't chaff as you like to do."

She stopped snipping.

"We should have discussed this months ago."

"We should have, but we didn't, so we are now," again, he reflexively turned his head, and she turned it back.

"No, stop cutting for a minute," Michael turned around in his chair and lowered her scissors. When discussing something so cardinal, he wanted eye contact.

"Do you?" Alma asked, taking a step back and shifting her weight around.

"I asked you first," he wanted her honest opinions, and didn't want her answer to be influenced by his.

"Yes, I do."

Michael had been told since adolescence that one day, he needed to marry and produce an heir. Until recently, he never thought of having children beyond that obligation, and he did not care one way or another. He enjoyed them, but at the moment, the idea mortally frightened him, and Alma's voice trembled when she answered.

"You really do? You desperately want them?"

"No, not desperately," she answered with more firmness that time. "But to raise children into good and honest people and leave the world a better place for it must be one of the most rewarding things you can do."

She always did look far into the future. *Somebody* had to. He often wondered if he would ever leave a lasting impression on the world, if only just a little piece of it. He was not sure he would even live past forty.

"You are smiling so strangely," she tilted her head. "Does my answer please you?"

"It does! I think I share your sentiment, Alma," Michael partially lied, and took her empty hand and brought it to his lips.

"Well not right *this minute,* and certainly not with that coiffure," she pulled her hand away and turned his head back, now having to wait until his fitful laughter subsided before she could finish cutting.

"It wasn't that funny. There! You are presentable now. Would you like to keep this hair?"

"What would I *keep* it for?"

"Maybe you'd like a moustache."

"Ah! I did at one time, but it would only draw attention to my banged up proboscis," he tapped the tip of his nose.

"I'll just put this in the compost box."

"Hair?" he turned to see her wrapping the trimmings up in cloth, and his stomach turned over.

"Yes. It breaks down just as manure, vegetables, or paper would."

He decided to take her word for it and make himself neat for Mrs. Webb's arrival, and not a moment too soon. The front door opened and shut just as Michael settled himself down in the parlour.

As she was in the pictures on the walls, Ellen Webb was about the same size and shape as her daughter, but with dark hair twisted up high, and a stern face lacking Alma's dreaming gaze. The eyes looked to be about the same colour, but heavier and etched with fine lines. She wore a trim and sober, yet very fashionable pearly grey dress and rosy kid gloves.

"You must be Mrs. Webb!" Michael nearly tripped over his own toes standing up, bowed, and offered his hand. "It is a pleasure to finally meet you. My name is Michael Bennett, as I'm sure you knew."

"Pleasure, indeed," the lady offered a thin and stiff smile with the handshake, then sat in Dr. Webb's usual chair, and Michael sat back in his place. "I understand you used to work for Dr. Webb."

"Oh, yes! He was a fair employer, though I worked at the docks for a minute, and currently, I work with animals in Bristol."

"Afternoon, madam," the doctor emerged from the hall and bowed to the lady that stole his seat, sitting on the couch beside Michael. "I hope coming here was no trouble."

"No, not all, Dr. Webb."

Michael sensed a degree of awkwardness, but no tension or animosity. They spoke easily, so he didn't have to carry the conversation, and needed only to answer any questions he was asked. Alma came in to greet her mother. Ellen Webb kissed Alma, and Michael observed that she merely leaned into the caress and tolerated it, and then she retreated to make coffee. James never came out to join.

Michael was interrogated by Alma's mother: his work, his interests, his parents, and even his credit. He offered to demonstrate his talent on the piano. Dr. Webb commented on his exceptional strength, but he wasn't sure how to demonstrate that except maybe to lift the doctor, which he decided against. His marksmanship? Not outstanding, and probably rusty by now.

Alma came in with coffee and toasted cakes to hand out, then sat between the two men. For Michael, she had just a glass of water.

Of course, the wedding ceremony was mentioned right away. Michael went over all that was planned for the day.

"It is customary that the bride's family pays for the arrangements," Mrs. Webb noted.

"Customary, perhaps, but not necessary!" Michael said. "It is a small affair."

"It is unusual for the groom to intrude."

"I would not say I'm intruding, only stepping in where I need to."

Alma was asked about her part in the preparations.

Before she could answer, the front door swung open and shut, startling everyone there.

A woman with a chestnut brown dress, pale yellow hair, and a sour expression stormed into the parlour.

"How dare you!" she marched forward with her eyes fixed on a perplexed Alma.

Michael had no idea what this lady was talking about, but he sprang up at once and intercepted her.

"Madam, what is this about?" he demanded as everyone stood up. Behind him, Alma stooped down to pick up the glass he knocked over.

"Now, Elisabeth—" Dr. Webb began.

"Stay out of this, it is none of your business!" Elisabeth Clarke snarled at her brother-in-law, then turned her attention back to Alma. "Just as my daughter is none of your business!"

Suddenly, he thought he knew what the fuss was, and maybe he wasn't supposed to, but he spoke up.

"Your daughter is *your* business!" Michael stepped back, because descending upon a woman half his size made him feel like some beast, and she didn't seem violent, just very loud. "Alma wouldn't be forced to meddle with Ida so much if you paid a mite of attention to her! She runs rampant with no guidance!"

She froze, as if just realising he was there.

"And who are you, telling me about my own family?" Mrs. Clarke now addressed him.

"Ah, sorry, I've forgotten my manners," he strained to soften his voice and offered a hand. "Well, ma'am, my name is Michael Bennett, and I'll be marrying your niece by the end of this year."

She didn't take his hand, only placed hers on her hips as a venomous smile spread across her face.

"It's not your place to tell me anything! Maybe nobody ever taught you how to behave, young man, but I'm not one of your chambermaids!"

"Elisabeth!" Mrs. Webb spoke up. "Don't tell people how to act when you come in here raising a storm as if you owned this house!"

Said owner of the house stood beside Michael with a grave and mildly disturbed expression. Alma looked like a cornered mouse for this entire ordeal. She'd not gotten a word in at all.

"Aunt Elisabeth, I'm sorry—" she squeaked.

"Don't apologise," her mother ordered her, and Michael had to agree with the sentiment.

Elisabeth turned on her sister next, and as she began shouting again, Mrs. Webb guided her out of the parlour so that they could argue apart from everyone else.

Michael had never come closer to striking a woman.

"Well… " he broke the new silence in the parlour. "You said this wasn't a trap!"

Alma mumbled under her breath and sat down with enough force to rattle the floor.

Even James came out to investigate.

"What did Bennett do this time? Is Alma alright?" he asked.

"Afternoon, Mr. Webb," Bennett huffed.

"Your Aunt Elisabeth came to visit," Dr. Webb explained. "Say hello if you see her, son."

James grunted and retreated back to his cave. Alma followed him to the hall.

"So, that was Ida's mother," Michael took out his handkerchief and sponged at the spilled water. "She's certainly a passionate creature."

Dr. Webb must have been stressed, as he lit his third pipe that day, and it was only four o'clock. He pursed his lips until they turned white, and he spoke in almost a whisper:

"Ah, um… she isn't normally like that. More often than not, she is rather *euphoric*, if inattentive. You see, soon after Ida was born, she was prescribed laudanum for her brooding and fatigue. She developed a sort of dependence on it. I suppose she did not partake today. In this state, only her sister could deal with her."

Michael shifted to conceal how he shuddered. He didn't fancy the idea of being dependent on anything other than food and water. Even coffee… Alma was peevish without it.

Alma... he excused himself and sought her in her room. He tapped on the door, and she nudged it open with her toe.

She was sitting at her toilette table, with her head hanging limp on her shoulder.

"I suppose she will not be attending the ceremony."

"It seems to me you wouldn't really want her there," he knelt by her chair. "Well, I'm sorry, but really!" he added when she glared over her glasses.

"She's angry at me for asking Ida if she'd like to go to boarding school without consulting her first. I undermined her authority. I didn't get to apologise."

"You don't owe her anything!" Michael protested. "Get angry, Alma, I know you want to. Better now than later."

She giggled and squeezed her eyes shut. A tear slipped down her nose.

"Ida does want to go to school, to be a lady, like *me*," she hid her face behind her fingers. "I discussed it with Mother, and she agreed to help facilitate it."

After a short interval, she growled:

"God, it's always the children who have to pay when people let themselves go to ruin."

"Yourself included," Michael took her hand and dabbed at her face with his shirt cuff. "I know you resent her. You never should have taken up her burdens as you did."

"Somebody had to. I mustn't complain about the hand I'd been dealt."

"Complain, Alma. Nobody dealt you that hand. I know I'm competing with a lifetime of conditioning, but don't martyr yourself because you're afraid of confrontation. What do you expect to accomplish for the world if you can't speak up even for yourself?"

Far better that you lament right then and there than become manic and stab somebody many years later, he added inwardly, as he knew what unchecked frustration could do to a person.

She lifted her head.

"What do you do when you're angry?"

"I chop wood, or run off into the forest to fight squirrels and fall out of trees."

Alma laughed and grabbed his other hand.

"Truly, Alma! Why do you think I took up boxing? Those squirrels really thrashed me."

He pulled her upright and tried to lead her to the threshold.

"Come, then, we have plans to sort out."

"You…" she stood where she was. A trembling little smile sprouted on her face. "You protected me from Aunt Elisabeth."

"I will protect you from anything."

Elisabeth Clarke was indeed not attending the wedding, but Mrs. Webb was still bringing Ida, and she was given one of Alma's old dresses to wear. As for boarding school, the two would continue to fight about the matter. Michael was told that Mrs. Clarke would likely forget her outburst soon, and then everything would return to the way it was before.

He went back to Brownwall three days later, and Alma would mostly be staying home for the coming weeks in order to prepare.

Abraham was ecstatic and always asking for something to do. Michael charged him with budgeting and handling mail, just because he pushed so much. He heard nothing of Peter Evans. Mr. Kelley did not want to attend (no surprises there), but sent his best wishes, and was excited to have Michael come back to work soon, *even* if he brought his bride.

Reservations for the journey to America were made, and for Abraham, Michael arranged a trip to the Irish countryside in the meantime. To his relief, he readily accepted the opportunity to have one last voyage by himself while he was still independent and able.

For the first time since last spring, Michael employed a tailor. Since Alma had gone to so much trouble to make a wonderful dress, he felt that a brand new suit was in order (there was no chance he'd learn to sew any time that year). Maybe he could hope to look half as fashionable as she would. New shoes and a winter coat were also needed.

There were no more preparations to make around Brownwall, except maybe to rename the property, because Alma couldn't get over how silly it sounded. Who wanted to be Lady Bennett, the nominal Baroness of Brownwall? It was becoming more grey than brown, anyway.

Her letters stopped coming in the final week, which did nothing to soothe his nerves.

Abraham assured him that she was just very busy, and if she had any reason to call off the wedding, she'd have told him.

<h1 style="text-align:center">XXXII</h1>

By the evening of December 17, he was all in knots. He chopped new wood until his shoulders ached, then he sat at the piano in the parlour but did not play, only stared into the fire until he saw blue and purple when he blinked.

"Will you have something to drink, Master Bennett?" Abraham sat beside him and offered him a glass of brandy.

Michael seldom touched alcohol for many months, but it was enticing now. He took a small sip, contemplated it, then swallowed the contents of the glass and asked for another.

"Thank you, old boy," he sighed. "I don't think I'll be getting much sleep."

"Oh, you must, sir. It won't do to have you swoon like a schoolgirl at the altar."

"Right. I'll save that for tomorrow night."

Abraham released a high-pitched, boyish cackle, then quickly sobered up, taking on a wistful air.

"You know… I always imagined both of your parents would see your wedding day… and then I hoped that at least your father would."

"As did I," Michael agreed and took the bottle to pour himself some more brandy. "I miss my parents."

"As do I. I tell you, though… you have done well for yourself, with all you've been given, and at only twenty."

"All of it was handed to me."

"But you handled it well, you sure did. And to show for it, you'll be bringing a lovely young bride home tomorrow, even though she is a degree better than you," Abraham took the bottle and nudged Michael's hand away. "So *go to bed!*"

"If you insist, Abraham," he retired to his room. Since he wasn't allowed to be intoxicated enough to collapse, maybe he could cry himself to sleep.

No such luck. He couldn't wring out even one tear, and his restless legs circled the chamber countless times until his eyelids suddenly turned to lead at about three o'clock. Naturally, he didn't sleep long enough to have any memorable dreams, as he was dragged out of bed at five to make himself ready. As soon as he remembered who he was and what he was doing, he was not the least bit drowsy.

Michael scrubbed himself raw before putting on his suit, and spent nearly half an hour carefully sculpting his whiskers before going downstairs for a light breakfast. His mother's locket went on under his tie, and his hair was combed away from his face. When he found Abraham, he asked for the linens on his bed to be replaced, as they likely smelled strongly of the alcohol he sweat off.

It was a beautiful day. The sky was a clear, deep crystal blue, with thin white clouds streaking towards the rising sun. It was all dazzling against the brown and grey landscape. The old chapel was within walking distance for Michael, but Abraham might have had trouble scaling the steep hill it sat upon after going that stretch. He offered to simply carry the old man, but he insisted they should simply get a ride when they passed through town.

Behind the chapel, he gazed upon the plot where his family was laid to rest— all except his parents and his sister. As inappropriate as it was on that day, he wondered when he would join them. Inside, Abraham sat with him and wiped the ever-accumulating dampness from his brow.

A few of the elderly tenants of the old village filed in. A wedding, especially between two very young people, was a rare occurrence. Michael didn't mind. It made his side look less empty, so he just greeted them and invited them to sit. Abraham went down to receive the guests as they came.

Ruth, her husband, and her sister-in-law were the first to arrive, so he met with them for a few minutes before they took their seats on the right-hand side.

"Do you fancy yourself a hypocrite, getting married in a sacred place, with you, yourself, being an unbeliever?" Ruth asked him, to his shock, and to the curiosity of the present pastor. "I've never seen you pray even once."

"A sacred place is open to all, I should say," Michael argued. "Mostly, I'm here in accordance with tradition, as this building has been in my family for hundreds of years. It has stood longer than Ashwood Hall, and my forefathers are buried here going back to the Tudor dynasty— um, sorry. And I never said I didn't believe there is a God! I suppose, though, that I've not done much with that knowledge."

"Maybe you should," she offered.

"Maybe I should," he echoed and stepped up to the altar.

Alma's relatives came in one at a time. Michael tried to smile and wave to them, but Abraham stopped him, telling him to look "stately."

John Briggs didn't come, even though he said he would. Pity.

His stomach dropped when he saw two little boys and a young girl shuffle into the chapel, followed by a woman with an infant in tow. He didn't expect there to be any small children. This put all of his plans in jeopardy.

"Who's that? Who's that, ma?" one of the boys pointed to Michael, and their mother pulled his hand down, and whispered something to him as they all took their seats.

Mrs. Webb came in with James and Ida, which meant Alma was due at any minute.

James had shaved, put on a tie, and combed down his hair, and he looked quite dignified. If he kept himself neat all the time, he'd have been a handsome man, and maybe been able to snag himself a wife.

Ida wore pale blue very well. Though it was Alma's dress, the colour suited Ida more with her

217

yellowish hair, though it pained him to admit it. She carried herself so demurely, probably only for this day, but it signified that she had the makings of a lady, after all.

Abraham rushed down the aisle, to Michael's side. Dr. Webb stepped in, looking as though he'd swallowed fire, and he brought Alma in behind him. She scampered up to his side, and when she realised that all eyes were on her, she straightened herself out and raised her chin high.

Alma caught the rays of the sun through the windows, and her graceful form swept over the floor. Her shining hair was arranged elegantly under a wreath of blossoms.

But this was not the dress that he remembered! What happened to it? He saw remnants of the original garment cut and arranged into the trim on her church suit. Thankfully, the colours went together beautifully.

And the length of lace he'd bought for her? It was the train, tailing behind her, dragging across the floor.

She seemed to stare listlessly into oblivion, and timidly toed her way down the aisle. He realised she wasn't wearing her eyeglasses. Where were they?

That walk was the longest minute of his life. Dr. Webb presented her, then moved her veil and kissed her hair.

Michael tried to discreetly square his shoulders and dry his palms— if only he'd worn gloves! The ceremony itself was solemn and still. They most often were. Every word echoed, and every breath was audible.

He almost dropped the ring as he put it on her little hand. His lips were numb from pinching them stiff and straight.

Alma's name signed on the licence was *Alma Temperance Webb*. He'd never learned her middle name before then.

"That's really pretty," he muttered as he watched over her shoulder.

Dr. Webb paid for a photographer in advance, and he arrived just in time. The bride and groom were stopped, and positioned as one might model decorative dolls for several minutes before they could leave the chapel. Michael didn't like having to face forward for some of those pictures.

Subdued whispers swelled into friendly clamouring once they exited the chapel. Now Michael could release all of the nervous titters he'd repressed. Instead of throwing her bouquet, Alma divided it evenly among the bachelorettes, and one of the small boys, just because he wanted a flower, too.

Michael was excited to greet all of Alma's relatives. They were wholly pleasant and gracious, save for one encounter with Uncle Frederick:

"Is it alright if I call you Mikey?" the balding man had a weak grip, but shook his hand violently enough to wrench it from his arm.

"Would you like me to call you Freddie?" *Michael* freed his hand and rolled his wrist a few times to make sure it was intact.

"No, no, it wouldn't suit me, I don't think. I'm a grown man, after all."

"The defence rests. Thank you for coming, sir."

He also thanked the random village folk who bore witness, though nobody knew them (Ruth definitely wanted to, but there was no time).

There was an unforeseen problem with planning and moving, partially because there were many extra children. Twenty people could not comfortably be transported in an old farmer's wagon. Some mumbled amongst themselves that bringing a pastor to the house and getting married there would have been easier. Now that he thought of it, he agreed…

About an hour's walk at an easy pace brought them to Brownwall, but the small children had to be carried. A girl, the oldest of the brood, maybe eight years old, carried her baby brother for quite a stretch, still clutching the flowers. They didn't seem to have good coats, and her little hands trembled.

Michael stepped back to the rear of the group. Two wee rosy faces peered up at him through wild ringlets.

"Hillo there, sweeting! You have a passenger, I see! Why don't you let me take him for you?" he plucked the little boy off of his sister, and he didn't fuss. He then knelt down and took her in his other arm. They would probably be warmer that way. "Well, I'm Michael. What are your names?"

"Emma Louise," the girl murmured, warming her hands in his coat.

"Emma Louise! How pretty! There's a lady here named Emma as well. Where did she run off to— ah, there she is. And what's this big man's name?" he pointed his nose at the baby.

"Jacob."

"Jacob is a wonderful name! Essentially, it means 'the overthrower.' I bet he'll be a powerful fellow one day."

"What does my name mean?"

"Sorry, I don't know about Emma. I do know that Louise is French, and it means 'great warrior.'"

Michael then had to tell her all of the name origins he could remember in the next hour, and try to explain some of the basics of French, Latin, and German.

The reception breakfast was light. Before he left, he had bread and butter set out, and he paid an elderly lady from town to make soup, tea, and coffee, and keep it hot for them. She was welcome to eat while she was there. The congregation extended into the drawing room, but everyone had a seat.

The little Emma had taken quite a liking to Michael, and tried to climb into his lap to listen to him speak more, but her mother, Alma's Aunt Erinn, called her away and told her not to bother him.

"I thought she said she wasn't bringing the children," he mentioned to Alma.

"She did. I suppose it's fortunate that she didn't bring all eight of them, but my mother was quite cross with her, anyway. Sorry, I didn't know."

"It's alright, they aren't any trouble. I was just taken aback, but they're well-behaved," Michael said, just as he heard two of the little boys yelling and swatting at each other. "For the most part… oh, and what happened to your eyeglasses?" he added, because at that moment, she had narrowed her eyes almost shut peering at the clock on the opposite wall.

"I have them with me, but Aunt Eliana told me I'd look better without them."

"Pish! You look no different. Can you see me?"

"Yes, I can see right in front of me, but I need them to focus on anything an arm's reach away."

"Well, I don't intend to be more than an arm's reach away from you," he pinched her ear. "But put them back on. It won't do to have you give yourself a headache trying to read a clock."

She produced her glasses from her sleeve and put them on, blinked several times, and then she looked more relaxed. Secretly, he enjoyed how they framed her face, but women never believed it when they were told that.

"And on the subject of your adornment," he continued. "What has happened to your dress? It doesn't look how I remembered."

He grimaced, recognising his error as soon as he finished speaking.

"You've never seen it— were you snooping?" she narrowed her eyes once more.

"Yes."

She huffed, but she seemed more flustered than angry.

"That's bad luck! No wonder my dress got ruined!"

"Ruined? What happened to it?"

"I… I spilled varnish on it," she mumbled.

"Hah! That has nothing to do with luck, you little bungler!" Michael chuckled. "But I've always fancied that green dress, and I daresay, the finished product is greater than the sum of its parts. Well done."

After the meal, they went to the parlour and took turns mucking about on the piano. Mrs. Webb sang while Dr. Webb played, but Alma wouldn't do the same for Michael in front of such a crowd. Abraham seemed delighted to speak to the doctor again. Ida loved running through the halls with the two older boys, and undoubtedly corrupting Emma Louise. Alma didn't even scold her for playing in her nice dress. James sat alone and read. Michael guessed that he only showed up because Dr. Webb prodded him.

Alma's friend Laura Baker called her *Ma*, and her explanation was that it was the only affectionate title you could derive from "Alma," it referred to her maternal inclinations, and lastly, "Alma mater" was too confusing in regular conversation. She seemed to be the only one of her acquaintances from London who approved of the marriage. Being married would take her away from her work in some capacity, and given that Michael was no longer exceptionally wealthy, it was not deemed advantageous enough to be worth the loss of independence.

At about noon, Michael considered that it was perhaps time for the guests to leave. He didn't want the small children to be out after dark when the temperature dropped. Alma also had this strange, glassy look in her eyes, and her cheeks were florid.

"You look flushed. Are you tired? I'll shoo them out if you want," he offered.

"I'm not really tired," she insisted. "But yes, I'm a bit fatigued from all the excitement."

"Alright. We'll break up the festivities," he nudged his lips behind her ear. "And then we can have the piano to ourselves."

She shuddered and rose from her seat, then started collecting cups and dishes.

"What do you think you're doing?" Aunt Sophia rushed towards her and took them out of her hands.

"I'm cleaning up—"

"Absolutely not. We will handle it. Entertain your husband."

Alma returned to Michael and took her seat at his left side.

"Entertain you, she says."

"Entertain me? Well, I'm tickled just by looking at you!" he replied, but got up from his seat to assist with clean-up, regardless of anyone's opinion.

One by one, the ladies began picking up dishes and cutlery, and the men put chairs and tables back where they belonged. Coats and hats went on. Lamps went out.

Ida was so preoccupied with her younger cousins that she didn't pester Alma very much at all, and took leaving without her surprisingly well. Dr. Webb and Mrs. Webb would be paying for decent lodging in town for all of the guests who didn't need to depart right away. Michael and Abraham quickly went through all the wardrobes in the house to find any spare coats or shawls for the children.

Affection for Alma was expected, but Michael received embraces as well. He even felt that he had a proper family again.

They departed, and the house was still once more. Aside from Abraham quietly ambling about, they were completely alone. The fire had died out. It would be getting dark soon.

Alma sat at the other end of the couch in the parlour. She kept her gaze low, and idly fingered at the pleats in her skirt.

"So, what about the piano?" Michael broke the silence.

"What about it?"

"Shall we play?" he reached over and took one of her hands. "Or, rather, shall I play, and be graced with your singing?"

"I don't much feel up to it," she admitted.

"What do you feel up to, then?"

"It's getting cold," Alma came close and pressed up against him.

"Actually, I was just thinking it's a little warm in here," he drew a cool breath to settle his uneasy stomach. His body was playing a cruel trick on him, and he was absolutely determined not to vomit on his wedding day.

He sprang up and swallowed down his nerves, and pulled out a little phial of clove oil that Abraham recommended for his ailing tooth; he found it did wonders for his nausea, and hopefully, it made his breath tolerable. He tasted a drop from his finger and returned it to his pocket.

"What do you say we take a walk?" Michael offered. "It's still light out, and not *that* cold yet."

Alma removed her veil, flowers, and the train on her dress before they set out. He took her down his usual path. The sky was now overcast. There was a stiff breeze that whipped at his hair.

"So, how do you like these woods now that winter approaches?" he asked.

"Right now, most of it is dead and grey," she answered. "But I like them perfectly well. It's very peaceful."

"I'm glad humans don't hibernate," he concluded. "We'd be missing out on such a fine winter afternoon, and I'd have to wait another three to four months to marry you."

"Those three to four months would surely fly by in an instant if you slept that whole time."

"And I bet you'd wake up with a lot of spiders making webs on you."

"You'd love that, wouldn't you?"

"Perhaps, though I'd prefer to wake up with a lot of Alma on me," he turned around (she was always behind him, after all), then seized her by the waist and set his cheek against hers.

She laughed sheepishly, and averted her eyes, but didn't retreat.

"Already regret marrying such a silly creature, do you?"

"No!" she spat, as if scolding a child for spouting something ludicrous. "All I am is nervous."

"Well, what is there to be nervous about?" Michael asked, knowing all of his nerves were in knots, and feeling he was the only man on Earth who could be genuinely sick from ardour.

"Your hands are shaking so much," she noted, as all that time, he'd been pretending that he wasn't nervous, and he definitely wasn't cold. If the wind continued, he couldn't conceal it for much longer.

"Why don't we go back inside and have some tea?"

"Already?"

"Yes! We can relax by a good fire and have something to drink. How about it?"

Reluctantly, she turned to walk back, placing herself behind him again. By the time they were inside, his fingers were numb.

"Oh!" Alma squeaked as they crossed paths with Abraham in the downstairs gallery. "Are we in your way?"

"No, no, my dear," he stepped to one side. "I believe I'm in your way. You came inside much earlier than I expected!"

"Mr. I-Don't-Get-Cold is freezing to death!" Alma chirped and removed Michael's hat. "I'm going to make a nice fire and prepare some tea. Would you like some?"

"No, no, I think I'll just read, play some cards, and pack for my trip. I'll turn in early, I imagine," the old man bowed and turned to head to his room. "Good night to you, *Lord and Lady Bennett*. You should settle into bed soon, as well. You'll be off to Liverpool in the morning."

Oh, Liverpool! They would be departing to New York from there, and they wouldn't be back for over two months. Most of the time would be spent on the ship. That, he both dreaded and anticipated.

She built up a hearty blaze in the parlour, then drew open the drapes to show a brilliant sliver of moon peeking out of the clouds.

"Alma, forget the tea, actually," Michael hurried into the kitchen for a bottle of young red wine, a nice glass, and a piece of the cake.

She knelt down on the rug in front of the fireplace, with her skirts spread about.

"You've never had wine, have you? I've never seen you drink alcohol," Michael sat beside her and filled the glass.

"No, I haven't."

"Any reason? Are you opposed to it?"

"No. I've just never had the chance."

"Really?" he took a sip, then presented the glass to his wife. "Here. It is a bit rough when you first taste it."

"You plan to get me soaked?"

Michael belted out a high, creaking laugh, but composed himself in an instant.

"No, that won't do. Try it, though. I think you'll like it."

She looked sceptical. If she liked black coffee, then surely a little wine couldn't be too strong for her.

Alma took the glass from his hand and held it up to her lips, hesitating for a second, and then taking a very small sip. She held it a moment.

"There we are. What do you think?"

"I don't know yet."

She took a substantial drink, and warmed up to it.

"That's quite nice," she decided, with wine glistening on her mouth.

She handed the glass back to him. He drained it, and then they finished two more, sharing the cake alongside it. It paired wonderfully with the wine.

Red wine did not fluster him, but he did feel giddy and warm, and maybe a bit stupid: stupid enough to wax poetic.

"I would be an abysmal lyricist, but if I were to describe you in song and poetry, I'd say you are the four seasons. Your skin is white and soft as snow."

"Are you really drunk on only one or two glasses of wine?"

"Your eyes," he continued, ignoring her remark. "Are the shining surface of a shallow creek when the sun melts the last crust of ice. Those blooming cheeks and lips are the warmth of summer, and newly opened blossoms. Your hair is the colour of falling leaves, and equally hypnotic when a September breeze catches it."

"And how would you describe me in plain, solid reality?" Alma still held the empty glass up between them. She was amused in a sardonic sort of way, but not moved or touched.

He knew flowered language did not reach her, but he enjoyed indulging in thoughtless prose every now and then.

"I'd say about the same," he set the glass down and leaned close. "You are an entire year as it changes and repeats. You are my life."

"You are mine," she declared.

Alma leaned against him. Her brooch dug into his breast. She was all flushed down to even her fingertips, and he wasn't sure if it was from the fire, the wine, or otherwise.

"You must be exhausted," he guessed.

"No," she protested. "I've been on my feet for an eighteen hour stretch before. All I did today was walk a little."

"Oh, I understand. Still," he sat upright with Alma still on him. "We should head to bed soon, as we shall leave for Liverpool in the morning."

"Alright," she picked up the bottle and dishes, placed them in the kitchen, and then placed her hand in his to be led upstairs.

XXXIII

Michael dreamed of water. This time, it wasn't a wailing storm or a crashing torrent; he was submerged in warm, still water, and felt it on his limbs. Vibrant marine plants tickled him as they danced in the gentle current. His head was weighed down by his wet hair. Storm clouds approached. He didn't fear them. He anticipated them and welcomed them. He saw a challenge.

Though his dreams were peaceful, his sleep was fragmented. He kept half-waking in a stupor, prodding at Alma, as if to make sure she still existed. At four o'clock, he finally rose up and stayed awake. He lit a lamp and watched Alma sleep for a while. She was stirring within half an hour.

"Alma! Good morning," Michael tried to take her hands, but she started and retreated into the bedding.

"What's the matter?" he pulled the linens away from her face. "I've seen just about as much of you as there is to see!"

"Don't say that so loud!" she hissed. "It was darker then."

"And you look even more lovely in this light!" he insisted. "Say, are you hungry? I bet I could make a palatable breakfast."

"Palatable, maybe, but not particularly appetising," she sat upright and stretched out her legs.

"I put your things next to the wardrobe," he pointed accordingly. "It's all still in the trunks, because I didn't know what you'd want unpacked, or where you'd want it."

"That's alright," she threw her old calico dress on over her head and stood up, letting the skirt cascade to the floor. She then put a large robe over it.

"You're taking that dress on our voyage, yes?"

"Yes. I'll go make breakfast. Would you please make up a fire and start water boiling?"

Michael did as he was asked, and Alma made tea and coffee with the water he set to boil. Breakfast was the turnips, onions, and carrots from yesterday's stew laid over fried potatoes: an odd combination. Abraham was usually out and about by this time, but he didn't come to the table until breakfast was almost over.

"What a wonderful sight first thing in the morning!" Abraham was gay as a songbird when he came into the dining hall.

Michael invited him to sit and eat, but he declined.

"No, no, that fried food don't sit well with me anymore, but I thank ye. I'll just have some tea and a little bread and jam, I think," he replied and reached for the tea kettle. "And good morning to you, little Lady Bennett! I trust you slept well?"

"Oh, yes!" Alma snatched up the kettle and poured his cup for him. "You're up a little late, according to Lord Bennett."

"Well, I'd say I was up and about at around nine o'clock last night. Couldn't quite get to sleep," Abraham took the tea, bowed his head, and excused himself from the dining hall.

Alma swallowed hard as though she'd just eaten a stone, and Michael did not know why.

"Alright, let's get washed up and get ready to leave," he left the table and took the kettle of water off of the stove.

Abraham stayed behind to lock the house up. He'd be leaving soon after them. They boarded their ship at nine o'clock, and an hour later, they departed for New York.

Michael had never spent three weeks on a ship before. He was dreadfully nervous about becoming ill, even though it was essentially a hotel on water. Alma was giddy with excitement, finally able to satiate that hunger for travel.

It didn't last for long. He did not get sick, but she, on the other hand, had a difficult time of it. It was the worst when she first woke up. If she wasn't moving, she was plagued with nausea and sweats. She couldn't even sit and read peacefully. They were both relieved to reach land at last, especially because the bed hardly fit the two of them.

They departed from Liverpool in 1889, and reached New York City in 1890. Michael made sure to get all of his *sensational* "I haven't seen dry land since last decade" jests out of the way at the dock.

After walking a short distance, stately hotels and lavish establishments beckoned to them with gaily decorated windows and shining facades. Alma's lack of appropriate conditioning would have barred her from many of the upper-class facilities, as they demanded a high standard of etiquette. He didn't want to take her somewhere

that would make her feel alienated. His home
training was largely neglected, as well.

None of it interested him, anyway. They went
north, as he was interested in an old cabin he'd
leased many miles away from any town. It was
the closest to camping that she would consent to
on short notice.

Once again, the excitement did not last long. It
was mercilessly cold, far colder than any
ordinary English winter. Thankfully, they'd
collected dry provisions before being blockaded
in by nearly three feet of snow in the hollows. In
order to leave the cabin, Michael had to plough
through it with a broad length of wood, and his
own body, and if he had to bring Alma, he
tethered her to his coat.

He'd caught exactly one pathetic little rabbit,
and that was the only meat they had for a month.
Other than that, they had beans and hard bread.
They didn't have a stick of furniture. They ate
their meals stooped over a box, and they slept
nesting in a heap of blankets and furs in front of
the stove. He thought it would be easy to collect
wood, but he went and bought coal as soon as
possible.

Michael went out to observe the flora and fauna
for as long as he could tolerate the weather.
Occasionally, he would get so bored, he would

forget how miserable it was outside. Cold as he was when he came in, he refused to drink the coffee Alma made; if he did, he would be unable to relax, but pacing throughout the one room they inhabited would drive her mad, and going outside for longer than he needed to wasn't worth it.

He wondered if he'd made a mistake by coming there, but talking by the fire for long hours with no choice but to huddle together for warmth was bliss. Of course, Alma noted that they could have done that in England, but the change of scenery was important. Michael hated being stuck indoors under most circumstances. With anybody else, he'd have possibly committed murder on day three. Alma made it not just bearable, but enjoyable.

He asked if she regretted making the trip. She said she did not, and that was probably a lie.

Being inside for such long stretches ruined their sleep. Sometimes, they were up and talking long into the wee hours of the morning until they couldn't keep their eyes open.

On one afternoon, a ghostly howl shocked them out of a deep sleep.

"What was that? What was that?" Alma anxiously pawed at Michael as he sat up.

"I think that was a coyote— I've never seen one of those!" he threw his clothes and boots on and made a wild, stumbling dash for the door, despite Alma's protests.

He desperately searched for the source of the sound, and found a trio of genuine coyotes prowling around in the hills. Even at dusk, their bodies stood out upon the blue-washed spread of snow. The awe that he felt almost made him forget the cold.

"Michael!" Alma squeaked from the door she held ajar. "You lunatic! Get back inside! It's going to bite your face off!"

"It'd be doing me a favour!" he called back.

Their shouting echoed through the woods and frightened the animals, and they darted off into the trees.

The thrill faded away, and then the temperature caught up to him.

"And what were you thinking, running out there without your coat, your gloves, your hat…" Alma grumbled. "You could have lost twelve of your fingers! Your hands are frozen."

"Well, warm me up," he held his arms out.

She ignored his request and began heating some
water.

"I think I'll make coffee."

"You're cruel," he teased and lay himself down
by the fire.

She heated some of the red wine he had from
their provisions, and added some dried allspice.
He withdrew his verdict, and told her exactly
how incredible she was.

"Do you still want to go to Africa?" he asked as
he sipped on wine and she pressed her mug of
hot coffee to her lips.

"I think at this time," she mused. "Even boiling
to death would be preferable to facing that wind.
You sure spent a pretty penny to live as a feudal
peasant."

"I know. I am sorry that I did not plan this very
well. I'm glad we came, though. I think we'll
appreciate being home so much more after this."

By the end of that two weeks, he was almost
sorry to leave.

"Well, it's time to return to real life," he announced as they shut up the cabin and set out on the path beaten through the snow.

Alma did better on the trip home. When she felt unwell, she lay on the floor of their chamber, claiming that it was more stable than being in bed. Michael had nothing against the floor, so he joined her.

Because night and day had merged together in that cabin, he often found himself pacing through the ship at odd hours, while few other inmates stirred, except two or three older gentlemen smoking or playing cards in the salon. He resisted the urge to touch the piano in the dining hall.

He definitely missed England's comparatively mild winters.

Abraham was waiting for them at Brownwall, and he was more vocal about how well he'd kept up the house upon his return than his own trip, but he was pleased to have them back.

Upon returning home, they had two weeks to settle into the house. Michael turned twenty-two in that time.

XXXIV

This next chapter of their life required a great deal of paper and patience. Alma became a physician's assistant, and was trying to get decent work closer to home. Additionally, she ministered to young mothers, and taught them about proper sanitation and hygiene— that, she did for free. She told him all about this, and he saved each of her letters.

In spring, Michael began spending weeks at a time in Bristol, working six days a week. Mr. Kelley really heaped a lot on his plate to make up for his time off, and it was much needed, as hibernation was ending for many animals.

As for Alma and Michael, they did their very best to coordinate their leisure time, and came together for an interval before returning to their work. Usually, he intercepted her at the train station and greeted her cordially, then descended upon her as soon as they were alone.

The arrangement was the best they could do with their differing occupations, but it wasn't perfect. They sometimes saw each other only one of eight weeks. He had to pull a lot of strings and work extra hours to be home on her birthday. He'd never gotten to celebrate it before, and twenty-one seemed a big deal. He bought her a big box of expensive chocolate.

He often ached to see her to the point of becoming sick and anxious, and sometimes they quarrelled when their plans failed and they could not make adequate time. Despite this, he was deliriously happy. He expected to quarrel sometimes.

But it was not sustainable in the long term.

In July, he brought Alma to Bristol and asked her to draw the salamanders for him, and supplied her with a set of fine pencils and chalk. They planned to spend the summer there, as she had decided to stop travelling for work. He had told her to think of it as a second attempt at a honeymoon… except he was still working.

The deal they struck was that if he picked up a chicken without panicking or making it panic, she would pick up a snake and let it slither on her, also without panicking. Michael held up his end of their deal in his own mind. Alma claimed that feeding chickens to a large python didn't count; they were dead. He insisted that they never specified in the arrangement that the chicken was supposed to be alive, and went to fetch an Asian vine snake.

"Oh! It's so pretty!" Alma marvelled at its slender body and dappled skin. He placed it carefully upon her shoulders and allowed it to take hold of her on its own. She trembled as it passed over her neck, but did not cry or jump.

She wasn't so enchanted after he plucked it off of her and then told her that it was venomous, but calmed down when he explained that its venom was very mild, and it was unlikely to bite. He also informed her that Mr. Kelley had many far more venomous creatures in his collection, and practically wore them as jewellery; that revelation did nothing to mollify her.

"But, congratulations, my dear," Michael put the snake back and watched it wind its way around a twisting branch. "You succeeded."

"And you did not," she insisted. "Expect me to pay you back in due time."

Michael worked very hard even while Alma was there. Mr. Kelley showed no mercy, for as long as he was there, he would be put to work. He woke before Alma, still adhering to the rigid schedule. Since Mr. Kelley cooked, and Alma was not permitted by Kelley to assist directly, all she was able to do was wash clothes, talk with Miss Gaye, and draw the salamanders. Alma and Mr. Kelley never seemed to get along, and she voiced great displeasure at Michael getting up for work at four o'clock in the morning, and coming to bed close to midnight.

They visited Dr. Webb in October. In that month, Alma withdrew from him a little, and that filled him with dread and fear. He tried to press her, but she insisted all was well. Indeed, she did not seem upset with him, but she was restless and spent a lot of time by herself. He was worried that all of the travelling was finally affecting her. Dr. Webb told him that it was merely a phase women go through once in a while, and he only needed to let it run its course.

Sure enough, she visited with a friend from London for a while, and returned to him just as easy and genial as she had been before. The reason for her sour mood is a mystery to this day.

While Michael was sitting on the front steps, shining his shoes, Alma approached him from behind. He excitedly dropped his brush and turned at the sound of her little footsteps, but found her kneeling at his side, with a slender brown hen nestled in her arms as if presenting a newborn child.

He swallowed hard.

"What is that?"

"What does it look like?"

"Want me to polish it, do you?"

"Take the chicken!" she beckoned and leaned forward to place it in his hands. "It's definitely not venomous."

"But it could easily remove my nose… or the rest of my eyebrow… They smell fear, I'm sure of it."

"She is young and acclimated to being touched. Look how sweet she is."

The hen seemed perfectly content in her arms, but Alma wasn't Michael. Chickens in particular had a tendency to hate him. Hesitantly, he let it rest on his hands. He could feel its clawed feet delicately clasping his fingers.

It was looking at Alma, then snapped its head around to look at him with those beady eyes, and he fought down the urge to throw it as hard as he could.

"I think she likes you," she said.

"I don't think she does," he handed it back to her, and continued working on his shoes, hoping she didn't notice how badly his arms quivered.

By winter, Michael and Alma had saved a substantial amount of money, and decided to stay settled at home for a long while to celebrate a year of marriage. Abraham was keeping the house all this time. He was slowing down, though he wouldn't admit it, and soon he wouldn't be able to handle it all by himself. It was also just good to be home.

Alma made many parcels of provisions to bring to unwed mothers that she used to minister to in London. She brought them cakes of soap and bundles of wool to make stockings for their babies (she did not do it herself, because she was not good at it). Michael even caught her ransacking the linen closets.

"They're beginning to dismantle their petticoats to clothe their children!" she explained.

"Well, if you'd asked me, I'd have simply given you some money. Go and buy them some pretty calico and warm fleece."

"It is my cross to bear, not yours."

"We are supposed to be sharing our burdens," he was already reaching into his pocket book. "Take ten, and give them what they need, and a bit of what they don't need."

In early March of 1891, Michael went back to spending only four days a week in Bristol. They were not wanting money, but it simply felt unnatural to not be working. Now that it was warm, he also went to work on his own property again. First, he cleared out all of the shrubbery that he did not want in the back garden so that blackberries and roses had more space to grow.

Some of the briar, he uprooted and moved to the front of the house, hoping it would climb the supports. After that, he purchased a large amount of wood and set to work on a stable so that he could finally have horses again. Halfway through, a beam he foolishly did not properly secure came loose and caught his cheek. The blow made a raw, swollen purple scrape on the side of his face, but did no permanent damage.

He also (reluctantly) made an enclosure for chickens, because Alma asked him to, with the understanding that she alone would be responsible for them. All of this construction took about two months. When he was finished, she bought four young hens and brought them home, and they feasted on an abundance of insects and weeds. Soon, they would have eggs.

Alma sectioned off a small plot of the cleared land for a vegetable garden. This occupied much of her time, so she was no longer working, but occasionally doing charity projects with church ladies.

Finally, he made the easternmost room of the attic into a study. From those large windows, he could see the sunrise through the trees, over the winding walkway up to the house. Did he have any particular need for a study at that time? No, not really, but it seemed proper to have one. Perhaps Alma would make good use of it.

All of this, he managed to finish by September, and by then, Alma was hard at work making preserves.

Ida did not get to go to boarding school as she wanted, but Mrs. Webb had taken her as an apprentice. She told Alma about becoming a seamstress and getting better at knitting. For practice, she made new dresses for her dolls, and showed her cousin when she visited for a week. Ruby, her cat, was fat and thriving. Judging by her letters, her grammar and vocabulary had not improved much.

Ruth still wrote him as well. She often said that she missed Peter and wished he would return her letters, wondering what he was doing in Europe and when he'd come home. Michael felt terrible for not telling her where he went, but he wanted to respect Peter's privacy.

It was still difficult to buy gifts for Alma. She considered the hen-house her birthday present, and most things that she liked, she could make for herself. Finally, after some prodding, she requested some chestnut brocade to make new drapes for the parlour, a project that she undertook with her mother's old sewing machine, which she received when Mrs. Webb bought a new one. He was surprised that she asked for such a sumptuous material, but pleased that she did so naturally and without a fuss.

"And what will you do with all that fabric?" Michael asked, watching her take down the old drapes. "It's a wonderful colour."

"Do you want a new waistcoat?"

"Pink wouldn't suit me."

"Nor would this particular hue suit me. I think this silk is in bad shape from neglect, anyway."

While Alma was replacing the drapes, Michael wandered into an unexplored stretch of wood, near another tiny hamlet. The dirt was boggy.

He heard some creature rustling through the brush and litter, and he followed the sounds, curious as to what creature he might find.

A greyish brown mass passed in and out of the shadows. There was a long snout and a short tail. It was too clumsy and ragged to be a fawn. It was a dog!

Michael stood at a distance and whistled. It perked its head up and stared at him.

"Ho!" he called, as if it could understand him. "Do you belong to anybody?"

It continued to amble about, and didn't seem terribly upset, so he approached.

"Here!" he whistled again, and it sheepishly came near. The dog was thin-flanked and unkempt, but it was obviously trained, so it must have been lost or abandoned— for at least a few weeks, from the looks of it. He realised that it wasn't actually brown, just filthy.

He held his hand out. It reflexively shrank away, kicking up debris as it leapt back, then approached once more and smelled him. There was a loose length of rope peeking out of the matted hair on its neck, and upon closer examination, Michael was pretty sure it was female.

"Who do you belong to?" he asked again. "Well, come on, then!"

He stepped back and tried to lead it towards the hamlet. It followed far behind him, very slowly.

Of course, he wasn't sure if anybody was home, but it was worth a try. The dog seemed to be roaming just outside the community, living off of scraps.

"Anybody lose a dog?" Michael interrogated everybody he came across. Nobody recognised her, and she didn't claim anybody they encountered.

Somebody tried to sell him some knitted wool stockings. He declined. A strange lady with bare feet and a mole on her nose asked if he wanted to try her jam, and he was not sure if the proposition was genuine or otherwise, but she didn't have a jar, a pot, or even a spoon close at hand. Again, he declined, and though he hadn't taken up her offer, the exchange left a foul taste in his mouth.

They were chased away by an old fisherman with a rifle, insisting he would shoot the "mad dog" if they got closer.

"Well, that settles it," he told her, as it was now time for him to be heading back to the house. "Anyone who wants you can come looking, but if you keep following me, you're mine."

She snuffled and nudged at his coat pocket, though there was no food in it.

"What, this?" Michael pulled a crumpled, smudged sheet of paper from his pocket. "It's just paper."

This revelation made no difference to her. She bit into the paper and tore off a corner.

"No!" he thrust it back into his pocket. "This isn't food! Don't eat it!"

She happily swallowed it anyway, and stared expectantly at his hand in his coat.

"My, you must really be famished. If you come with me, I'll feed you something substantial.

She followed at his heels as he stomped back through the woods. Now she excitedly trembled and wagged her tail when he spoke to her. He needed to name her, and he chose her name in a very careful and contemplative way, by shouting out whatever came to mind and seeing which utterance made her tremble the hardest.

She decided that her name was Jeannine.

Alma was not amused by the dirty dog nosing around in the hall, and even less amused to learn that he essentially stole her, but since she seemed pretty much abandoned, he believed it would be cruel to leave her to her own devices. Furthermore, he explained that he would train her, and she could be useful for guarding the house and keeping foxes away from the chickens.

"Are you certain that you can train her?" she asked.

"Absolutely. Dogs love me."

She relented, but demanded that Jeannine be bathed before she came back inside.

Michael first took a piece of cheese from the larder, as he thought he should feed her before he gave her a bath. Jeannine didn't mind being wet, but she wouldn't get in the wash tub. He poured cupfuls over her and washed out the knotted masses in her coat until she shined. She had a few ticks, which he removed with oil and a fine-toothed comb. He then trimmed some of the hair around her face and feet, and ran races with her until she was dry enough to be brought back inside.

Alma was happy with Jeannine now. Abraham accepted her right away, and cheerfully reminisced about the fine hunting dogs that the former lords owned. At dinner, Michael brought her a plate of scraps in broth, and she licked it clean, then sprang up and licked his face.

Jeannine was not welcome in bed. Michael had to lay out a nest of old rags and sneak upstairs once she was fast asleep. Until he rid himself of the dog's aroma, he wasn't welcome in bed, either.

When he woke and went downstairs the next morning, he found her lying in a heap of shredded books pulled from a table in the main hall. They weren't valuable or treasured relics, so he hurried to clean up the mess before his wife saw it. Now he had to make sure that all the paper in the house was out of her reach.

"You're going to get me in trouble!" Michael scolded her, and took her outside to find sticks for her to chew.

The next coming December marked two years of marriage. The inevitable waning of the honeymoon must have been some bitter fabrication, or at best a self-fulfilling prophecy to those who believe that affection and excitement can and therefore must be tarnished. Six months was reportedly the average lifespan of the tenderness between a husband and wife, but after well over a year, she was still a captivating presence and a sensory delight. Every day, he courted her all over again.

He never tired of her company, even if they didn't say a word. Her aura was warm and relaxing. Sometimes when he sat and read (he finally found books that interested him) she would go to wherever he went and merely sit close by, sewing, drawing, or reading herself. It was like a conversation. For that reason alone, he could fully believe in something spiritual because he was sure there was no other explanation for it.

One of Michael's favourite things to do was always to take Alma on long, long walks into the woods. On that day, their anniversary, they skipped breakfast and set out at nine o'clock, eating bread and cold butter as they walked. Jeannine followed, kicking up detritus and sticking her nose into crevices in the rocks. Her enthusiasm broke the stillness of that gorgeously sunny day.

Alma spied a beautiful doe creeping through the woods, and tried to alert Michael to its presence with a quiet nudge, but Jeannine gleefully chased it into the brush before he could call her back, breathless with laughter. There was no murderous intent in her antics. She just loved to chase. Clearly, she was not meant to be a hunting dog, but her sheer size was a good deterrent for foxes. While she explored, she brought them presents: sticks, bunches of leaves, and sometimes smooth stones from the banks of the creek, and she was not happy until they accepted them.

By the time they returned, it was so dark that they had to toe around carefully to keep their footing. The moon was full, but not yet shining bright enough to light their path. Jeannine had no issue. It was as though she simply smelled her previous steps.

Mail was waiting inside. Mr. Kelley was welcoming Michael, Alma, and even Abraham to a charity exhibition lasting only one day at his garden in March of the next year, and it was his particular wish that Michael greet and lecture guests.

Needless to say, it had been many years since he'd attended any such event, and Alma said she'd never been to one at all. Abraham still did not want to go, even as a valet, much to Michael's unvoiced disappointment.

He warned his wife that she may have to dress for the daytime and the evening on that day, and she prepared to update her wardrobe. Most of the people attending would have valets and ladies' maids, but she said she could do without one.

"Why don't you dress me yourself?" she teased and threw a glove at him.

"I wouldn't know how. I'd find a way to be a burden instead of a helper."

"Will there be dancing?"

"I don't think so. There will undoubtedly be a lot of people our parents' age, or older, who may expect it, but knowing Mr. Kelley, it's unlikely. Can you dance?"

"No."

"Good. Neither can I."

Michael had essentially been appointed the spokesman for Mr. Kelley's operations so that he could lurk in the shadows and reap the benefits of the patronage (Michael really couldn't complain, since it contributed to his salary). As such, he expected that he and Alma would be heavily scrutinised, especially because of their youth. He expressed a desire to shield her from as much of it as he could, but she took his protective intentions as a slight.

"I have seven aunts," she asserted, curling her lip over the pot of soup that she watched. "There's nothing any exacting old woman could say that should upset me."

"Exacting old men?"

"Even less so. Most of them don't have it in them to confront a small young lady, lest my tender little heart crack under the strain. If they take issue with me, it's *you* that they'll complain to."

With that, she batted her eyelashes and smiled so rosily.

"So I suppose I'll be on my best behaviour just for you."

While she prepared dinner, he cudgelled his brain trying to make sense of his instructions. He'd never given a lecture before, but it had to be something intellectually stimulating and maybe a little impassioned. After all, he was meant to appeal to their magnanimity, if they had any. Anything he had to say would be lacklustre compared to Mr. Kelley's adventures deep in the heart of the jungle.

Additionally, Michael's charisma was found wanting, though Mr. Kelley himself was no charmer, either. Speaking in front of so many people was a chore, not because he was timid or reclusive, but because he'd always had a tendency to stammer, especially when reciting something written down. His first tutor called

him a moron, and his father threatened the man
with violence…

He went for his books on amphibians, and his
and Alma's notes. With these, he could surely
form a compelling case.

Alma chastised him for writing at the kitchen
table, with his papers over his food. In his
trance, he poured the soup back into the pot, and
took his work upstairs with a crust of bread in
his teeth.

At ten o'clock that night, he came downstairs at
last and threw on his coat to run outside with
Jeannine, then came back inside and brought his
lecture notes to Alma. She didn't look upset, and
told him that she didn't stop him from leaving
the table because he wouldn't have done so
without good reason. That being so, he knew his
work would be held to very high standards.

The subject was how amphibians reflected the
health of the environment around them, and how
they responded to polluted waters. She took it
into the parlour and pored over it for nearly half
an hour, with a pen ready. He watched her
scribble all over it, and then she handed it back
to him.

"First of all, it is one massive sentence,
completely disorganised and lacking

punctuation. I suppose that suits your character, but clean it up and save it, and speak on something else."

"What for?"

"There is good material here, but it won't stimulate a large audience that is unacquainted with the subject. I don't know what half of these words mean. It would do better in an academic environment once it is fixed and enriched. In fact, it needs some more research."

Since he wanted her to be frank, he curtailed his reproach and took the papers away.

"What should I speak of, then?"

"Pathos. You love that garden. Make them feel as strongly about it as you do. They enjoy feeling guilty and writing cheques to mollify themselves. Do not try to rush. You have three months, you know."

But since he had already started, he could not retire until he was finished.

It would have been rude to wake up Abraham to force him to read his thesis, so he went back upstairs, but sitting up in the study and staring at those books didn't help him. He'd gotten what he needed from them already, and Alma told him it wasn't right for the job.

"Why can't he hire some professor to do this, or track down one of his old associates?" he grumbled to himself as he stared glumly at the illustrations on the pages. "I'm not a teacher."

Alma went to bed. Michael followed, but didn't stay for long. He lit a lantern and went out into the back garden, even as cold as it was. The stars were out now, so he really didn't need the light, but he enjoyed its warm glow. On his path, he passed by the cluster of stones where Ida found that grass snake. He remembered having to teach her quite a lot. Now that he thought of it, the average person probably didn't know much more than she did. Many people feared snakes, even though the ones in England were almost completely harmless. If his demonstration was enough to charm Ida…

Michael turned and ran back towards the house, then quickly stopped to extinguish his lantern before he could trip and light himself on fire.

"Alma! I have it!" he called to her as he ran into the chamber and threw open the bed curtains. There was a candle burning out on the table, and it seemed she had just settled when he came in.

"I don't care if you want to be inside or outside, but pick one and stay," she mumbled and sat up with her hair tucked up in a cap, cream on her face, and a book in her lap. "What do you have?"

"I have my lecture! It's so simple! I'll demonstrate common European snakes!" Michael climbed into bed fully clothed and curled up against his wife.

"I think there's one in my bed."

He went ahead and took that as a compliment, and put out the candle.

"Thank you for spurning my thesis. I'll start writing a new one tomorrow."

XXXV

Christmas and the New Year were mostly
overshadowed by preparations for the event, but
Alma made a rich fruit cake and asked for a
sumptuous crimson velvet to make a simple
evening dress. It was his delight to be entreated,
and he was glad to purchase something frivolous
at her request. She never let him watch when she
made her clothes, insisting they were a surprise,
but she was exceptionally sharp when he asked
this time, and shut herself up in her sewing room
for a long stretch.

When she was finished with it, she stored it
away in her locked wardrobe, and yet, she kept
going back to it and trying it on over and over,
as if she just couldn't get it to fit quite right. He
suggested that she hire a seamstress if she
struggled, and she declined. He asked if he could
see how it fit, and she became sharp with him. Is
this how he was when *he* was inspired to work?

After it was finished and she (presumably) put it
away for good, she suddenly came into the
parlour and climbed straight into his lap.

"What's this?" Michael asked, positioning her
head to rest under his chin. "I could hardly get a
hold on you the past fortnight, and now it seems
I've picked up a little hatchling."

"Now that I've stopped working, I can relax."

Though she said that, she seemed tense and pensive thereafter, and spent a great deal of time sitting at the window, practically comatose. He brought her his revised paper, and she only barely looked over it and said it was "alright," then rose up like an automaton to go prepare dinner.

"Alma, are you alright?" he chased after her.

"I'm fine. I'm only a little tired."

He relented, deciding it would do no good to molest her right that minute, and went to Abraham to see if he could read his paper and maybe give him any clue if he knew what was wrong with her.

Abraham froze and stared up at him from his seat, opening his mouth, then closing it again, as if he'd had a *geas* put on him.

"I don't know that there is anything wrong with her," he sighed and adjusted his reading glasses. "But I believe I saw her going over the same letter at least four times in the past few days. It's possible that there is family trouble."

"Something she can't tell me?"

"If she wants to tell you, she will in her own time. Don't try to force it out of her, just be ready to listen."

And he was determined to be, so he reminded her that she could write him at any time while he went back to work. He tried not to let it distract him, though as most of the animals were hibernating, there was nothing that could bite him if he messed up. Mr. Kelley warned him that his wife had inevitably "gone sour" after two years. He was a well-meaning and amiable fellow who didn't mean any offence, but he had no tact to speak of.

He finished up the necessary maintenance in two weeks, presented his new lecture to Mr. Kelley, who probably did not read it, and went home. Alma was not there when he returned, and Abraham told him that she was seeing family.

Without telling or inviting him?

Michael could hardly sleep. At least Abraham knew where she was, but he had anticipated seeing her at home, and the house did not feel quite right without her presence. Eventually, his eyes simply surrendered to fatigue.

She came back early the next morning; he was awoken by her climbing into bed and twining her hands around his neck. Now he was aching to talk to her. Her letters to him had been cheery, but vague. She promised they would have a little visit later, but not until she rested, because she couldn't sleep on the train. There was a jovial gleam in her eyes as they fell shut, so surely she was back with good news, and all was well.

The suspense was tormenting him! While she slept, he threw some sticks for Jeannine, sat and watched the chickens (from a distance), scolded Jeannine for trying to play with them, and then went inside to find something to eat.

Michael prepared little sandwiches of cold duck meat and brought a plate to Abraham. He'd hunted the ducks himself; his preferred game was birds. Perhaps that was why they hated him. He brought his food to the parlour to play the piano.

He had fully mastered Mozart's *Piano Sonata No. 16,* and it was a nice piece to play when he wanted to relax and shut his brain off. This composition, he did not have the sheet music for… he'd heard it several times before, and simply banged on the piano until he found the notes he wanted. He could copy sounds from memory as a phonograph might, yet he forgot his own address.

Alma was finally awake! He hadn't even finished the first movement. She came in with her basket and sat near the piano. This wasn't new, but it stuck out to him because she sat facing him on the stool, and seemed to make a show of pulling out her needles as she greeted him. She was studiously working on a little pale blue square in her lap.

He stopped playing.

"Practising your knitting, are you?"

"Yes," she answered without looking up.

He continued.

"What is it going to be?" Michael asked as he played.

"A blanket."

"Seems like it'll take quite a while."

"No, no. It's a small blanket."

"Ah."

"Very small."

"Ah! Very small."

"Maybe I'll put little ducks on it."

"Oh, little ducks!"

And then his playing became slow and staggered as his thoughts fragmented. Alma hated knitting. The few times that she did, she used a machine, and yet, here she was, making a blanket entirely by hand, and smiling while she worked.

"Where does this song end?" she asked at last, and he realised he'd been repeating the same measure this whole time.

It probably took him far too long to put the puzzle together, but after all, he had just shut off his brain.

"Alma!" he turned around and snatched up her needles. "You're *having a baby*?"

She at first started when he sprang upon her, but now her expression was somewhat pleased.

"Well, you can't blame only me. I'm told it takes at least two people."

"Blame you!" he dropped the needles as his hands trembled, and he grabbed onto hers, which shook just as badly as his.

"My needles—"

Michael responded with an incomprehensible squeal that he couldn't translate, and strained her against him so tightly that he could feel her pulse.

"Mich— you'll squish him into my spine!" she gasped.

He released her.

"Oh, I'm sorry," he stooped down to pick up her knitting, handed it back to her, and paced around the room a few times, followed by Jeannine, as she had been drawn over by his squeaking. There were a million thoughts clamouring in his head all at once, and half of them were fearful. He couldn't put his feelings into words.

"You're not angry?" Alma asked timidly, and placed herself in front of him to stop him in his tracks.

Angry was the very last thing that he felt.

"What would I be angry for?" now he was anxious, wondering if he'd done anything to make her fear confiding in him.

"Well—" she wove her fingers into the holes in her blanket, averting her eyes. "I don't know why I thought that, but maybe you think this isn't the right time."

"I don't think there is a better time," Michael answered, and he meant it. "We have plenty saved up, and an established household. And we aren't travelling a great deal, either."

"You're alright with that?"

"Yes! Mr. Kelley's garden isn't far off. Daily train rides wouldn't be very economical, but I can still be home three or four days in a week."

She relaxed and fluttered her eyelashes as she looked every which way.

"Here," he took her gently into his arms this time and sat with her perched on his knee. "Are you happy with it?"

"Yes," she made herself small and nestled her head under his chin, and she trembled hard enough to rattle his teeth.

"Good. Then I am, too, and mostly I'm relieved that everything is well."

She lifted up her head.

"What do you mean?"

"You'd been acting rather strangely the past few weeks. I almost thought you were sick, or that something bad might have happened."

"No, no. I didn't mean to trouble you."

"I'm guessing Abraham knew before I did. He caught himself when I asked if he thought anything was wrong with you."

"Oh! Well he's been in your household for so long, and… I wanted to know, for example, how your father or grandfather handled such news. And then I visited my mother and my aunt. They have ten children between the two of them, so if anybody could confirm my suspicions, I was sure they could… you aren't angry?"

"No, Alma, no, I'm not angry!" Michael threw up his hands. In fact, he was already trying to imagine the sensation of a newborn placed in his arms, wondering how big it would grow, and whether he would comb lustrous titian locks or wild auburn ringlets. "This is a lot for sure, but I think it's the best news I've ever received."

She was now contently working on the blanket once again.

"Oh! You really were working on something?"

"Of course I was."

"You hate knitting."

"I want to make him something with my own hands."

"Him?" Michael raised an eyebrow.

"Yes. It's a boy," she declared.

"Hmm…"

"You don't think so?"

"I don't," he decided. "I think it'll be a little girl, and just as pretty as her mother."

"Well, he's in *me,* so I ought to know," Alma insisted, and now her feathers were ruffled.

"Think of it as a contingency plan," he reasoned with her. "One of us must be correct, and if it's you, you can gloat about it later. If not, we won't be floundering to think of names."

"Do you have a preference one way or the other?"

"I do not. Just a strong feeling."

"Your feelings are wrong."

"Anyway, you like to crochet more. Why don't you do that?"

"The knitting got your attention, didn't it?" she smiled. "I'll knit the border on this centre square and crochet the rest."

Well, Michael wanted to make something, too. Almost right away, he set to work constructing a cradle: a tall one with a sturdy bottom, that could easily be reached from the bedside.

Working with his hands always distracted him from his crippling feelings of terror and inadequacy. Of course, they were financially in a perfect position for children, and at a prime age, but Michael knew beyond a shadow of a doubt that he was not fit to be a father. Any child deserved better than him. For that matter, Alma deserved better. He felt that all he had to offer was the fruits of his strength.

As with the last piece of furniture he constructed, he was told it looked "rugged." Abraham called it "an admirable attempt." It took on a more pleasing shape once he sanded it down and painted it, and he ruined one of his shirts because he was too impatient to let it dry.

"So, how can you chaff me about getting varnish on my dress?" Alma prodded him.

"This is a work shirt. I wasn't wearing my wedding dress while painting, simpleton! Why were you doing chores in it?" he twisted her ear with his clean hand.

"I just liked the feeling of wearing it. I felt that it would turn my dreams into reality."

"And did it?"

"Yes, but the dress was sacrificed."

"Well, wee alchemist, hasten to finish that blanket, so we can stage it."

When Alma finished the little blue and yellow blanket, he placed it in the cradle to see how it looked. It was big enough to contain a child for two or three years. They placed it next to their bed. The sight made Michael sick with fear, but he made an effort to repress it, as he knew he would have to get used to it.

Or perhaps not...

That line of thought was far more ghastly than the former, and he pushed it out of his mind so that it could not be realised.

By the time he finished the cradle, March had already come upon them. Michael and Alma had gotten so swept up in the whirlwind of feverish preparation, that they'd neglected to pack for the trip until the weekend before. He packed his finest suits, knowing he probably wouldn't even wear them.

He went to see how Alma was faring with her packing, and found her sitting on the floor in front of her trunk, stripped down to her drawers, and clutching her crimson gown with the faintest glimmer of tears in her eyes.

"Something wrong?" he sat across from her.

"My dress barely fits," she didn't look up at him. "I just made it, and it barely fits."

"Oh…" his heart sank, thinking he wouldn't ever get to see her wear it. "Is there any way you can fix that?"

She shook her head.

"No point. I'll take apart the bodice and alter it, have the baby, and then need to fix it again, after I wore it only once. Anyway, I won't be able to fix it in time."

"There's nothing you can do?"

"I'll see," she stood and gathered up the dress.

"Well, how about I pack what you laid out over here?" he offered.

"No. I know exactly where I want everything."

Her solution was to shorten the skirt waist, and attach many roses around the shoulders to conceal that her bodice was too snug (not that he minded it).

Now he had to ask her for something she might not like, and made sure to do so after she had eaten breakfast and washed up, and went into the parlour, while she was comfortable and content.

"Ah, Alma!" he knelt in front of her and began taking off her shoes so that she could recline on the couch. "How do you feel this morning?"

"You asked me at breakfast. I feel just as well now as I did less than an hour ago."

He didn't see how anybody could feel well after eating only curds and jam for breakfast, but she refused him when he tried to fork some of his ham onto her plate.

"That's good, that's good! Well… about the exhibition, I have a favour to ask of you."

"Yes?"

"Could I use you in my demonstration?"

She raised an eyebrow and didn't reply, so he elaborated:

"I'd like to place some snakes on you—"

"No, Michael!" she squeaked.

"*Harmless* snakes, Alma! It's to make people aware of the nature of non-venomous snakes! They won't be any threat to you, and if they show the slightest sign of fear or hostility, I'll take them off immediately! Just consider it, please, my dear," he'd taken her hands and had his chin rested on her bosom.

"Don't lean on my chest. It's sore."

"I'm sorry," he placed his head in her lap instead. "But do consider it. I'd appreciate it a lot."

"I'll consider it," she laid herself out on the couch and opened up a book.

Alma did not give him a definite answer until they'd already boarded the train, but at least it was a favourable answer. She would consent to have them placed on her, but she would not pick them up.

"But why can't Mr. Kelley be the demonstration?" she asked as they stopped in Bristol.

"Because they're his. One might assume he trained them."

"Did he?"

"I don't think so, but if anybody could do it, it'd be him. Additionally," he pinched her nose. "You are much nicer to look at than either of us."

XXXVI

They arrived with only half an hour to throw on their formal clothes. Alma's dress was delightfully simple and elegant, and the roses on her dress and in her hair were the perfect touch. Michael's nerves were so overworked already, he swallowed down two glasses of whiskey before they'd even left their room.

He was absolutely forbidden to tell everybody about her condition, no matter how tempting it was. It was too early. Besides, it was not a proper subject to cast upon a crowd of strangers.

Luckily, it was not as rigid as the average gentry gathering, as Mr. Kelley most certainly would not have approved of it. Michael's manners had atrophied, and he was possibly passed the point that he could integrate into their ranks.

Mr. Kelley was there to help receive the guests when they arrived, and explain the purpose of the exhibition. That was the extent of his involvement. He then retreated to the private section of the property to undoubtedly work until his body gave out.

Michael was disappointed to learn that those with children had elected to keep them at home. He was always the most excited when children came to the garden; their wonder was unmatched, and they were easier to impress. In front of this crowd, he felt a great deal of pressure.

It was more of a guided tour than a lecture. He did not deliver an emotional and sympathetic speech, as Alma had instructed him to do. Instead, he began with a simple introduction, and as he picked up his creature of choice, he became excited, and spoke from pure enthusiasm, and then he was more comfortable. Really, it was little different from how he spoke to guests on a regular day, except he was a bit more scientific in his explanations, and he tried to emphasise the potential for education and research.

He presented Alma to the crowd, and then when she was prepared, he placed a large and mellow European rat snake on her shoulders.

"And this beauty— not Mrs. Bennett, the snake— is not of the venomous sort," he began. "Don't be intimidated by its size. As she— that is, as this woman is quite still and calm, it has no reason to strike."

Alma was still, yes, but her expression was pinched and strained. She slowly relaxed and shared the guests' fascination as it wound its way over her arms and around her neck.

He took it off of her and placed it on himself.

"So you see here," he continued while it twined round his arm. "It's not— ah, it does not mind being lifted with gentle hands, and will not bite."

The prickling needle sensation in his left arm signified that it did, indeed, bite him. Alma saw it before he did, and her eyes grew wide as saucers.

"It's alright," he murmured through his teeth as it bit him a second time. His credibility hinged on her not panicking.

"That is, unless they become a little impatient!" Michael chuckled nervously, and luckily, they laughed with him. "But if one reacts calmly, then it realises you're not— ah, you won't— you aren't a threat. See, now, it has let me go, and that didn't even hurt."

He put it back and scolded it for trying to embarrass him, knowing well and good that it couldn't hear him, and then he moved on to other specimens: lizards, toads, newts, and their newly acquired bats. Those, he was most excited about. Bats made up a substantial portion of England's mammals, so their preservation should have surely been a priority, especially for their role in curbing the mosquito population. Now, he could

speak with emotion, ensuring his listeners that
their efforts were not simply for profits, but for
the salvation of many of the creatures in their
care, and for mankind.

With that, he circled them back to the entrance,
and that concluded the exhibition. It lasted for
only two hours, and ended at three o'clock. The
crowd dispersed, though some lingered to ask
questions on their way out, which he answered
as best as he could. Mr. Kelley emerged from the
shadows and spoke highly of his little
performance.

They had dinner at four, washed his bites, and
came back to do it a second time, in front of
even more people. He used a different snake to
place on Alma, and it was calm enough for him
to wear it for quite a stretch. He'd never spoken
so much in his entire life. It was exhausting. He
didn't dislike it, but he wished he'd had some
practice. That was his own fault.

After that, they had a light supper and settled in
for the night. Alma praised him, though he didn't
feel he'd done anything praiseworthy. It wasn't
something he'd enjoy doing every single day,
and it likely didn't even make much of a
difference.

"Next time he wants to butter up some gentry, he
should call upon a professor," he rasped and

heaped a brimming spoonful of honey into his tea. "Or an actor. They're loud, and better-looking."

They went home the next morning. The event did not draw in many donations right away, but more and more visitors began to trickle in, as people wanted to see the mysterious white snake charmer. This meant more work for Michael, but luckily more money as well. Visitors inquired about his ancestry, insisting he must have some Indian blood in him: none that he knew of, and he didn't even consider his feats to be impressive, but they pressed even more upon learning he was, at some point, a nobleman.

This led to newspapers printing his name. He did not read one scrap of what they wrote about him. It was all pomp, he was sure of it.

Regardless, it drew even more people, but to his disappointment, most had no desire to learn and only wanted to see him play with the reptiles.

"This isn't a circus," he grumbled to Mr. Kelley when they were alone. "I can't do tricks all day."

"Vexing, isn't it?" he chuckled. "Most people don't want to be educated, they want to be entertained. Bread and circuses, you know. Few out there share our passion."

"Is that supposed to make me feel enlightened? I feel like a fool."

"You are enlightened. And a fool."

XXXVII

He saved every little bit of that money that they didn't use right away. His work sped up, and Alma's slowed down. By May, she was in a nesting sort of way, and was always at home, making preparations for their child— they expected her late that summer (that is, Michael expected *her*, and Alma expected *him)*.

Alma said it was a boy because her complexion was clear and sunny, whereas a girl syphons her mother's beauty. Michael reasoned that it was still a girl, because Alma had so much beauty to share.

Furthermore, she made her case that a boy would exhaust his father just as much as his mother, and Michael had grown more fat and lazy recently.

"Fat and lazy!" he huffed. "I only became so because work is gruelling in warmer months, and I must eat enough of your cooking to sustain me for many days away from home… do you really think I'm fat?" he added at the end of his rant.

"*More* fat and lazy, simply more so than before!" she corrected him. "You must admit you've gotten a bit softer than you once were."

"And is that a problem? I tell you, I can still lift three times your weight! This is muscle!"

"Well, if you are pleased with it, and still able to work, then it is not a problem."

After that discussion, Alma gave him more generous portions at dinner. It always tickled her when he praised her cooking. Still, she would not waver in her opinions.

Abraham said that when a mother and father can't agree on whether to anticipate a boy or a girl, that meant they would likely have twins. Michael hoped not— he'd only made one cradle.

What they did agree on was that her indigestion signified a full head of hair. They discussed it at breakfast. Her mother and aunts passed this information on to her, and he had no reason to deny it.

"Mother and aunts—" he remembered. "Does Dr. Webb know about it?"

Alma's face blanched as white as the curds she was eating.

"I meant to tell him last month. I have a letter for him somewhere, but I'd never remembered to post it, and sometimes my feet hurt too much to walk to the post office."

"Dig it up later today and give it to me," Michael thought that was the obvious solution.

That being said, she forgot to do so, he forgot to ask her, and the letter was soon buried.

Alma still tended to her vegetables, even though he was always entreating her to go easy on her feet. Her eyes were getting strained much more easily, so reading and writing too much gave her a headache. Sometimes she needed somebody to write her letters for her.

"You only want me to write your letters because my writing is nicer!" he teased.

"Not so. Your penmanship is inefficient."

"Let me have my small victory. It is all that I have that is prettier than yours."

Additionally, she was sleeping a lot more, but the quality of her slumber seemed to have diminished, which may have been the cause of her cloudy vision. She tossed and kicked, and was always switching sides. He knew she needed undisturbed sleep, so when the battering was too much of a nuisance, he just spent the rest of the night on the couch in the study. Sometimes, he slept on the floor with Jeannine.

She had less patience for Jeannine, as well, shouting at her for jumping up on her and grabbing things in her hands— especially if they were clothes she was taking off of the line. Michael took responsibility for her behaviour and took time away from work to rigorously train her.

As it all unfolded, he wrote it down. He never imagined he would be the type to keep diaries, but he developed the habit years ago when he started writing down his dreams and feelings. Now, there was a drawer of filled books in his study, which he went about without ever expecting them to see the light of day.

Mr. Kelley did not allow Michael to be home for Alma's birthday, which she said she did not mind, since she had plenty, and she was much more occupied with someone else's birth…

He still had boxes of roses and jammy sweets sent to her on that day.

Michael came home in the middle of June to see a small carriage by the walkway, and a tawny horse tethered up in the stable he'd built long ago.

He was not expecting company, and did not know that horse.

He patted Jeannine, and then he went to greet
the horse that she seemed so excited about.

"Hello, ah— sir," he observed, and saw he had a
good supply of water and vegetables. "You have
been set up well, I see. What brings you here?"

Coming up the steps, he heard the chatter of
three people inside: Abraham and his wife, and a
voice he didn't recognise. Did she bring a friend,
or a colleague?

He let himself in and followed the sounds into
the parlour, and found Alma and Abraham
sitting across from a large middle-aged woman
clad in red and blue, with her back to the door. A
young lady in plain brown dress stood at her
side.

Alma saw him first, sending him a look of relief
and total exhaustion forced behind a cordial
grin.

The colourful mystery woman turned around,
and beholding her was uncanny, because the
features were so familiar, and yet so alien.

"Michael!" she called out and rushed at him.
"Michael Bennett! So it is you!"

"Madam, who am I that you believe I must be?" he asked, realising immediately that his question made no sense.

"I am Hannah Lavigne— Hannah Bennett, the sister of Samuel Bennett, your father," she stated outright, bowing her head and offering her hand. He detected a lilting hint of French in her accent, signifying, alongside what was presumably her married name, that she had been in France for a long while.

But his heart raced to the point of bursting when he heard his father's name, as it had not been uttered in so long, and certainly not by anybody claiming kinship.

"It's true, I am Michael Bennett. How do you do, madam?" Michael took her hand, prepared and possibly hoping for the possibility that she was blood, but too sceptical to accept her outright.

"I am well, and so much the better now that I've found you!" she beamed and gathered both his hands to her bosom, eyeing him up and down. "I can hardly believe it! My, you look just like your grandfather, you certainly do!"

"And how did you find me?" he led her to the parlour and took Alma's seat, as she'd silently excused herself to flee upstairs.

"You're in the papers, my lad."

She drew in a great big breath and began a long recounting of her experience.

Basically, she had been estranged from the Bennetts for many years after running off with a French merchant at sixteen, and had been living in France ever since— now independently wealthy and a widow.

As news travelled to her slowly, she discovered only last year that Samuel Bennett had passed away, and rushed back to England to find his surviving son, the last remnants of her dear brother. Finding the estate was no more, she began desperately combing the countryside until she came to Brownwall, pleased to find it was not abandoned, and ecstatic to reunite with sweet Abraham. He confirmed her identity himself, saying he remembered her vividly and asserting the validity of her records. He couldn't see her very well, but he must have known better than any of them.

Michael was more at ease now, and she must not have been looking to get her hands on the estate, now that she knew very little remained of it, and was likely much wealthier than her nephew.

He sought a likeness in her: the eyes and hair were the same as those in the portraits of Berthe

Bennett hanging up in the house. The mouth was firm and grim, as he saw in the Bennett men. She was certainly fairly tall and strongly-built, if a bit on the corpulent side. She might have been gorgeously plump in her youth. At present, she had a big ruffled bodice pushing out her bosom and pinching her waist down to a preposterous circumference.

On one hand, this was a complete stranger that he had no feelings for, but on the other hand, he was now able to believe she was family, after so many years of thinking he was the last of his kind.

Additionally, she had many children for him to meet: cousins, all about his age.

"And on the subject of children," she continued, after pausing for the very first time— now she was holding hands with Michael and Abraham. "I've met your wife. She is an enchanting lady, though a bit timid— uncharacteristic of a Bennett woman, but she is young, after all, and I admit that I never did meet Mary Glasse. She tells me that you expect your son in September. As she doesn't have one, I've informed her that I will be her midwife!"

"I suppose that is well, but did she consent to have you?" Michael asked, as he saw Alma flee as soon as he arrived.

"She at first insisted she didn't need one, but decided I could at least be of some help when the time to deliver draws near— after all, I am a practised midwife, and I've had nine of them myself. I say, though, she's quite thin. You need to fatten her up, or she won't have a healthy baby!"

He was excited to have more family, but she was being awfully hasty about inserting herself into their lives.

Hannah Lavinge would be staying with them for the night, then leave to make more permanent arrangements and return to them in late August. That night, she toured the house and commented on all that had changed, and exchanged a few words in French with Michael— whereas hers was casual and natural, she told him that his was too formal: too "academic."

"Do you really have no servants?" she asked as she watched Alma busy herself in the kitchen.

"Alma didn't want any, as she isn't used to them, and she's quite conscious of our spending," Michael explained. "Besides, we get all of the work done just fine between the two of us."

"Hmph! She'll appreciate the extra help after she has the child."

She ordered Sandra, her lady's maid, to assist with supper, and Alma's cheeks flushed deep red as she worked. He noticed she kept her head low, and spoke only when prompted.

He volunteered to take the horse for a walk before bed. His name was Sebastian, and he was old and mellow, gentle enough to tolerate Jeannine running circles around him. Michael enjoyed feeding him radishes from the garden.

"I suppose that is my aunt," Michael declared as he settled into bed. "What do you think of her?"

Alma prepared to speak, but bit her lip and chose her words with caution.

"I think she is quite… impetuous, though that is not surprising."

"Ha! She really insists upon herself, doesn't she?"

"I don't think I'll need help delivering the baby. I've had more midwife offers than I can count— even from Ruth White! I don't want to be crowded."

"I understand how you feel, but I do think we should at least have somebody on hand who knows what she's doing, and I think you should have at least one attendant as it is."

"No relatives," she insisted. "I've already selected Laura. She will be here in September."

"But you don't mind Mrs. Lavigne being there?"

"I suppose we would call upon her if we absolutely must, but no sooner."

"That will suffice."

While Alma stayed at home and filled a trunk with little toys and linens, Abraham, of course, was wild with glee, as he'd not welcomed a new baby in the house since… Baby Berthe. He feverishly searched the attic for any relics that could be of use, even though Michael had already scoured it while transforming it into his study.

And how would Mr. Kelley take this news? The birth was expected to be in late September, and Michael intended to take the remainder of the year off, if it was allowed.

He brought it to his employer in July, hoping that was plenty of notice.

The announcement that he so jovially shared at the end of his shift did not land in the way that he thought it would.

Mr. Kelley was sifting through papers in Miss Gaye's office. He did not look up even once.

"Ah, most astounding!" he finally said. "September… so, you're sure it will survive?"

"What— I'm certain!" Michael huffed. "Alma is in good health, breathing clean air, and has lightened her load significantly as of late. I make sure that she stays off of her feet."

"Well, if her work is not so demanding, I fail to see why she should need you. Out in the wild, most offspring know only their mothers, after all."

He brushed off Mr. Kelley's statement about wild animals. It did not apply, and he knew it. Why did he need to cite the laws of nature to justify his intentions?

"Do we not make a point to care for all living things under our care?"

"Yes, indeed, that is our purpose!" Mr. Kelley shouted into the open drawer, still avoiding his gaze. "And you've lost sight of it! Did I not tell you that men such as we are unfit for marriage and conventional life? Your *wife's* use could be taken up by any whore on the street!"

Michael thrust his hands into his pockets and clenched the seams of his clothes, or he might have swung on this old man. He glared down at his employer that he had always revered as an example to mankind, and he saw something that he did not want to become.

"I *will* be taking my leave," he stated, as softly as he could manage. "I will return in no sooner than three months, and things will continue as they always have, because you *need* me. I do not need you."

He began to sweat as soon as he finished that sentence. He took a great gamble in saying it, because with his current set of skills, this was the closest, best-paying job he was likely to get. His family's future hung on Mr. Kelley's answer. He even felt a bit sore afterwards, as there was no need for him to add that last biting remark.

"Then it shall be so," was all that was said.

"Thank you, sir," he tried to be cordial on his way out, but some evil spirit possessed him. "And penguin fathers raise their young!"

Michael went home and gladly told Alma that he had his leave approved for three months. No papers? Well, it was an informal environment, after all.

He returned to work with just as much enthusiasm as ever, and Mr. Kelley fed him and directed him accordingly.

It was admittedly difficult to focus as September drew closer and closer. The closer it was, the more he imagined something bad might happen, and then he scolded himself for doing so.

One early morning, a visitor came up to the entrance with an unusual inquiry: a young lady probably no older than Ida asked if one of them would come and examine a dog that was having strange convulsions. Mr. Kelley had a history as a veterinary, so he readily volunteered, and took Michael just in case another pair of hands was needed.

"He followed me a little ways very slowly," she testified. "He didn't seem mean."

Near the end of a secluded street, they saw the animal in question: a raggedy stray dog held its head skyward, and had severe spasms of the neck. The jaws hung open and nipped at the air. Michael inched closer for a better look, then jumped back when it found him out and slumped forward in a pitiful attempt to lunge.

Undeterred, it picked itself back up and ambled towards them with no fear.

Mr. Kelley's whole mein seemed to lose its vigour.

"Oh, no," Michael murmured, as they were both thinking the same thing.

"Aye, I think he's mad, lad," his employer sighed. "Did you bring your pistol?"

His heart raced. He knew what that meant.

"I did," he replied.

"Let's have it," he reached out, and Michael delivered, inwardly relieved that he was not being elected to do it himself.

"Ah! You're going to shoot it, Mister?" the lady cried, grasping at Michael's clothes. "You're supposed to help animals! This is cruel!"

Clearly, she had never ventured far out of the city.

"My dear, we have no choice. Rabies is a wasting disease. It won't get any better; only suffer and possibly make other people sick. It's kinder this way."

Mr. Kelley waited until the very last second, when its glassy eyes were plainly visible.

"Step back, madam," Micuael put himself between the girl and Mr. Kelley, and she fled the scene. He squeezed his eyes shut, preparing for the gunshot.

The dog fell, and continued to flounder even with a bullet in its neck. He shot it once more in the head. As it went down, Mr. Kelley heaved a deathly rattle as if it was he who'd been shot.

"I've never gotten used to it," he handed Michael his pistol, with his eyes downcast. "It is always distressing, but it can't be helped... when I stop being affected by it... I'll give up my animals."

Which will never happen, Michael thought to himself, and put away the pistol to assist in moving the corpse.

He'd hunted before. The image of that dog as it was shot should not have stuck with him, but for the next few days, he saw it every time he shut his eyes, and its blood on the pavement painted his vision. He saw Jeannine succumbing to the same fate, and he hated the idea so much, he couldn't fall asleep at night.

She was well and happy when he returned to
Brownwall, and merrily bounded down the
walkway to greet him. Now he was at ease.

There were more guests when he arrived home,
and this time, he knew them: Henry and Ellen
Webb, and Ida.

"Michael!" Dr. Webb called the moment he had
both feet in the door. "You have some explaining
to do, both of you."

"Explaining, sir?" he shrank back towards the
threshold.

"Absolutely, you do!" he gestured to Alma, who
had occupied the entire sofa, and had Ida's head
in her lap, fixed to her midsection. "You would
conceal this from me— my first grandchild!"

"Sir, we've been quite busy, and we simply
forgot— we didn't mean anything by it!" he set
his things down in the hall and scampered over
to the parlour. "There's a letter somewhere, I
know it, but I suppose that won't do any good
now."

"No, it wouldn't. You've at least been keeping
her off her feet?"

"To the best of my abilities," he replied and greeted everyone in turn— even kissed Ida— before he seated himself on a stool by said feet.

"Ida, I can't believe I'm saying it myself, but you seem to have grown into a very nice and pretty young lady!" Michael felt he had to admire how still and proper she was at the moment. "Did you make that dress yourself?"

She hissed at him to be quiet and continued listening to Alma's abdomen.

"Trying to hear the ocean?" he asked.

"He does it, too," Alma whispered to Ida and shifted to put her feet on the floor so that her cousin could sit.

Ida brought a blanket with a very ugly embroidery of Ruby, and Michael pretended he liked it. With all of the gifts brought to them, they had more baby clothes than they knew what to do with. There was more than enough room to house them comfortably, so he invited them to stay for a few days.

They voluntarily took up most of Alma's workload. She appreciated it, but she hated it. Her parents kept her confined to the sofa for much of the day, only allowing her to get up every few hours. If she wanted fresh air, they just opened a window.

Hannah Lavigne was due to arrive on August 25; that was the date she gave in her letter. She was late. They stayed up after dark to greet her when she came, and she never turned up. Michael even sat on the doorstep with Jeannine until midnight.

He came back inside and snuck Jeannine some scraps from the kitchen. Once inside, he got about three hours of fitful sleep.

Whatever roused him from his slumber, he did not know. Some presentment drew him awake and alert at once. He groped around in the dark and lit a candle.

It was about four o'clock, and the air was balmy and warm, yet it was heavily charged, as if lightning was about to strike, but as the curtains were drawn, and a window was open, he saw that the sky was clear. He could hear crickets.

Alma was up, with her head against the bedroom window. He came up behind her and beheld a sliver of moon sinking below the treetops.

"You can't sleep?" he asked.

She shook her head, and turned towards him. Her eyes were red and heavy.

"It's hot. I'm going to walk," she threw on a robe and passed him on her way to the door.

"Should you?" he followed her with the candle he had. "You shouldn't try to go down the stairs on your own. It's dark."

"I won't!" she snapped and took his candle. "I'm going to walk the gallery.

He allowed it, but stood and watched her pace around from one end to the other.

"You need some water?" he offered.

"No."

She paced maybe twenty rounds. Though he knew it was vexing to her, he stood by, in case he was wanted. He rarely voiced it, but in those days, he was so very afraid of her falling. Her unshod feet didn't make a sound. When she came back his way, she snatched at his robe; sweat glistened like embers on her face, and she was ghostly pale.

"Get my mother," she ordered him.

"Do you have a fever?"

"Go and get my mother now!" she turned him towards the stairs.

"Alright, alright, but don't go anywhere!" he snatched the candle from her hand. As he turned, he nearly slipped on… something.

He didn't question her, and did as he was told. It was always a queer feeling to go knocking on a woman's bedroom door, but of course he had no choice.

"Mrs. Webb!" he rapped on the door and wrestled with the handle. "Ma'am, come out!"

As soon as he spoke, the door swung open, almost right into his face. Apparently, she was a light sleeper.

"What's the matter, you?" Ellen Webb hissed, tying her robe as she came out.

"Alma needs you upstairs," he guided her to the staircase without taking no for an answer, and soon she was rushing up with his candle in her hand. He stood at the bottom stair and watched the little flame dance away into the darkness, throwing trembling shadows across the walls. A door opened, closed, and opened again.

He followed as frenzied whispering rose from the second storey. Mrs. Webb intercepted him on the staircase.

"Is everything alright?" he asked.

"She is in the beginning stages of her travail, and fast approaching delivery," she affirmed, already taking hold of his sleeves.

"You mean— it's too early!" he tried to hurry up the stairs, but Mrs. Webb pulled on his robe. He heard stitches split and shed the garment, continuing in just his bedclothes.

"Michael Bennett!" she threw the robe at him. "Get back here, you won't be any help!"

"Five minutes! You said it's the beginning, so give me just five minutes!"

"No more!" she called. "Then get right back down here so that I can make use of you."

Mrs. Webb had plundered the spare room upstairs. Three chairs were set apart, and Alma was seated in the middle, with her feet up on the two others. Tears and sweat streaked her face.

"Does it hurt?" Michael knelt at her feet.

"It's too early," she puled feebly. "I expected to wait another month, I'm not ready."

"Well, we were just wrong, then," he used his robe to sponge at her face. "But I'm certainly glad I came home when I did."

"Laura isn't even here!"

"Your mother is here, and so is the doctor."

"I don't want them stooping over me, looking at me…" Alma's sentence trailed off, and she leaned so far back into the chair that it creaked and groaned.

"If you have any troubles, *somebody* has to look at you, and I don't know what's happening!"

She only huffed and braced her feet against the chairs.

"Does it hurt now?"

"No," she lied. "It's speeding up. Started at nine o'clock. Thought I could sleep through it. At two, I couldn't go back to sleep."

She surely did not need to be confined to a wooden chair throughout the entire ordeal, so he plucked her out of it and cradled her, sitting on the floor.

"Think, though," he reminded her. "We're about to find out whether it's a boy or a girl, aren't we?"

"It's a boy," she insisted, now looking more relaxed, and a little amused.

"Care to make a wager? If you're right, I'll buy you anything you want."

"And what do you want from me if you're right?"

"I'd like you to sing for me."

She raised an eyebrow.

"Is that all?"

"That's all I want. And what could I get for you?"

Alma took the hem of his robe in her fingers.

"I'd like a new stove."

"Is that all?"

A self-satisfied little smile bloomed in her features.

"A stove is useful, and that thing we have is older than my parents. I want a new one."

"Understood. And I'll deliver, when *you* deliver," he kissed her forehead, which was already damp again. "Would you like me to go and get your eyeglasses? I'll fetch whatever you'd like."

"I don't think I shall need them, but I think, soon, I'll want some coffee… some chocolate…"

People were stirring downstairs. Alma's mother evidently alerted the entire house.

"Just what she needs," he mumbled, and he gently set her down, and went to the door. Mrs. Webb was there, thrusting an armful of linens onto him.

"Your five minutes has passed."

"It has *not!*" he protested.

"Put those over there," she pointed to the chair on the left. "And go downstairs."

"Maybe I should stay here."

"You will do no such thing—"

"I'll leave if Alma wants me to."

"I won't have any distractions; you're of no use here. Go downstairs and start a kettle of water boiling."

Michael looked back at Alma. She wasn't paying attention to him.

"He's not going to wait for us, so do *something*, or get out of my way!" Mrs. Webb pushed him towards the door. "And when you've done that, I'll be wanting another lamp and Dr. Webb's tools."

"Now, wait!" he kept his footing. "What are you doing, ordering me around in *my* house, tearing me from *my* wife?"

"She was *my* daughter first, and there was no thought of pleasing *you* when she was born!" Ellen Webb snapped back.

"Just you explain to me what I'm meant to do, and why I'm doing it!"

"It is obvious that I need these things, or I wouldn't ask for them, but you're a *man*, and have no business knowing, nor could you possibly. If you're interested in helping *your* wife, then do as I tell you! This may be *your* house, but I am *your* elder, and I have experience that *you* don't!"

Michael swallowed his words, as when he looked back at Alma, he saw her growing more restless, and having a shouting match with her mother did nothing for her nerves.

It was easier to do what he was told, so he hurried downstairs and filled the largest kettle they had.

He brought the lamp, and a rattled, hastily dressed Dr. Webb came upstairs with his tools.

Mrs. Webb seized Michael's arm.

"Rending your plumage will do no good," she said with surprising softness. "I have attended all of my sisters' births. Everybody will be fine, you do not need to watch— you do not *want* to watch, I promise."

"Does Alma want me to leave?"

"I want *everybody* to leave!" Alma snarled.

Dr. Webb deposited his tools and retreated at once, but Michael stood and watched for just a moment.

Mrs. Webb hovered over her daughter and muttered something Michael couldn't hear.

"But I want to get up!" Alma protested and writhed in her seat.

"You mustn't. You need to sit still."

"It hurts when I sit still!" she growled.

That wasn't an outburst brought on by pain, but fear. Her muscles were relaxed, but she still trembled and wept. Her mother heaved a sharp, rasping sigh, and Michael expected her to lose her temper, but she continued to speak gently.

Now even Dr. Webb was dismissing Michael from the room.

"You're not going to sit in with Alma?" he asked as he was escorted downstairs.

"Not unless somebody's life depends on it. She'd never forgive me."

The water had started to boil. He let it cool down to merely scalding hot and took it upstairs. Some of it spilled onto his wrist. The pain nearly caused him to drop the kettle, but he set his teeth and rallied.

He peeked through the doorway and saw the tools spread out on the table, glistening under the lamps.

"Say, there, those are for surgery!" Michael squeaked, suddenly feeling as though he might faint, vomit, or both. "What are you doing with them?"

"I doubt they will be necessary, but I want them sanitised," Mrs. Webb explained. "Begone."

With that, he was locked out. Foolish woman, thinking a mere wooden door would contain him.

Dawn was approaching. He decided he may as well get dressed, and made up a fire, not for the warmth, but to look at it and relax. Abraham brought tea and cold sandwiches, and everybody herded into the parlour with Michael. He didn't feel he could keep any food down at the moment. Now he somewhat understood why Alma wanted to be left alone, because for all their good intentions, being crowded didn't mollify him one bit.

"Why are you in knots?" Ida demanded. "You're not the one having a baby!"

Michael ignored her and decided he'd go on a little walk with Jeannine. She happily licked his hands, oblivious to the commotion inside. He brought his old straw hat and threw it for her to catch a few times, since Alma was not present to scold him. He'd just made it down the walkway with her when he saw a familiar carriage clattering up to the house. He took his hat off and waved it over his head.

"Ho, there, dear boy!" Aunt Hannah called out when she stepped out of the carriage with her lady's maid.

"You're late!" Michael called back, momentarily forgetting his manners. "And Alma is in confinement as we speak!"

"Sacré dieu!" she cried and hurried up the walkway, with her maid barely able to keep up, and her driver carrying her things. "She was due for September! How long has it been?"

Instead of checking his watch, he looked at the sun. That was stupid.

"She said she started at around nine o'clock last night. It is close to six now."

Hannah Lavigne gave a shriek of alarm and hiked up her skirt.

"She could deliver any minute! Who's with her?"

"Her mother," Michael passed and took the bags from the driver, still blinking the purple out of his eyes. He recklessly deposited them in the hall and chased her down to make sure she didn't cause a disruption and grieve his wife.

"Who are you?" Mrs. Webb checked them at the threshold upstairs.

"I am Madame Hannah Lavigne, Lord Bennett's aunt, and that makes us family!" she answered sweetly. "I can assist in the birth."

She still blocked the door.

"And what makes you qualified?" she asked coolly.

"I've had nine of my own, and been a midwife to a dozen more!" Mrs. Lavigne insisted. "All are living and well— listen, you'll need an additional set of hands very soon, so allow me to attend!"

Michael watched two of reportedly the most stubborn women on the planet stare each other down.

"Hurry up!" he ordered them, and he knew he was prodding an alligator with a stick, but now he was vexed.

"You may come in and stand to one side," Ellen Webb relented, and stepped aside.

"Does anybody need something to eat?" Michael offered.

"Alma has been begging for a cup of coffee for nearly an hour. Bring us all some coffee."

"And why was nothing said for nearly an hour?" he demanded.

"My, you are stubborn as a mule! No wonder Alma acts the way that she does. Just go and get it now, please."

Aunt Hannah was already upon Alma, lavishing her with a repetitive deluge of *"ma chérie,"* and *"petite maman."*

He brought up a tray with three cups, and some bread and butter, then he was ordered to fetch a clean smock and more sheets.

"Alma!" he called into the room. "Do your best!"

As soon as it escaped his lips, he realised how stupid it sounded. She was not playing a game of chess.

Alma released an awful, throaty groan, but when he tried to peer inside and talk to her, the door was shut in his face and locked. The strong scent of blood made him feel faint, and he fled downstairs.

As his foot touched the threshold of the parlour, what sounded like a sobbing wail raised the hairs on his arms, and he turned and went straight back to the staircase.

"Sir, you cannot go up there!" Sandra intercepted him and snatched at his waistcoat.

"Don't touch me! *Don't touch me!*" he bellowed as he spun on his heels so fast, he almost threw her to the floor. "This is *still my house,* and you are *no family of mine, so stay in your place!*"

He should have turned his attention away from her and continued on his way, but instead, his nerves were wrought paper-thin, and he spent his fury on the first thing to cross his path, until Abraham and Dr. Webb both came to retrieve him.

"Michael!" Abraham cried gently, but as he spoke, he struck him across the face, hard, and led him back to the parlour while Dr. Webb tended to Sandra.

"Michael, compose yourself! It is not this poor girl's fault, and you know it! And your shouting will only distress Mrs. Bennett, you know! She's right, you really should stay out of their way unless they call for assistance. You know that they will not harm Alma, they would never!"

His anger cooled with each word, and he was successfully, though reluctantly, subdued.

"Come on, then, and sit down," Abraham forcefully sat them both down on the couch.

"It's been nearly ten hours," Michael observed to Abraham, who began stroking his head as if he was the one giving birth.

"Sometimes it takes much longer. Nothing to be afraid of."

Whereas Dr. Webb appeared cool and serene, Abraham was as sunny as could be, completely undisturbed by current events. Michael sheepishly apologised to Sandra, who had calmed down considerably, and did not seem slighted.

Ida was sent outside to tend to the chickens and play with Jeannine. Hannah Lavigne's driver went out to water the horse.

Since he had nothing else to do and could think of no other way to settle his nerves, Michael began to play the piano again.

By the time he had breezed through a handful of Mozart's sonatas, the neglected fire was only a heap of coals, and the sun lit up the whole parlour. Ida coming back inside pulled him out of his trance. He put the music away.

"No, no!" Dr. Webb stopped him, lighting up his fifth pipe that morning. "Keep playing. Music is medicine."

"You only want me to play so that we can't hear them."

"No, I mean it. It's calming, and everybody needs it now, especially her," he put the pipe to his quivering lips, but didn't inhale. "Though I admit, since there's currently nothing I can do either way, I'd prefer not to hear."

"Why don't you pray?"

"I have this entire time."

"Well, how about you pray and I play?"

"You're white as ash, and your hands are trembling worse than mine. I haven't seen you eat or drink anything today."

"I couldn't."

"You must," he nudged the plate of remaining sandwiches towards him. "You want to collapse before you can hold your child for the first time?"

That didn't make him any hungrier than before, but agreed to eat, and did so while he played.

When mid-day was upon them, he paused in his playing only to send Ida upstairs with cool water; it was getting quite hot, and it must have been damp as a marsh up in that room.

Ida went to the second storey and returned, looking solemn and determined like she never had been before. Since she claimed she was allowed inside, Michael interrogated her. How was Alma doing? Did Ida speak to her? How were the ladies treating her? Did they say anything? Was the room dry? Did she need anything?

"It was horrid in there!" was her answer to all of it. "I never want to have children."

"So all is well," he concluded, and continued playing for another stretch.

"Stop that racket!" Hannah Lavigne shouted from the top of the stairs at ten until noon. "Come up and listen to a real song!"

Sure enough, Michael turned away from the piano, and strained his ears to hear a small cry that was frightfully similar to that of a cat.

He stumbled over every stair on the way up to the second storey, and the rest of the inmates followed close behind him.

"I think it's a girl!" Ida chirped and gayly skipped up to his side.

"You're disagreeing with Alma?"

"Girls are just better."

"Non, non, non!" his aunt stopped them. "Only the father! You lot can wait until she's revived. Away with you!"

Of course, Ida protested the loudest. Even Michael was stopped, and ordered to wash his hands and face first.

"You waited this long," Alma's mother presented him with a basin of warm water. "One more minute is nothing."

One more minute was *torturous*. He counted fifteen hours, and he was not about to wait one second more than he needed to. Still, after he washed, he was checked to make sure his hands and face were free of residue and bone-dry, then his hair was moved to the side, and his watch confiscated. He didn't know why they took his watch, but one minute became three, and if he had to wait any longer, he was liable to swoon, so he let them have it without a fuss.

Mrs. Webb finally opened the door and stepped to one side.

"Born at 11:43 in the morning, on August, the twenty-sixth. *'Friday's child is loving and giving,'*" she declared.

XXXVIII

The room was a shambles. Soiled sheets made a heap in the far corner, and everything smelled musty and metallic. Several vessels of water laid about. There was evidence of some hastily-mopped splashes. To his immense relief, the surgical tools appeared to be untouched.

And Alma, in a fresh gown— weary, lovely, and very damp— triumphantly held her prize to her bare bosom.

He tended to her first, combing her hair out of her eyes with his fingers.

"Oh, you did it, you did it! I knew you could!" he kissed every bit of exposed skin. She was alarmingly warm, so he ran to open a window.

"Well, who is this?" Michael returned and sank to the floor at her knees, reaching for this fascinating pink thing. It breathed, it grasped, and it had a full head of fair hair. He stroked that little head; it left a waxy sensation on his fingers. Even the scent was enticing. What an unearthly creature it was!

"If I had to make a guess," she still found the energy to be dry with him. "I would say this is our daughter."

"It is our daughter! It's a little girl!" he exclaimed wildly and victoriously: not because he was correct (he'd forgotten their wager in that moment) but because she was theirs.

Alma brought the child down to be level with him. Tiny fingers groped at his face, apparently just as curious about him as he was of her. The eyes shone like black-grey gems. He shook one of those little hands so that they were formally introduced.

"What happened to your wrist?" Alma touched his burn, which he'd forgotten until then because it no longer stung.

"I spilled some water this morning," he waved it away and reached out. "Let me have her— let me have her!" he entreated softly; she'd grimaced at how loud he was.

Taking her into his arms made her fully real, and she was frightening. He released a primal huff, unsure of what to say.

"Is she how you imagined her?" Alma asked.

"No," he admitted. "It passes me. I could never dream of this."

"She's bigger than I thought she'd be."

"So, what's her name?"

Alma bit her lip and darted her eyes every which way.

"Ah, I didn't think of any girl's names."

"No?" he laughed. "Well, that's all right. I know what we'll call her."

"What will we call her?"

"Her name is Autumn," he decided.

"Autumn?" Alma's features contorted, as if he'd just confessed to murder. "It's August, Michael."

"It's pretty and singular. And I always knew she should be Autumn because I knew she would have your hair."

She smiled. He'd never seen her smile so fondly at anything before, even though her eyelids were florid and fluttered half shut.

"Not quite. Hers is lighter. But she can be Autumn."

"It's a lot like yours is when you're out in the sun often. It turns sort of rosy and golden."

He noticed that Alma wasn't really listening anymore. She was fighting hard to stay awake that entire time.

"How do you feel?" he asked.

"I feel many things. Mostly, I'm relieved."

"You should rest," Michael drew Autumn closer to him.

She weakly shook her drooping head.

"I cannot yet. She must be fed, and I don't think I could sleep in this chair, so I'll stay here until I feed her."

"If you must, then by all means," he handed Autumn back to her mother. "You should be fed, too. I know you have not eaten much. Would you like me to fetch anything? What do you want?"

She rallied a bit at the mention of eating.

"I think I'd really like berries, and some cream."

"You mean… mixed together?"

"Yes! And maybe a bit of honey."

"Nothing else?"

"Nothing else."

He went downstairs, though he didn't want to take his eyes off of them for even a moment (yet what was the worst that could happen if he left for only twenty minutes?) and steered himself straight towards the back garden.

People intercepted him and asked about Alma and the baby.

"Her name is Autumn!" was all he said.

"Her? My grandson's a girl!" Dr. Webb exclaimed.

"She sure is," he replied. "Are you disappointed?"

"Oh, no, I'm not disappointed. Just surprised, as Alma was so set on having a boy," he shrugged and lit yet another pipe. "Well, this is wonderful! And how is Alma?"

She was well, yes. She was only a bit tired and quite hungry, and he needed to go fetch what she asked for. Yes, she found her attendants satisfactory. He really needed to go.

When they asked subsequent questions, he only gave an unintelligible squeal (mostly to make them leave him alone) and hurried outside. In the meantime, they helped themselves to the wine to celebrate, and the two women took their shoes off, got into some clean clothes, and relaxed. Hannah Lavigne was already gushing endlessly about the "perfect baby."

Given her temperament, she probably said that about all babies. As for Alma, Mrs. Lavigne still maintained that she was too small, and that was why they miscalculated her delivery by a whole month.

It took longer than he thought, as he had to pick some particularly stubborn crawlers off of the berries. All he had to do was put them in a bowl, mash them up a bit, and drown them in cream and honey. He took it upstairs and grabbed some cushions out of the bedroom.

"Here! That chair can't be comfortable," he tucked them underneath Alma's back, and under Autumn so that she could have a free hand. "Why didn't you labour in bed or on a sofa?

"These chairs are easier to clean."

"When can we move you?"

"I think I'll try to sleep after I feed her, but I don't know if I feel ready to get up."

"I'll carry you there whenever you want."

"This room needs to be cleaned."

"You needn't be doing anything, except feeding this baby. You've done quite enough today."

It seemed Alma needed both hands to get Autumn to latch onto her breast, and so Michael just fed her himself.

"I can't imagine this red pulp is particularly appetising after what you've endured, and being in this rank air," he said. "Why don't you let me go ahead and put you to bed?"

"Eat in bed?"

"Yes, let's allow it today, shall we?"

She agreed to be taken to bed, and then she finished what he offered her, and he brought her water, even though she didn't ask for it. He also had to promise to wake her if the baby had to be fed again, but he guessed she would do that herself when the time came.

It took her a while to fall asleep, because Autumn was alert and curious those first few hours. Michael curled up around them both. He took her from Alma as she began to drop, and seated himself near the bed.

"I'm glad she was born in the summer. I don't want her sleeping in our bed yet… she's too little," she mumbled with the last of her energy, and then she couldn't summon the resolve to say any more.

"What an eventful day!" he cooed and brought her downy little head to his lips. "You can meet everybody after Mama gets some sleep."

Somehow, Michael stayed still in that seat for hours. She was mesmerising. Eventually, she, too, fell asleep. He wrapped her up in the blanket that Alma made, and he was probably supposed to place her in her cradle, but he couldn't seem to put her down.

Michael nearly leapt out of his own skin when he realised he'd nodded off, and the baby was starting to fuss. It was getting dark. He frantically pawed at Autumn, even though he knew where she was.

"Michael!" Alma was stirring. "Give her here."

He passed the child over, and took a deep breath to steady himself.

"How are you feeling?" he asked.

"More rested than I thought I would be," she declared.

After feeding Autumn once more, Alma decided she wanted to get up and walk, so he took them downstairs.

Ida was calmer than anticipated, only looked, and didn't grab at her.

"You can't name her Autumn," she protested. "It's summer."

"It's winter in the southern hemisphere."

"That has nothing to do with the baby."

"Neither does the fact that it's summer here."

"She's lovely," Abraham gushed over her, though he squinted and couldn't quite seem to focus on her face. "She's bigger than you were, but you had so much hair that it had to be cut straight away!"

"Alma had dark hair when she was born," Dr. Webb noted. "But it fell out, and grew back light as champagne, then it darkened again. Maybe that will happen to her."

"It's a good thing she has hair!" Hannah Lavigne added. "Most of my babies were bald!"

Alma agreed to pass Autumn to the others for a little while. Michael hovered over them and nudged them along when he felt they'd had their time. The family stayed with them for a week and did most of Alma's household work for her. In between hanging the washing and polishing every bit of metal in the house, Aunt Hannah hung over Alma and burdened her with endless advice about Autumn, whether she asked for it or not. Aside from being visibly annoyed with all of her relatives, she adjusted well to motherhood. Ida was always looking for any excuse to hold Autumn.

The doctor once again hired a photographer, but only when Alma felt that she was ready to look presentable, as she spent most of that first week in no corset, and no shoes. Her mother had the foresight to gift her with several new garments that fastened in the front, but she did not want to wear them in the portraits. Before they were positioned for the camera, Michael had a thought to run and find his mother's locket to put it on Alma. It seemed appropriate.

Laura was informed that the baby had already been delivered, and she came at once to see her.

The real challenge would be introducing her to Jeannine. Michael had been training her to be calm around people, and had begun bringing out

Autumn's blankets and hats for her to smell, but it was possible that she'd never even seen a baby before.

Once she reached two weeks old, he had Alma bring her outside, with the dog tethered. Gradually, she brought her close, until Jeannine could just smell her. Once she had a sniff, she wriggled and strained against the lead, craning her neck to lick the baby, but Michael had a good hold on her.

Autumn sneezed, and Jeannine excitedly dropped her front half, wagging her tail in the air.

Thus opened up another chapter of great trial, but it was blissful nonetheless.

With trial, there is inevitably error. Sometimes, Autumn's crying late at night had no immediately apparent cause, and when she didn't want to be fed, Michael was awoken and elected to help solve the problem, and they blamed each other when it couldn't be resolved, but were too tired to argue. There were days that she would not sleep at all unless she was held.

For nearly three months, they had only four or five hours of sleep between the two of them each night. Alma was never in the habit of napping in the daytime, but she began soon after Autumn was born. She tried to get an hour or two of sleep before she needed to prepare dinner, while Michael or Abraham walked the gallery with the baby.

And since Autumn consumed so much of her waking hours, Michael took full charge of the gardens, and at the peak of harvest season, thought he could still not brave entering the chicken enclosure on his own.

By her third month, things began to slow down, and she began eating more and sleeping longer, and could contently sleep in the cradle.

Upon first glance, many may assume that once you'd seen one small baby, you'd seen them all, but Michael knew for a fact that he could find Autumn in a packed nursery. He knew her face and the scent of her hair as intimately as he knew his own hands, and as she grew, and grew very rapidly, these singular features became more and more prominent. She had Michael's eye shape, but her eyes were still deep blue. Her hair was starting to form coils on her head. She had round little ears like Alma, and she was pink, pretty, and perfect.

When that three months' time elapsed, Michael knew that he would need to return to work. Alma told him that they were nowhere near running out of money, but he insisted that he did not want to wait until the well had run dry, because anything could happen.

Moreover, he was inwardly deeply worried about keeping his position secure with Mr. Kelley, despite his prideful departure, but he did not voice these concerns, as Alma had enough to worry about.

He ran over a handful of lists numerous times to make sure that nobody would need to frequently leave the house while he was gone: there was enough coal, cut wood, and preserved foods to last all of winter, if needed.

Michael's eyes were wet when he departed for Bristol. These three months passed in the time it took him to blink, and he already knew as he left that he would be missing so much of Autumn's life.

XXXIX

Mr. Kelley carried on as though no time had passed, and was glad to put him to work at once, as December was days away, and preparations to pack up the animals had to be made in great haste.

"Welcome back to doing what you were made for, old boy!" he said.

Michael returned with many conflicting feelings quelling within. He did, indeed, miss Mr. Kelley, somewhat, and most definitely missed the animals, but he yearned to go back home almost as soon as he started work.

And once more, he had to choke down Mr. Kelley's flavourless repast three times a day. He did not look forward to his weight fluctuating each month again.

As shameful as it was to admit, even being worked to the bone by Mr. Kelley was easier than rearing a child. At least here, there was a schedule, and a full night's sleep was guaranteed. His body was relieved… his heart and soul were consumed by guilt that made it hard to take advantage of the repose. He was making good money, but he'd be gone for days, and Abraham was a faithful friend who would help in any way that he could, but he was in his twilight years, and could not be reasonably asked to do so much. The distance made him want to pull his hair out.

Exactly a year ago, he couldn't even imagine being a father, and didn't care to, but now, he kept a picture of her little face in his watch, and every hour or so, he would take it out and melt into snivelling slop.

And before he knew it, the usual four days had lapsed, and Mr. Kelley still entreated him to stay, as he had fallen behind, and had so much work to do before it became too cold.

"I had gotten so used to your hard work!" he explained. "You were quite right, lad, I do need you around! Please stay a little while longer and help an old man out. Help these animals out. I am sure nothing dire will happen in only a few more days."

Michael relented, but first, he wrote to Alma to explain the delay. That few more days quickly became two weeks, three, and he finally resisted right at the weekend of his third anniversary. He simply had to go home.

In his spare time, he arranged for a shiny new stove to arrive at the same time he did.

He came home on Saturday evening, ready to devour some sweet little fingers and then install a new stove.

When he went inside, he found Alma with Autumn on her knee, gazing into a low fire, and she did not greet him, but Autumn still knew his voice and shrieked with delight when he announced himself. It seemed she'd just about doubled in size in less than a month.

He sat down and heaved them both onto his lap.

"Alma, did you see the new stove?" he asked.

"But I was wrong," was all that she said, with her eyes still on the fire.

"I suppose so, but you were correct in saying that we do need a new stove! Anything to make things easier for you, and it will be our third anniversary tomorrow besides! You should also think on what you will want for Christmas. I'm sure I could get some oranges or fine chocolate."

She only squeezed her eyes shut, and trembled.

"I just about thought you wouldn't come back," she admitted.

"What!" he cried. "Of course I was going to come back. I did write that I would be a few days late."

"Nearly a month! You can not miss entire months of Autumn's life, not when she's so little!" now her face was growing flushed and her breath quickened. " I can't do it. I thought I could, but I can't manage for so many days like this. It's not fair!"

"I know it isn't. I am sorry, and I assure you, it will not happen again!" Michael drew her close against his bosom and nestled his face into her hair. "What's important now is that we all catch up, wouldn't you say? I'll make it up to you in any way that I can."

Alma lifted up her head at once.

"You could prepare me a bath," she began. "A hot one, and hold onto Autumn while I soak."

"Anything to get my hands on this little peach," he chuckled, and placed them back down so that he could go out and draw water.

Her spirits were lifted after steeping in hot, perfumed water for a good hour, and Michael's cup was refilled when he had Autumn all to himself after weeks away from home.

When she finished her bath, she decided to take advantage of Michael and Autumn both being occupied and helped herself to some coffee and freshly toasted tea cakes. Michael prepared some tea for himself and ate what was left over when he handed her back.

He then ran with Jeannine, as usual, played a very slow game of cards with Abraham at his request, and started to get settled for bed.

Autumn now slept for most of the night, but Michael still rose before Alma did, so he tried to have the stove installed before she came downstairs.

He thought he was doing her a favour, and yes, he did want a "good boy" and a pat on the head for it, but Alma came down in a sour mood because he was not in bed when she awoke.

"I wanted to surprise you! You asked for this stove months ago!'

"I want you here!" she answered, with Autumn on her hip. "When I woke, I thought you'd left again!"

"On our anniversary? I wouldn't dream of it, and certainly not without telling you!" Michael was just finishing up. "It's all finished, so why don't I start some water for your coffee?"

"I'll do it myself, just as I do everything," she huffed and handed Autumn off to Michael.

"Oh, Alma, really, I just built a stove!" he protested. "Happy anniversary."

Alma made her coffee, and breakfast was only bread and butter and the remains of a soup from yesterday. As much as he missed her fresh cooking, he gladly ate a cold meal. He did not want to step on her toes any more than he already had after coming home later than promised and scaring her out of her skin the next morning. He was told that it was normal for new mothers to be feeling blue, but it still worried him, especially as he would be leaving again so soon.

At dinner, he proposed that they finally hire a housekeeper. She seemed to be in better spirits, and made an excellent stew.

"Am I not doing enough?" she asked.

"You are doing perfectly well!" Michael spat quickly. "But I think both you and Abraham should have a helper and companion while I am away—"

"You said that you would not be gone for so long again."

"And I will not! However, we can indeed afford it, and it would take a lot from your plate. If you agree, we can begin advertising whenever you please… besides, it would put my mind at ease."

Alma cleaned her plate, heaped another serving onto some bread, and then made her decision: "Yes, I will send you the applications that I like while you are at work."

When he went back to Bristol, he and Mr. Kelley compromised and decided that he would spend every other week at home, no matter what, and he was firm in his request. In the meantime, Alma sent him applications, as she said she would.

He selected a woman named Mary Jones, who had twenty-four years of experience as a housekeeper. At sixty years of age, Michael considered her still able-bodied enough to be a great help, especially with laundry and gardening, but old enough to be an appropriate companion for Abraham, who undoubtedly was overwhelmed by all of the young people around him.

She began work in February. As Michael suspected, Abraham took a liking to her immediately, though he was momentarily confused about a Mary being in the house. He thought of Mary Bennett when he heard that name.

The alternating weeks were much more agreeable to Michael, as he was less worried about balancing his days, and he was still making good money. Alma was not thrilled about it, and wished he could simply take up a profession that could see him home every evening, but she considered it an acceptable compromise.

And having Mary Jones at Brownwall meant considerably less strain on their marriage. With less work to do while juggling a baby, Alma was not squeezed dry when Michael came home, and was beginning to enjoy the things that she used to. She even started to dress herself up all pretty again, after voicing concerns for several months that her figure did not look the way it once did.

All he had to say to her about all of it was, "It will be alright, but it will be different," and he believed it to be true.

"So why is it that you hardly touch me anymore?" she asked, twisting up her hair for the night. "You don't caress me at all."

"What?" Michael sat up in bed. She had the lit candle, and her face was in the shadows. "I figured that you would not appreciate me molesting you when you had time to rest."

"You could have asked me."

"Likewise, you could have asked me. You have to tell me what you want, woman!"

That got a hearty laugh out of her for the first time in months.

Things gradually began to smooth out a little at home, so he was less anxious about his absence, but he still lamented it from time to time. He'd take longer hours if it meant that he could be home every day.

But a part of it was selfish… he could have gone back to the docks, and traded Mary Jones for time at home, but he did, indeed, feel that he was made for this line of work. Unlike Mr. Kelley, however, he felt that he was made for it, and so much more. He longed to bring his life at home closer to his occupation, but of course, Alma likely would never consent to going to Bristol with him. He knew it was not a reasonable request, and he also knew that she could not tolerate Mr. Kelley.

He just missed them when he was gone.

XL

Michael had contemplated before that to miss somebody is to slowly notice the little things that are gone in their absence, but it was even stranger to miss somebody who was present.

Abraham was there, and yet bits of him were disappearing. At first, he was only forgetting things around the house, and they didn't pay it any mind, because everybody was a little careless sometimes. Soon, he was leaving kettles unattended on the stove, and lamps lit all through the night. Mary was instructed to watch him closely.

Next, it was names. Half of the time, he called Michael his father's name, and Alma by his mother's name. Autumn could have been Michael, Berthe, Samuel, Gabriel, or Hannah. This had been lasting for many months, and again, they overlooked it until it was too frequent for them to ignore, but by then, he was slipping in other ways.

It wasn't ever unusual for Abraham to scold Michael, but now he was upbraiding him for coming in late for his lessons and threatening to tell his father, and shouting orders at Mary Jones or even Alma as if they were kitchen maids.

He was still very stubborn, and not easily corrected. That had not changed. All they could really do was be patient with him.

Some days, he was his jovial self, merely needing a gentle reminder, and doted on Autumn no matter who he saw in her. Others, he wanted nothing to do with her, and did not have any recollection of her, even as Michael or Berthe.

On one occasion, Alma came upstairs in tears, clutching Autumn to her shoulder, and she explained that Abraham had called her a harlot and a thief for trying to claim Master Bennett's paternity for her bastard spawn; she deserved to be flogged for preying on her employer's son in such a way.

And worst of all, Michael did not feel angry or injured, only sick, knowing that such foul words came from the sweetest man who ever lived—or, somebody with the same name. Who was this strange man in his house?

She wiped away her tears on her sleeve. Autumn was undisturbed.

"He doesn't mean what he says, you know. He does not know what he's doing," was all he could think to tell her.

"I know," she insisted, and tittered softly. "I feel silly. It should not affect me. I've seen such behaviour before, and had far worse shouted at me."

He took Autumn and sent Alma to rest. Abraham seemed to have no recollection of his remarks, and was very pleased to see the child, though he had to be told her name once more. Alma decided she would keep her distance from him, and Michael understood.

In recent days, he mostly just sat in his chamber and stared at his cards, seemingly unaware of the world around him, until he was told when to eat or wash. He could not carry a full pitcher himself.

Michael informed Mr. Kelley of the circumstances. He merely said that it was to be expected, and to persevere.

Even so, it happened that he was unable to predict when Abraham made a sharp decline. In April, Alma informed Michael that he was acutely ill, and it was urgent enough that she had sent a telegram at Alma's request.

Michael did not ask for leave, he only went to Miss Gaye, as she was closest, and announced that he was going home, for there was no time to waste. He was on the first train that he could catch, no matter what anyone had to say about it.

A doctor intercepted him at the door. Any physician other than Dr. Webb made Michael nervous, but he tolerated his presence.

He warned Michael before he could go see that Abraham had fallen yesterday, and was now completely unresponsive. The doctor determined that he had a bleed in his brain. Mary Jones reported that he mentioned a recurring headache three days prior, thus he concluded that it caused the fall, not the other way around. As it was, he was unlikely to wake up.

"I'd say he has only a few days left. Best I can do is try to ease his passing," he concluded, pointing to Abraham's chamber.

Alma was insistent about going in ahead of him, claiming she'd seen such things many times before. As he had no idea what he would see, Michael had to stop and prepare himself, anyway.

Abraham looked just like he was sleeping. He was much easier to look at than Samuel Bennett; he looked like a corpse before he was even dead.

Admittedly, Michael had begun to mourn Abraham months ago. He knew he'd been slipping away for a while. Somehow, the fact that he had already lost both of his parents made it easier.

"Do you want me to write Hannah Lavigne?" Alma sat behind him. "She may want to know about it."

"I'll do it later," he mumbled.

Autumn slowly fell asleep, and she gazed with such a passionless and untroubled expression. In a way, he was glad that she was too young to understand. Alma took her upstairs and put her to bed.

Michael thanked Mary Jones and the doctor that was there, and offered him something to eat and a spare room to spend the night in.

Now, what?

This was a sensitive matter. It was best that he acted with a (relatively) clear and sound mind. Normally, he'd go out and run with Jeannine, but she was also asleep, and he did not want to disturb her.

He headed outside with a lantern to blow off steam, chopping up firewood. It was a relaxing chore in all seasons. Soon, his lantern was fizzling out, and he was surrounded by heaps of wood. He carried them to the cellar and went back inside.

After that, he went up to the study and hurriedly penned three very smudged letters: one to Dr. Webb, one to Hannah Lavigne, and one to Mr. Kelley; he felt they all had a reason to be informed. By then, it was nearly midnight. The letters would have to be posted tomorrow. Hopefully, they arrived in time for… whatever happened next.

He went downstairs and sat beside Abraham once more. He knew he likely couldn't hear, and for the sake of his sanity, he resolved not to entertain the prospect, but he felt compelled to speak to him anyway.

"I thought I had a bit more time," he admitted. "I know I should have been home more often— well, of course you wouldn't say so… you'd scold me, and tell me to continue to work to the best of my abilities. I wouldn't mind being scolded right this minute… I'd like if you said anything at all… anyway, it's too late now, isn't it?"

Abraham, of course, said nothing. Once he'd rattled off the nonsense in his head, he started saying what was far less comfortable.

"Hannah Lavigne is family… I suppose… but she is practically a stranger. I'm more familiar with my in-laws than her, but you—" he steeled himself. Why did it matter if he wept? Nobody could see him.

"I love my father. I still miss him more than I can say— and my mother, of course… but I've learned more about life from you than from either of them. You are just as important to me, and well—"

No longer caring to contain himself, Michael let the tears fall, and wiped his eyes. He'd never seen his father cry. He spent his whole youth trying to be like him, but he just wasn't made for it.

"Now I know my youth is behind me," he declared. "You don't need to look after me anymore, Abraham."

He stood up and quitted the room, and softly shut the door. Alma was standing behind him with a candle.

"Oh…" he wasn't embarrassed, but he blushed anyway. "How much of that did you hear?"

"Enough," she took his arm and led him towards the parlour, where there was a nice fire.

"I don't suppose it's quite the same thing," she offered. "But my grandfather passed when I was ten, and in a similar way."

"I never met Nathaniel Bennett. Abraham essentially was my grandfather… I need to handle his will— not that he had many material possessions, nor close relatives to claim him. He was a simple man."

"You can take care of it later! He hasn't even gone anywhere yet!"

"That's true," he admitted. "Though I do like to be prepared."

"And I am sure you will be more equipped to deal with that strain once you have rested and taken time to process the situation at hand. Just sit and relax for a little."

Michael tried. He really did. He was able to force himself into bed early in the morning, but he slept poorly, and woke in two hours, with baby feet on the back of his head.

Alma was asleep; these days, he always awoke before she did. He lay there and tried to keep Autumn quiet until she began to stir. She rose and dressed herself, spoke with Michael about small and unimportant things while she nursed Autumn, then went downstairs.

Michael was still in bed and undressed when he smelled that food was being prepared. He simply could not bring himself to go down… *he* was down there.

Luckily, Alma knew of his ailment and never came up to ask about his mood. She'd learned to tell what was a good or bad time to press him.

By eight o'clock, there was a hushed bustle downstairs. Since it sounded as though they had company, Michael decided he'd better get washed and dressed.

He found himself missing breakfast and wandering to Abraham's chamber. He never expected to be intercepted by Mr. Kelley, of all people. The situation at hand must have been dire, because his coat matched his trousers.

"Ah, Michael Ashley Bennett," he observed, standing at the old man's door. "Your housekeeper let me in, and you're certainly up late, it seems."

"I'm not sure that I really slept," Michael admitted, still trying to realise his employer's unannounced presence. "What brings you here?"

"Of course, I was concerned when I saw you'd left so suddenly, and was told that somebody was dreadfully ill— Abraham Reed, yes? I know him well— or at least, I used to. How is he faring?"

"Not well at all. He's fallen into a deep sleep, it seems, and may never wake up. He likely doesn't have long."

"I see," he nodded. "We might not have agreed on many things, but I consider him a valuable person. May I go into his room?"

"I'm not sure how it would help anything, but you are welcome to. Where is the doctor? Did you see him?"

"Alma Webb tells me that he left soon after breakfast."

Michael stepped aside. Maybe Mr. Kelley had some history with Abraham that he didn't know about, so he decided to allow him to have time alone with him, and went to go take Autumn outside.

It was a lovely day, but he could not enjoy that morning's stillness; in light of the ongoing ordeal, it made him feel taut and apprehensive. Even the bugs and birds were quiet.

He found movement behind the house. Alma was tending to her garden, with Jeannine

excitedly bounding after her, needing to be
nudged away from the plants that she tried to
eat. Autumn shrieked with delight and writhed
to be released. Michael lowered her down for
Jeannine to affectionately nose at her ears and
hair.

"You aren't going to sit with Abraham?" he
asked Alma.

"I don't mean to sound heartless," she began.
"But it won't do any good. It won't even make
me feel better, and I don't suppose I have
anything more to say to him that would help
now. I may as well continue working and hope
for the best— whatever that is."

After all, she hadn't known him for nearly as
long as Michael had. He understood, and did not
take offence.

"I admire your work ethic, and your practical
mind," he noted. "It has always been one of my
favourite things about you."

"Take this to the cellar, please," she handed him
her sack full of carrots. "And give her to me."

Michael exchanged Autumn for the vegetables.
She trilled and played with Alma's bonnet
strings.

"What a scam! You got the better end of the deal, I think."

"I'll give her back when you come inside," she stood up and headed towards the house with Jeannine at her heels, and Autumn straining to reach for Michael— truly the most rapturous feeling there was. He deposited the sack quickly.

Crossing the threshold into the house reminded him of death. The air was heavy, but he tried to shake it off and brave the discomfort.

Mr. Kelley was now standing in the gallery outside of Abraham's chamber, sporting the most dour expression Michael had ever seen him wear.

Michael put on water and offered him anything he wanted from the kitchen. He declined, claiming he could not eat at a time such as this; just as Michael was about to go upstairs and tend to his girls, his employer stopped him.

"Before you leave me," he beckoned. "I think we should discuss some pressing matters that pertaineth to the near future, and possibly your well-being."

His blood froze. Was he about to be dismissed? Now, and in his own house?

"Very well," Michael consented. Mr. Kelley wandered outside without waiting for him, so he quickly breathed a draught of his near-empty phial of clove oil (now only the scent was enough to settle him, anyway) before he followed.

He still hadn't gotten to play with Autumn. He'd do that later.

If he asked what the damage was, it would have probably been seen as an indirect admission of guilt or incompetence, so he left his insecurities at the door.

"Sir?" was all that he said.

Mr. Kelley gazed into the trees for many minutes.

"You know, it is unlikely that Mr. Reed will ever wake up. As it is, he is as good as dead."

Though true, that was not what Michael expected to hear, at all.

"It is so, yes."

"With this in mind, I think it would not do to prolong his stay."

"What are you getting at, sir?"

"I think you know," he continued, still facing the trees. "If I may make a rather unconventional proposal, I'd say that we… that is, Abraham Reed should be granted a swift and peaceful end to his life."

Michael could not believe what had just been suggested to him. Was Mr. Kelley asking him to kill somebody?

He turned at last, with a disturbingly smooth and untroubled countenance, and an inquisitive raised brow.

"Hah! I don't know what I expected," he noted, as if Michael's stunned silence amused him. "But I mean what I say."

"You're t—" Michael stammered. "Suggesting that we k— that we take another man's life."

"No. He is already dead, no matter what we do. I am suggesting that we merely put an end to his suffering."

"No matter how noble you make it sound, it is still murder!" he caught himself at the end of his sentence, as he did not want anyone else to hear them.

"And allowing him to waste away is the lesser of two evils? When we come across a mad dog, we shoot it, because that is the merciful thing to do."

"Shoot Abraham?"

"Don't be obtuse, boy!" Mr. Kelley shook his head. "I don't intend to harm a hair on his head. Any number of medicines could be administered to hasten the process, and would not incriminate you in any way, if done carefully."

"He is not able to consent to such a thing."

"And he never will be again. You must be his proxy, and choose what is best for him."

"Maybe... he will rally! He could wake up, I'm sure of it!"

"You don't believe that," Mr. Kelley concluded, and headed towards trees. "While you think about it, I'll take a stroll through these magnificent woods. I will not do anything you do not want me to do, but I will ask you one thing: are you keeping him around for his own sake, or for yours?"

His gaze pierced Michael. In his eyes was normally all action and wild energy, but at that moment, he was passive and thoughtful, in a way Michael had never seen before. It was unnerving.

And the question cut him even deeper. He was not ready to face the answer, so he went inside and tended to his family.

He lay himself on the rug in the parlour and let Autumn climb him. She was crawling now. Never in his life did he feel so beholden to somebody. She was here because of him, not of her own will, and everything he did, she was watching, learning from him. He owed her the very best that he could offer: not just her toys (though it delighted him to see her features light up when she received these gifts), but everything that he did not get from his parents.

As he gazed upon his wife sewing, and his daughter, he felt he was a stronghold encompassing them, and he sensed (at least, he imagined) that he made them feel safe. Yet, as he was a protective wall, he felt they were his foundation. It was a strange feeling… he needed them to need him, or he could not live.

And it was then that he put himself in his proper place in the world. He was his own master and caretaker, and now he was depended on.

There was a little hand mashed onto his eye, and he was pulled from his stupor by a very authoritative string of babbling.

"Yes, ma'am," Michael took the hand out of his eye and placed Autumn on the floor beside him. He quickly wiped his tears when he noticed them.

She shrieked with discontent, so he picked her back up. It was perplexing, and sometimes a bit taxing, and it was why he got out of bed every morning.

Michael had her until Alma finished making an early dinner, and then she was taken to be fed. She was still nursed, but just now starting to be fed food from the table.

He'd never once fed her, bathed her, or combed her hair; he was told it was simply the duty of the mother, and he had no choice but to accept this as fact, and swallow down the bitterness he tasted. It made him feel that he was not doing the best he could. Now that he was with them on all days of the week, it only became more apparent.

Even though Dr. Webb had shown himself to be perfectly competent and trustworthy with babies, Michael was never invited to partake in these basic needs, and Mrs. Webb even discouraged him, because he was not "required."

On that day, he asserted himself.

"Let me have her," he pushed his dinner to one side as Alma was just sitting down with hers. "You eat your food while it's hot for once."

"You don't have to."

It took a great amount of effort to not be angered by this. She likely thought she was doing him a favour, but at the expense of them both, and she may have resented her workload, but would never say so until she was near her wit's end. He had been trying to coax that behaviour out of her.

"I would like to," he insisted, leaning towards Autumn, who had just settled into her little seat. "Can you think of any reason I *shouldn't?*"

That sounded more aggressive than he intended.

But she relented peacefully, and he could tell that she enjoyed taking her dinner slowly and undisturbed.

Autumn's dinner was a bit of potato mashed very soft.

It all appeared to be effortless when Alma did it, but needless to say, it was a bit of a challenge. He felt triumphant when he'd gotten her to finish her meal. Most of what he offered from the spoon ended up in other places, but even Alma was pleased with his efforts.

Michael did not know when (or if) Mr. Kelley would return that evening, so he laid out food for him if he wanted it, and then he walked around with Jeanine and put Autumn to bed upstairs— she was always sleepy after she ate. He then checked Abraham, who had not changed, and gave Mary Jones her usual instructions.

He tried to pay special attention to Alma…tried.

He asked what she wanted to do, but her first answer was a question, and the second wasn't any help:

"What did you have in mind?"

"I'm asking *you!*"

"Whatever you want."

He knew she wasn't being difficult on purpose. They were both distracted and worn thin. He was worked up into a taut ball of nerves.

Firstly, he sat across from her in the parlour, ready to spark a nice conversation. He couldn't think of anything to say. Alma spoke to him, but he only heard half of it. He built up a good, low fire, poured wine, and set up a game of cards. Normally, he was a passive card player; he would partake if he was invited, and wasn't that good. That was all he could think to do with his wife at the time. It was pathetic.

Though the desire was there, his thoughts were fragmented, and drawn to one thing. He'd been trying to push it down and deny its presence.

At first, it tickled at the back of his head, then it sunk its claws into his skull, until he could not focus on anything else. Alma commented that he had the greatest poker face of all time, and then he realised he'd been staring at his unchanged hand for that entire stretch.

Michael excused himself and abandoned their game.

Mary Jones was not in Abraham's chamber. He let himself in and shut the door behind him.

"You can go," he declared, though he nearly choked on those words. "If you're holding on because you're worried, you don't need to. You don't need to worry about me— you don't! I'm a man. You have done well for me, but you don't need to do any more."

Was there truly no recognition stirring within him? Was Abraham Reed really no more, and Michael was talking to little more than a plant?

"You're free to go," he repeated, and his voice threatened to break. "I don't need you anymore."

Naturally, he got no response. What was he expecting? That Abraham would feel slighted enough to awaken whole and vigorous, ready to prove him wrong?

He did not know what he was angry at, but he was furious, and then not one second later, he was fearful. He knelt down at Abraham's face and kissed his white, papery cheek. It was cold, as if he was already dead. The eyes did not flutter, nor did the lips part. There was barely a heartbeat.

But there were tears on his face. They were Michael's, of course.

The front door opened and closed. He quitted Abraham's chamber at once.

Mr. Kelley had just wandered into the house, with Jeannine behind him. It was not yet dark out.

"Mr. Bennett?" he asked quite plainly.

"Do what you will, and don't tell me what it is," Michael answered him.

XLI

Nothing that he'd just said made any sense, and yet as if possessing clairvoyance, Mr. Kelley understood. He nodded, and asked for Michael to fetch his carpet bag that he left in a spare bedroom.

Trying to be quick and discreet, he found Mr. Kelley at Abraham's bedside, and handed the bag to him.

"Get out," he ordered Michael, in a deathly cold tone he'd never used before.

"Mr. Kelley?"

"Get out, Michael," he said once more. "You are not needed here."

He turned around without question, unable to cast one last look at Abraham Reed.

"What's going on?" Alma had collected the cards and was shuffling them. The wine was untouched.

"I thought we might take a walk, just the two of us," he offered, and inhaled both glasses of wine. "Grab your hat. If Autumn is still asleep, leave her be."

Her spirits lifted at once, and she sprang up to fetch her little straw hat and put on practical shoes. Michael didn't bother to wear a hat or coat.

There was still enough daylight left for a brisk stroll through the country. The walk revived him, but he felt the need to put up a facade. He didn't like concealment, but what transpired on that evening, Alma did not need to know, not yet. He felt that he didn't even need to know, and would have liked to pretend it was not happening; perhaps he would tell her some day.

At least Alma enjoyed their walk. She said that she liked doing things alone with him once in a while, and that she hoped he was feeling better.

Michael kept himself well-knit and sturdy until they came back inside. Autumn had not awoken yet, so she would probably sleep through the night. Mary Jones was tidying up the kitchen. Nobody had asked her to, but if a mess was left behind and forgotten long enough, she would tend to it herself.

The house was so still, as if it held its breath. Even Jeannine was quiet.

Mr. Kelley sat in the downstairs gallery, pale and grave.

"Sir! Is something the matter?" Michael asked theatrically.

"Ah, well," the old man tugged at his fingers—Abraham used to do that. "I'm sorry to tell you lot, but Mr. Reed seems to have passed away."

"Why, so soon!" Alma exclaimed. "Are you sure?"

"Aye, madam. I went unto his chamber earlier, and his breathing was unsteady, hardly there at all, so I sat with him. He drew his last breath at about ten past six o'clock," he pointed to the stopped clock on the wall behind him.

He sold it well enough to fool even Alma. Michael himself was inclined to buy it.

"I'm sorry that you were not there when it happened," Mr. Kelley lied.

"So am I," he lied as well. "I'm sorry it had to be you to bear witness."

Alma examined him herself, as if she did not trust anyone else's judgement on the matter. Her eyes were shining when she emerged.

"It is so," she announced.

Michael forced himself to go see. There was no change to Abraham, except that his face was blanched more greyish-white. He smoothed that thinning wisp of silver hair and pulled the linens over his head. Likewise, he found a sheet to cover the vanity mirror. He did not know why he did this, but he remembered that Abraham did any time somebody passed.

"We must make funeral preparations first thing in the morning," said Mr. Kelley, stumbling towards the doors, without his cane. "For now, I'm quite fatigued, and would bid the two of you good night."

"Sir, do you mean to go home at this hour? There's plenty of room here!" Michael pointed to the empty chamber beside Abraham's.

"Nay, I never did sleep well on goose feathers and horse hair," he chuckled, averting his gaze. "It's so mellow out, I think I'll roost under the stars tonight! Care to join me?"

"Not tonight, sir," he declined, and his wavering tone warned him that he ought to keep his reply short. "Good night, then. I will see to these affairs tomorrow."

With that, he went upstairs with his wife. Neither said a word as they scaled the staircase.

Autumn still slept peacefully in her cradle. Michael was able to quietly lie down in the dark and steady himself, pretending to sleep until Alma simply placed a hand on the back of his head; upon which, he probably wept into her gown until midnight.

Mr. Kelley had vanished before the sun came up. Michael forced himself out of bed at dawn and wandered the property, then departed on his own without breakfast to begin all the necessary arrangements.

While he was out, Alma and Mary Jones made Abraham pretty— his hair was combed, he was slipped into his best evening ensemble that was probably older than Michael, and his face was dusted with a light coating of powder that Alma never used anymore.

As he had to do many times before in his life, and possibly would continue to do, he was forced to drink in one final gaze at Abraham Reed before he would be received by the earth. That must have been the hardest part: telling oneself that this is, for sure, the last time you will lay your eyes on somebody. It never feels real at first.

Michael gave a short speech for, in his mind, one of the greatest men that had ever lived, and he granted him the honour of being buried among the Bennetts. As expected, few attended his funeral, as no surviving relatives claimed him (if there were any), and as he truly lived for his career, he had few friends.

Most of the guests that he knew were Alma's family, but Hannah Lavigne also brought some of her children for Michael to meet: three ladies of equal size and stature to their mother, all clamouring to hold the "pretty baby" rather than meet their cousins, and one young gentleman who did not seem to know why he was there.

The oldest stood out in that she led a Bohemian sort of lifestyle, as a traveller living with her mother, with six children from five different men, and only four of them living with her. Why she decided to share all of this at a funeral with a cousin she'd just met, he had no clue. The youngest was almost fifteen. Michael took a quick liking to him, and taught him how to whistle through a blade of grass. Even approaching manhood, his three sisters, as well as the rest of his siblings, considered him "the baby," and he never had to do anything himself. Michael knew first-hand that they were not doing him any favours.

Mr. Kelley was not present, not that he was expected. Michael wrote him a letter and even sent a telegram saying that he truly could not come back to work until June. He never got an answer, and he tried not to let it affect him, because in those days, he could only worry about things as they came to him. Very little was planned.

Brownwall had lost some of its soul. Little bits of the past were always slipping through his fingers.

But Alma and Autumn were his present and his future. Though a lesser man would have thrown himself into his work to forget all of his woes, he knew that they needed him there. He had to make sure they were settled before anything else, and he was fortunate to have that luxury.

Abraham owned very little, and his room was plain and white, the way he liked it. There was hardly anything that needed to be moved, even if he wanted to, He was not sure he could use this chamber for anything else, not for many years. The air was too hard to breathe in there.

Intellectually, Michael knew that Abraham would soon die, as all men must, but inwardly, in his core, he had the sensation that he would simply always be there.

And yet, the picture he hung on the wall in that room and the memories were all that remained. Would Autumn even remember him?

Even Jeannine had grown gloomy. Michael often found her in the hall, with her nose under Abraham's door, as if waiting for him to come out.

"I know, Pigeon," he sat beside her on the floor. "I miss him, too. He loved having a dog in the house again. Thank you for keeping an old man company."

Alma made his favourite breakfast for two consecutive weeks, and was so wonderful in many other ways. Just her presence was a great comfort, as it was all the time. With Autumn now sleeping at regular intervals, they found time to have their late night talks in the parlour, as they had done years ago— back then, they may as well have been children, but some things never changed.

One mild spring afternoon, while he already had too much to think about as it was, Michael received a letter from an address he did not recognise. Mary Jones handed it to him soon after he arrived home. It came from Germany, allegedly from a Father Gabriel. He had no German associates that he knew of, certainly no Catholics. The letter was in English:

'My dear Michael Bennett,

I am well. I do not know how or when this letter finds you, but as you read it, I live a life of pious solitude.

You knew me as Peter Evans...'

Michael's heart nearly leapt out of his chest. Peter was alive! Or at least he was recently… He just hadn't expected to hear from him again, as not even Ruth had much to say about him. This discovery conjured up many mixed feelings. He read on.

'If you remember me, I perhaps owe an explanation to us both, as part of achieving true devotion and enlightenment is relieving oneself of cumbersome and worldly burdens in order to strive for a sinless existence and a closer relationship with our Maker.'

"And relieving oneself of punctuation, apparently," Michael mumbled.

"Pardon?" Alma asked across the table.

"No, nothing," he replied. "I'm just reading a strange letter."

'I had at one point harboured unsavoury feelings towards you— your peculiar way of manliness, your generosity, and your will— they fascinated me, and fascination unchecked can create

obsession. You did not reciprocate, I sensed as much, and that was how I fully realised my feelings are perverse and unnatural: worse than even the corruption of a woman.

In order to remedy this unholy burden, I sought routine and prayer to rid myself of all worldly temptation. I have contemplated this for many years, and I do so in good conscience, knowing that Ruth is being supported. She will understand. I wash my hands of the outside world, and all it entails, for better or worse; this is my farewell to all that is in it.

So farewell, Michael Bennett. God be with you.

Father Gabriel.'

It was good that Michael had not yet started eating dinner, because his insides churned like a mountain river. This was neither a pleasant nor unpleasant feeling, merely a confusing shock that he could not quite understand.

Most of all, he ached— both for poor Ruth, who undoubtedly felt discarded, and Peter, who must have been terribly troubled.

Regardless, his sentiment towards Peter's situation stayed the same: he wished him luck, hoped he would be content, and was still grateful to him. He did tell Alma, only because it was too outlandish to keep to himself. She was equally perplexed, and disappointed that it was now set in stone, she would never get to meet Peter Evans.

"Perhaps that is for the best," he admitted. "There are similarities between the two of you, but I feel you would not have gotten along."

He soon wrote Ruth to make sure she was handling it well, and she visited often. She claimed that she always knew inwardly that he wouldn't come back, and she had grieved a long time ago. It turned out that her new life was comfortable and peaceful, and she loved being a stepmother.

"It's one child that I didn't have to give birth to!" Ruth said in jest, and Alma gave a strained, grimacing laugh.

Additionally, they adopted two more little ones. She considered Michael their uncle; this, he thought, was the highest honour a friend could bestow upon him.

Alma's own brother scarcely talked to her either, though presumably for the opposite reason; she was convinced that he still *hated* Michael.

"You know… I never was terribly close to him," she admitted. "When we were younger, he didn't really want anything to do with me, and had no patience for me, especially because I always gave our mother a hard time. As long as he is well, I can handle not talking to him."

As he had no surviving siblings, he could not offer any advice, and trusted that she must have known the situation better than he. Michael had hand-picked his brothers and sisters. If she wanted to speak of it, he was ready to listen.

Now that the house had settled, he knew he had to go back to Bristol, whatever awaited him, and wrote one more letter to Mr. Kelley to announce his return. He departed in early June.

Nothing could have prepared Michael for what received him when he arrived.

XLII

He was not greeted at the garden. Every animal he passed on the avenue was in its place, but all was eerily still. The shrubbery was wilder than usual, and the air was heavy, with a peculiar smell. He attributed it to the compost heap. It was piled quite high, but even that was not normal. It looked neglected.

Mr. Kelley could have been just about anywhere during the daytime, so Michael expected to intercept him naturally. He decided to seek out Miss Gaye first to announce his presence, so he strolled over to her office building, still carrying his belongings. He heard a lot of clattering and huffing before he let himself in.

He found her feverishly packing a stack of papers into a case, and hangings had been taken off of the wall.

"Oh, Miss Gaye!" he called. "What is that you are doing? Are you leaving us?"

"I was dismissed, Mr. Bennett," she replied sharply.

"By Mr. Kelley?" he asked, as if anybody else could have been the culprit. "Where is he?"

"I have not seen him, only a note on my desk telling me that I am no longer needed."

Michael's heart dropped into his feet. He would likely be next.

"Good God! He cut you loose without even coming to face you? He must be around here somewhere."

"There was a note for you, as well, I think," Miss Gaye pointed to a folded paper on the far end of the table.

"What does it say?" he reached for it.

"I do not know. I have manners, unlike some people."

Michael ignored her little jab and broke the seal on the note.

It read:

'Michael Ashley Bennett,

As you know, I am most certainly getting up in years. There are a great deal of things I can not do anymore. You were right. You do not need me, and cannot be controlled.

In the hopes that you would choose the right path, I have henceforth entrusted the garden to you, and you will be its sole caretaker. It is yours now.

It is time that you go one way, and I go another. If you are reading this now, I have already left, embarking on an adventure into uncharted waters.

Remember your purpose in life, and there will indeed be hope for the earth.

Until we meet again,

Adam Gregory Allan Kelley.'

Michael had to read the letter three or four times for it to take. His heart never settled, and it all hit him like a blow to the neck when he drew his next breath.

"No, no, *no, no!*" he frantically scoured the paper for some hidden text. "This isn't happening, it can't happen! This is an awful trick! This is insane!"

He dashed out of the office and searched the entire compound, but it was as if Mr. Kelley had never been there. He could not have vanished too long ago, as the animals were all well… so, where was he hiding? How long would he keep Michael waiting?

The sun began its descent towards the horizon, and there was still no trace of him. Unsure of what else to do, he returned to the office, barely able to fight off the urge to vomit.

"Miss Gaye, Miss Gaye!" he cried out on half a breath. "Please do not leave! I need you! I need you desperately, I need help!"

She stopped packing.

"Is this a trick?"

"I wish it were so," he puffed. "But many lives depend on your cooperation. Stay with me, and we will both remain employed."

"I could take employment at any office in Bristol. Why must I believe you, anyway?"

"Madam, I know I am eccentric, but have you ever known me to lie? Stay and help me, and nobody needs to go anywhere."

It was completely desperate, and there was no plan, but Dolores Gaye reluctantly agreed to assist.

First, he locked up the zoological garden so it was inaccessible to outsiders, went ahead and let himself be sick in a ditch, and then he dictated a series of telegrams for Miss Gaye to send out: to his banker, to his solicitor, to Hannah Lavigne, and most importantly, to Alma.

He knew what had to be done, and there was even a chance for it to benefit everyone, but he did not know where to begin.

Giving immediate care to the animals was paramount, and he was able to carry on these tasks without guidance.

Next, he raided Mr. Kelley's house, half hoping that he would be lurking in the shadows. The damned crook had cleaned out the building. There was not one scrap of instructions, and not one penny. Miss Gaye confirmed that most of the financial documents were gone. He would have to start from scratch.

"You turncoat! You scoundrel! *Du verräter! Lâche!*" Michael cursed the old man in every tongue that he knew, as well as some more severe oaths, as he sorted through the stack of papers in vain.

Alma was to take Autumn and come to Bristol straight away. These were uncertain times, and he wanted them near. Mary Jones would mind the house for the time being.

When he received her the next morning, he could tell that she was holding back hysterics as well as she could. Michael brought them to the garden and latched onto them for about an hour, because he badly needed it, and then he had more work to do.

He'd set up appointments with a banker and a solicitor as soon as possible, and they discussed the financial condition of the property as well as they could with the resources at their disposal.

He couldn't believe it had come to this yet again, but the writing was on the wall: he had to sell his house.

Michael agonised over it for hours, and he could not think of how to tell Alma. His options were to sell Brownwall or the Kelley Zoological Garden, and both were grim, but the animals falling into the hands of the exotic trade was a horrid thought, and would undermine decades of work. Not to mention, the livelihood of a decent handful of people depended on it.

This time, for sure, he believed it was the only course of action, and the morally right thing to do.

Alma was hard to convince, of course.

"I don't believe what I'm hearing," she began. "Lord Bennett of Ashwood Hall, who fought tooth and nail to retain any piece of land with the Bennett name on it, is selling it once again. It is your home, Michael."

"Anywhere that you lay your head is my home," he replied. "There is much more at stake here than a duty to people who are already dead. This is an investment in the *future*. This is Autumn's future."

"And you truly believe this is what is best for her?"

"I do, wholeheartedly!" said he. "When she grows older, she will have access to so much more, and besides… if I remain here and sell Brownwall, I will always be home, close at hand. Please trust in me to care for you, as I have done for nearly four years now."

Her breathing was getting heavy again.

"You can have your vegetable garden and your chickens here," he promised. "As big a garden as you want."

She smiled.

"Well, don't make me regret this," she said.

With Alma's compliance, Michael met with Hannah Lavigne to sell her the property. He imagined that she would have more of an attachment to it than he would. She leapt at the opportunity to have it exactly as it was, and liquidated many assets in France to make a payment up front. They agreed on six thousand pounds, which was much more than what he paid for it.

Additionally, he had both Alma and Madame Lavigne take what they wanted to keep of the heirloom jewellery, and he sold most of that, as well. A good portion of it would go towards Autumn's education.

And after that, he ventured deep into the cellar, where the wine was stored, and moved the case to the side to reveal a secret cabinet.

Reportedly, Great Great Grandmother Adelaide Allard Bennett loved her fire-water, and had quite a monumental stash of expensive whiskey when she passed in 1805, at only forty-one. Over the years, it had undoubtedly been chipped away at, but Michael could not believe his senses when he produced a lone crate of liquor with the date marked at 1802. It was nearly one hundred years old!

He gave two bottles to Hannah Lavigne, kept one for himself, and sold the rest. Some high-class simpletons paid good money for the novelty of drinking whiskey older than anyone alive.

"And what are you doing with it, since you laugh at the buyers?" Alma looked over her glasses at him.

"This is an emblem of longevity," he declared. "On our thirtieth anniversary, we shall drink a toast to our marriage, if I even live that long."

"Don't speak of such things!" she spat. "You will likely outlive me."

"Pish! Not so, I will make sure of it."

"Oh? Then, suppose we both die before thirty years pass."

"Then Autumn can have this most exquisite liquor all to herself."

He locked the bottle away, and it was to remain in hiding once again for another twenty-six years. After that, he officially parted with Brownwall, but Hannah Lavigne made it known that they would always be welcome there.

The train did not allow such a massive hound, so Michael sent Alma, Autumn, and Mary Jones by train back to Bristol, and he would meet them there later in the day, catching a ride in the back of a labourer's wagon with Jeannine. It was not the most hasty mode of travel, and Alma did not want to be separated from him, but she most *certainly* would not have wanted to spend half a day in an uncovered wagon with a large dog and an impatient baby. Still, he found nodding off in a heap of feed and straw much more relaxing than trying to nap in a train.

It took a month to move all of the things they wanted out of it and into Bristol, with the help of Mary Jones. Though she was wary and dragged her feet at first, Alma was quick to make Kelley's house her own, having already staked out her new vegetable gardens and hung all of her ornaments exactly where she wanted. It seemed she'd had her mind made up about decorating for quite some time. Despite her penchant for practically, she always had an inclination towards making her surroundings pretty, first and foremost. It gave her a sense of order and impetus, so as long as it helped her settle into a new space, Michael didn't complain.

The house was about the size of Brownwall: maybe a bit smaller. He'd never been to the second storey before, and almost never made it there; while hauling a sofa up the steep staircase, he lost his footing on the steps. The couch stayed put and stopped him from tumbling to certain death, but did not stop Alma from nearly dying of shock. Jeannine thought it was a game, and leapt onto the couch. He had to order her off before he could continue dragging it.

Michael simply refused to part with his faithful old bed, so he brought that, too, and bought a new piano. Every home needed one.

Of course, he'd been tending to the animals all this time, but he'd not yet opened the property back up to the public. Now that he had the means, Michael was going to do something that he'd wanted to do for years.

It was time to bring this facility into the modern era.

XLIII

Michael had been scheming in secret for a long time, but now, he put his plans on paper. The infrastructure and layout were a sprawling logistical nightmare, and the enclosures were hardly enforced. It was well on its way to being a hazard.

He'd never loathed Mr. Kelley more than he did then as he painstakingly relocated dozens of creatures while mapping out and rebuilding their homes. His skills with wood were finally being put to good use, and he'd even managed to begin teaching himself how to solder. He bought good steel and wrought iron to work with, and dug out many ditches. It was truly back-breaking labour. To save money, he consulted people who knew what they were doing, and applied their advice himself.

Even as his own employer, he found himself waking at four o'clock, and working until it was dark. There was just too much to be done, and not a lot of time. It nearly drove Alma insane. He was missing dinner, coming to bed late, and waking her, demanding that she ram her elbow into his back in order for him to fall asleep. The request confused her, but he felt that his spine needed to be put back into place.

Despite Alma's insistence, it was not until late November that he actually hired help, even if it was not from experts, but only extra sets of hands.

The process of doing so was rather informal. A handful of young men shouted over the gate, "Are you digging a hole?"

"Yes!" he cried back. "Come and pick up a shovel, and I'll pay you!"

And that was how he hired four employees in one day, and Alma considered it a good deed, as those young fellows were not mudlarking or resorting to crime.

He hired them as young as fourteen, and trained them primarily in the less hazardous duties to start with. It was mainly young men who were willing to risk their limbs, and that was both good and bad. Their attitudes needed to be checked before they were permitted to handle wild animals. He wanted them just timid enough to be cautious, but not enough to freeze up. Michael was not good at giving instructions at first, but he was excellent at demonstrating.

What he lacked in finesse, he hoped he made up for in enthusiasm. This may have worked out in his favour, as most of these lads were rather rough around the edges, and didn't handle formality well. At the very least, his apprentices matched his energy, and respected him.

Once in a while, they took turns trying to ambush and overpower Michael just for fun. He usually didn't mind, but they understood perfectly well not to try it on Mrs. Bennett, because she did not like being surprised, and she didn't put up a fair fight, thus he was not responsible for them getting an ear bitten off.

The girls wanted to be recruited for safer assignments. They mainly worked in the office with Miss Gaye, fed birds, or talked to visitors. If they had very small children (which some of them did), they could leave them with Alma or Mrs. Jones at no cost, and Autumn had no shortage of playmates.

There were often babies, too. Alma, in correspondence with Ruth and Aunt Hannah, often allowed new unwed or widowed mothers, and the occasional young widower (Michael couldn't even imagine!) to stay for a few weeks and save up money. This made them unwitting matchmakers, as occasionally, some of them paired off and married for the sake of convenience. Sometimes, the same people they sent off returned a few months later, be it from trying circumstances or poor choices, but they were always allowed to return.

Alma also expressed that it would be good for Autumn to grow accustomed to the presence of smaller babies, but that was for another time.

Though she did all of this in good faith, she also made a habit of hiding all of the fine furnishings in the house, and locking up even the cheapest jewellery.

"Don't you feel awful, to think of them all as potential thieves?" Ruth asked, when Alma told her this.

"As I've said before, even the righteous are tempted when they become desperate," she explained. "If they need a little extra money, they know they can ask."

He of course aided his wife in her efforts whenever he could. She had begun to mingle with the local church-goers and put together an efficient network of charitable entities throughout southern England. Dr. Webb believed in her cause, and sponsored her efforts with the little money he could spare. Even Mrs. Webb and Ida contributed. By the age of sixteen, Ida was a professional seamstress, making a modest income alongside her Aunt Ellen.

And since there were multiple sponsors for the church efforts, they always had a shilling to spare. However, it was understood that the

money for the people and the money for the
animals stayed separate. Michael had no
problem with this, because he did not consider
one need greater than the other.

At first, workers came and went rapidly when
they learned exactly what they'd signed up for;
Michael didn't understand how they would
refuse such a position in favour of pitiful wages
dipping matchsticks and sweeping chimneys, but
in a few months, the numbers stabilised.

The garden was suitable to be open to the public
by winter, not that there was much out and about
for them to see. Most of the animals were
indoors. There were now ten people working for
Michael. The majority of them were very young,
and required rigorous training in order to be
allowed to work with the animals.

With a little more time on his hands, Michael
finally had time to mourn Mr. Kelley.

On a surface level, he hardly knew the man. He
knew nothing about his family, his childhood,
his taste in music, or even his favourite food.

But he knew enough.

Mr. Kelley's garden now belonged to him. He
did not feel entitled to it. It did not feel right to
claim ownership, so he still told people that it

was Kelley's, and that he was the one who built it all by himself, with his own two hands; that was the truth, after all. They were only the caretakers.

Most surreal of all was that Miss Gaye had agreed to stay on, and was now employed by him. As their relationship was always strictly a professional one, though, the transition was smooth, and she found him to be equally as agreeable as Mr. Kelley, so long as the pay stayed the same.

Working on these massive projects did not take Michael away from his family. He merely slept fewer hours for most of the week. That wasn't difficult; before Autumn slept through the night, he was used to getting five, or even as little as two hours of sleep. Once in a while, however, when there wasn't much to do, he'd lie down for a quick nap and wake up in fourteen hours, irritated that nobody had roused him.

Dr. Webb warned that he only felt alright now because he was young. Once he approached his forties, he would not be so agile, and his health would rapidly deteriorate.

Michael, in his usual way, reasoned that he'd better just do as much as he could, while he could.

It was only troublesome when he was too stubborn to leave a task unfinished, and he tried to work through the night under oil lamps. Sometimes, a few people volunteered to help past their regular hours.

On one occasion in winter, this proved to do more harm than good, to say the least. He'd hired contractors to lay down pipes for him at a specific date, but due to a particularly heavy frost, they fell behind schedule, and he and four others resumed digging as soon as the ground had begun to thaw, shovelling away well into the wee hours.

A lamp had been knocked over and broken, into a shallow ditch, and the fire spread quickly. One boy— his name was William— panicked and ran off. The other three stood and marvelled at the blaze.

"Alright, stand back, this is all well! I'll handle it, just stand to the side!" Michael insisted, reaching for a shovel, as he meant to heap soil over the flames and smother them.

Those three did as they were told. William returned, and cried out:

"Don't worry, sir!"

Then there was a great splash and a roaring hiss, and Michael only had time to turn to one side before he was splattered with an inferno of burning oil. A frenzy of awful shrieks rang out into the night.

"You killed Mr. Bennett!" a young girl screeched.

He was not dead, of course, but he was petrified and unable to think. He just barely managed to roll onto his face and tried to crawl away from the fire. Somebody lifted him sharply by his collar and mashed a wool coat into his face, so now he could not breathe in addition to being burned and blinded.

"What are you doing to him!" came a muffled cry from the same girl.

"A fire needs air!" his attacker declared.

"So does he!"

Fortunately, somebody was smart enough to extinguish the ditch fire correctly, and soon he stopped burning as well, and their wailing died out.

Then he felt it.

At first, it was freezing cold, and then it was as if he'd been stuck with thousands of hot needles on his hands and his left side from his face to his sternum. The pain was so intense, he couldn't even scream or cry, because he could hardly breathe. He still couldn't open his eyes, and seemed to have forgotten how to stand up.

Still shouting and trying to blame somebody, two of the kids picked him up between them, and the rest followed at their heels. Every touch on his skin was like he'd been burned again, and as it slowly worsened, the cooling night wind was all that made it bearable. He could feel that blisters erupted on his fingers. They brought him to the house and banged on the door. Jeannine barked and pawed at it from the other side. It must have been past one o'clock by that time.

Alma invited one fellow into the house and drove the rest of them away. Mary Jones was summoned to fetch cool, clean water, and Jeannine was sent out because she kept nervously pacing and trying to lick the burns. Michael could walk, but he had to be guided (one eye had blistered shut), and would have preferred to be left to curl up on the floor and die. He was brought to the closest bedroom, and undressed by Alma and one of the young men. They then inspected his burns. She was astoundingly collected, gently asking him to explain what exactly had happened.

"Then the fire was contained?" she asked, now sponging at Michael's burns with a damp rag.

"Yes, ma'am. We put dirt on it, as we were supposed to."

"Thank you. You don't need to stay, it's all taken care of. Why don't you go on home?"

"Will Mr. Bennett be all well?"

"Yes, he will. Go on and get to sleep. There's no work tomorrow."

Michael started upon hearing her say that.

"No, there is!" he insisted, finally able to open his mouth. "We will open at the usual time, so anybody who wishes to come can continue with business as usual. Instructions will be posted."

The boy left.

"You can't work tomorrow!" Alma insisted. "It will be light out in a few hours, and I've not even dressed your burns— or fully inspected them!"

"Somebody has to finish digging so that the people can come and lay the pipe!"

"Then it will simply need to be postponed nonetheless," she answered. "And how has your plan come into fruition with this foolishness? You need a doctor, anyway."

Michael didn't want any doctor except Henry Webb. Alma said she would see what she could do about that, and then began applying her menthol paste. The worst of it was on his hands, the left side of his face, and down his neck. His clothes had shielded him from most of it. His arm and side were only lightly scalded. He'd lost yet another coat.

"My left hand doesn't hurt as much as my right," he murmured through one corner of his mouth.

"That isn't good," she replied, just now showing her distress in her tone. "There has been significant damage to the nerves. My father will see about what will happen to it, and I know I don't need to tell you the error of your ways."

"No gloves."

Until Dr. Webb could come to Bristol, Michael could only sit in agony that was lessened when his skin was dabbed with a damp rag; it peaked in the first eight hours, and by day two, he could tolerate the burns on his arm and neck without the cool water. Blisters oozed on his face. Even the fleeting pleasure of laughter was painful. He refused opium in any form, because it frightened him no matter how much pain he was in. Soon, the sting was gone, and it became a dull throb.

He could not work, or play with his daughter. He could not do anything by himself. The best he could do was listen and give instructions, and have Alma or Mary Jones dictate writing for him.

On the fourth day, Dr. Webb arrived and first examined his hands, at Alma's insistence.

The right hand, he decided, would make a full recovery in two or three weeks. The left hand had deep tissue damage, and may not even be useful; it was possibly better off amputated. Michael refused. Unless it began to rot, he was keeping his hand. After surveying the damage, the doctor stayed and watched him for several weeks, as he was at risk of developing blood poisoning.

Since he was heartless enough to do it, unlike Alma, Dr. Webb pried his eyes open at last so that they could be washed and examined. Reportedly, and as predicted, the left eye looked far worse, and could scarcely discern fine details, but the doctor told him he was lucky that he could see at all.

He only had to suffer the degradation of being fed, washed, and dressed by Alma and Dr. Webb for three weeks. It was difficult not to fuss with them. He hated being a burden, but they tended to him tirelessly, and without complaint.

When his hair was combed, some of it came out in scorched clumps at the ends, so Alma took the liberty of cutting most of it off, reasoning that it would be easier to tend to his burns that way.

His left hand had seized up. It could not fully straighten out or perform fine tasks, like playing the piano or buttoning a shirt. His fingertips were sloughing off.

His left eye stayed cloudy and sensitive to light changes. He could still carry out most of the tasks at work, but had to mostly give up boxing. Alma took him to a specialist in London, who said he would likely never regain full vision in that eye. He often wore a patch so that he did not get headaches.

Worst of all— much to his own surprise— was his face. The left side was mottled and rough. His eyelid and corner of his mouth drooped, and the brow was mostly gone.

In about two months, he resumed work as normal, but was quite anxious about being seen.

He definitely looked monstrous. His workers cringed and averted their eyes when he addressed him. Guests stared and whispered, circulating rumours that some animal had done this to him, or even suggesting that he was another creature on display. It was harder to take pleasure in talking to guests, which used to be one of his favourite things to do. Now they rarely approached him, only looked. He had a greater understanding of Mr. Kelley, now. At least animals did not gawp at him.

Once, when a young boy cast a curious glance his way, Michael told him, "This is what happens to you when you stay up past your bedtime."

Even Alma and Autumn looked at him with pained expressions in the first few months. He tried to look sunny, and convinced himself to feel so. After all, he could still see and use his hands.

But all of the people he lived with and worked with nonetheless looked delighted when he put himself out again. They loved him all the same.

Naturally, Autumn adjusted to it the best. She likely didn't quite know how bad it was, so as long as he smiled, so did she.

Alma asked if she could draw him, which he thought was the last thing he needed, but he consented, and as he saw her face light up as she pored over his picture, he felt at ease. She gave him the finished product; seeing himself through her eyes, in her smudged charcoal sketch made him feel special. She chose not to hang it, and shut it up in her book of drawings she thought were too precious to put on display. It was theirs. He never grew fond of his disfigurement in the way she had, but he learned to live with it. It even nullified some of his older insecurities. Being shy about his crooked nose seemed silly, now.

Mr. Kelley's garden continued to flourish, even if Michael's role was now limited. It maintained a modest but steady yield. Every farthing that Michael did not need to survive and spoil his girls went into it and its staff, whom Michael considered his brothers and sisters— yes, even William. He was not angry at William, and he had been horrified just enough to never do something so silly again, so he could continue working there.

He continued writing papers on his research and observations, even though nobody wanted them. He offered them to specialists and scientists, but they were deemed too unrefined, and not very useful, even when he hired people to edit them until they were unrecognisable. After all, he was no scholar. Nobody even wanted to steal them.

When he was not doing anything particularly dangerous, he brought Autumn to work with him, and she loved it, not simply because she was his little pocket mouse, but because she had that untainted innocent wonder.

Her very first glimmer of fascination with the animals appeared when she was enchanted by a massive boa coiling around its meal.

"That's what they do!" Michael told her, seeing her awestruck little face. "They catch their prey and *crush* the air out of it, like this!" he entwined her into his arms and squeezed until she was breathless with delighted squeals.

"Michael, that's so morbid…" Alma murmured behind them.

XLIV

One day, a very handsome and excited young man speaking in quite a refined accent intercepted him with a book and pencil in hand, asking if he could perhaps pick up some of the Asian snakes.

"As it stands now, I cannot let you, old boy," Michael replied. "Sorry, even under close watch, it would be quite dangerous."

That was only partially true, but he did not have the willpower to go into great detail at the moment.

"Ah—I understand, sir," the fellow was graceful about being rejected.

"May I ask why you want them?"

"Ah, you see," he became even gayer, straightened himself out, and waved his book. "I am an author writing about a young traveller in India, and to fully immerse myself, I'd like a first-hand experience of the jungle's fearsome beasts!"

"Oh, an author!" Michael was at once intrigued, because very rarely did somebody artistically inclined come to the establishment. He always believed that professional authors didn't actually go outside. "Good for you, wanting to go out and enrich your work! I'm almost sorry I cannot let you play with the snakes— ah, what is your name, then?"

"My name is Grant Abernathy," he offered his left hand. "T'is a pleasure to make your acquaintance."

"Oh, no, no, the pleasure is mine!" Michael grasped his hand as best as he could. "Well, I'm Michael Bennett. Grant Abernathy? Why, that even sounds like an author's name! I imagine I'll see it on the cover of some sensational epic tale some day! In fact, would you care to describe this story? I have time. Come and walk with me!"

Michael turned, without waiting to see if he would follow.

"Capital!" Grant Abernathy trailed behind him, already enthusiastically describing a romantic narrative about a handsome and stalwart adventurer of noble birth leaving home to wander the earth.

"A nobleman?" Michael's ears burned. "Well, I was one of those not so long ago. I could perhaps examine your manuscript and see just how close to reality it is."

"Oh, how splendid!" Abernathy gazed up at him with a starry sort of look in his steely and ambitious blue eyes. "Tell me everything! You look as though you've had quite an exciting life! If you don't mind me asking, where did you get those scars?"

"This?" an incredulous blush bloomed in his face, and he raised a hand to his concealed eye. "This happened right here, and it was no fantastic journey, only a little mishap."

"Oh, is that so? And when will they ever heal? They look ghastly."

"It has been many months. I believe they are about as healed as they'll ever be."

Still, Michael was somewhat pleased that this fellow did not cringe away from his injuries, and was bold enough to ask about them himself. He appreciated a forthright man.

Mr. Abernathy talked with Michael even as he was finishing up his work, so he invited him inside for tea.

"My dear, we have company!" Michael called into the main hall as he took his guest's coat.

"How splendid!" Abernathy marvelled at the house and peered into the parlour. "What a fine home befitting a man of status! Such tall and grand windows! And these sumptuous drapes! Capital!"

This man was either an expert flatterer, or he'd never even been outside of Bristol.

Alma gladly greeted Mr. Abernathy, and went to finish preparing tea.

"And what a fine Missus!" he added as the two men took their seats in the parlour. "So humble and lovely, but with spirit— befitting a great adventurer!"

"Ah, well, that's hardly the case," Michael finally managed to explain that he really had never even been further east than Germany, was not very rich at all, certainly wasn't exceptionally handsome, and would simply not be a suitable muse.

"No? Well, I like you just as well! You're good company, you sure are!" tea was being served.

Michael *did*, however, describe Dr. Webb and Mr. Kelley, in his eyes, two of the most impressive men he knew, especially if you didn't know too much about them. Abernathy greedily ate up his words— and Alma's superb cooking. She supplemented his retelling with her own

413

knowledge as she came and went, and their guest was quite charmed by her.

Michael kept unconsciously steering the discussion towards his animals and his girls—including Jeannine, who was now in his lap. No, Jeannine was not a stately hunting dog. She was a happy dolt who could now barely get up the steps without help. In fact, Michael was not far behind; his right knee had been giving him a great deal of trouble.

Autumn, who was now walking, came to Michael after an interval, and he made room on his lap for her.

"And who is this wee dumpling? What a little angel!" Abernathy beamed and held his arms out to Autumn, briefly casting a curious glance at Michael, no doubt trying to piece together how a rock formation such as he had the privilege of fathering such a little pet.

"Oh, well this is Autumn, my little girl," he wove his fingers into her shining ringlets while she wriggled on his knee and stroked Jeannine. "Her mother believes she will turn out just like me—I say she should have a bit more faith in her than that! Ah, Autumn, say hello to this man, Mr. Abernathy!"

She waved a hand at him without a word, and continued to sit and play with the dog's woolly ears.

"Mmm, she is a bit tired, I imagine," Michael concluded.

"How sweet!" Grant Abernathy squealed. "What a lovely family you have, Mr. Bennett! It is enviable, to have accomplished so much at your age— you are about thirty-five?"

"Twenty-five, almost twenty-six. The sun has aged me. I don't often wear hats."

"Ah! I'm twenty-four, myself— right behind you!"

"Is that so? Well, you'll never catch me."

As they'd talked late into the night, Michael invited him to stay until morning.

"Here, there's a nice uninhabited guest chamber to the left of my study," he climbed up to the second storey, with Autumn sleeping draped over his shoulder. Most of the young girls they occasionally fostered shared the down-stairs rooms so that they did not have to scale the staircase with their small babies. "Mind these stairs— they are quite treacherous."

"Hah! An athletic young man such as I shall not be defeated by stairs."

"Mrs. Bennett would never forgive me if I didn't warn you. She hates them."

Just as easy as that, the two men clung fast to one another. Grant Abernathy was quite a visionary; he spoke endlessly about his work, and even seemed to enjoy Michael talking about his family; he adored Autumn and took a liking to Alma's art, even asking to be drawn by her, which she eagerly accepted, and likened him to Apollo. He became a regular visitor, and was always describing his latest project. It seemed he had several going all at once.

As for his life, Michael gleaned that he was indeed from Bristol, the youngest of four children and only son, who received a charitable education in London (which explained his knack for flattery), and returned with big ideas: songs, poetry, literature, and theatre. He hoped to turn his books into stage productions and star in them himself. His ambitions had true talent behind them, which he demonstrated by singing with Michael's piano playing, and he had a fine baritone voice. He wanted to save up money to eventually go to India himself, but in the meantime, he would look at these fantastic creatures behind bars, and worked for a local publisher as a way to get his foot in the door.

The talent was there, and sometimes the drive
was as well, but sometimes it wasn't. Whereas
Michael could not leave a project unfinished,
Grant couldn't seem to finish them. Every time
he came to Michael with a new idea, he had a
different one less than a week later. His
reasoning was that he simply had so many
passions and ideas that he simply couldn't focus
on them all at once. The ones he no longer
discussed were not abandoned entirely, merely
placed on hold.

That being said, some of them were never
mentioned again.

As it turned out, he was also an avid boxer and
rugby player. They would spar on occasion, and
Grant was a gentlemanly opponent, favouring
Michael's stronger right side.

His speech was eloquent, but his mannerisms
were rough. He, too, had been in numerous
fights in his youth, as he possessed a hot temper,
yet an air of manly energy.

Soon, Michael even let him handle a few of the
snakes under close supervision. He wrote about
the animals, and Michael wrote to himself about
his new friend. They went on hunting trips, and
shared more and more stories. He knew that Mr.
Abernathy would eventually go to Asia, but he

held on to his hope that he would return and perhaps remain a life-long friend.

That was not to say he didn't get along well with his workers and his friends of the female sort, but there was a shortage of men his age in his life. Most who started work were nearly ten years his junior, and he had little in common with them aside from playful grappling.

Mr. Abernathy remained constant.

Michael buried Jeannine in the spring of 1897. He found her on the back steps, and it seemed she died in her sleep. Since he never did know exactly how old she was, he prepared for her passing ever since she began to slow down.

She was his first real pet. Many dogs would follow, but none replaced its predecessors.

Thanks to Alma, there were also cats. She fed a handful of strays until they were hers, and followed her home. Now Michael had to step around them every morning before work.

Aside from being involved with the church ladies and having some sort of social meetings at the library (no men allowed), Alma was entirely at home. She was informally employed as a greeter, alongside Autumn, whose charm lured in more visitors. Autumn was the very picture of an angelic child. Her hair grew out as shining golden curls making pretty coils around her ears, and she had plump, rosy cheeks. She was sharp from a very young age— essentially, she didn't get *anything* from her father.

Alma's newest interest was exotic plants. Out of curiosity, Michael once purchased a cactus, and she became enamoured with them, immediately harvesting grafts and nursing them into little sprouts, all the while diligently reading about their upkeep. That process entailed a lot of waiting and doing nothing with them, but she was patient. Most people would not have found them so delightful, but he was not surprised that she'd taken a liking to them. She'd finally grown to enjoy toads and lizards, as well.

In 1898, when Autumn was six years old, Alma gave Michael a son.

Autumn was so wildly enraptured by the idea of having siblings, because she loved the babies that the young ladies brought— and because the prospect had been an increasingly maddening topic of hushed discussions for nearly two years prior. She wanted to be a part of all of the planning, and she was not just content, but proud that this new baby was inheriting her cradle.

They both agreed that they were expecting a little boy. Alma claimed intuition again, because she apparently hadn't learned her lesson, whereas Michael was only guessing, and they happened to have the same idea. In addition, they both planned on him coming a month sooner than their initial estimation.

Alma had her wish that time: nobody meddled with her, except for one of the church ladies sitting by. Nobody stopped Michael from bringing her anything she asked for.

He was still a tightly-wound bundle of nerves. That could not be helped.

Unlike his sister, he chose a more convenient time of day to come into the world: Alma's confinement began at around ten o'clock in the morning on November 7; word came to Michael within an hour, and he rushed home. He hadn't left work in such a hurry since he'd been set on fire.

Autumn could not be contained. He kept her busy on the piano and explained to her that the child would not be ready to play with her, but she could look all she wanted— not right that minute. Mammy needed privacy, and she'd see her later.

Ashley Samuel Bennett (it was Alma's idea) was placed into Michael's arms at half past seven that evening. He smelled different from Autumn, and had more hair. Though Alma put on more weight with this one, he was smaller; Hannah Lavigne would have been tying herself in knots over this mystery.

Michael presented him to Autumn, and she was taken with him at once. He warned her that Ashley was very delicate and needed to be handled gently; she heeded his word without question. In fact, she watched him as a hawk might have done if he was ever held by anybody other than his parents. Even Great Aunt Hannah was forbidden to touch him. It was a blessing that she was set on being such a good sister, though he knew she would be.

She was almost too good of a sister. Once he began to grow too big for her liking, she howled and wept upon realising that he would not be little and cute anymore. Admittedly, Michael and Alma had a good laugh at her expense, even as they tried to mollify her.

Worse yet, though, was when she considered Michael's height and realised that Ashley would likely be taller. Since she came first, she felt entitled to be the taller one.

Michael suggested that they heap bricks on Ashley's head. Alma didn't laugh, only shook her head, but she smiled a little.

He was a more reserved child than Autumn. He was every bit as adventurous, but he hid his face from people for quite a while, and it took him longer to begin to talk. Autumn spoke for him in the meantime, as she believed she knew him better than anyone in the world. They had to discourage her, or he'd never learn.

His hair was different, as well. Curiously, it was almost coal-black when he was born, then grew out blond, just as thick and wavy as hers, but it darkened to chestnut by the time he was walking. They were both born with large, dark blue eyes, but Autumn's turned hazel, and Ashley's stayed blue.

Grant Abernathy had no children and no wife yet, but was always doting on Michael's little ones; they even called him Uncle Grant, and he wore this title proudly. When he finally went to India, he was always sending letters. Michael demanded pictures of monkeys, cobras, and gharials.

At long last, 1899 drew to a close, and Michael was prepared and armed with a barrage of "-since the last century!" that only he and Autumn laughed at.

At the turn of the century, the world was in a massive hurry. Motorcars were spoken of as a passing fad only ten years ago, but now, they could sometimes be found on the streets. Some still speculated that they would not last long, but Michael found them fascinating nonetheless. Wireless transmissions were now possible, opening up endless possibilities for communication. The Ashwood estate was now part of a suburb. A wave of social reform like no other seized the world, but most bewildering of all in Michael's eyes was women's fashion.

Women's hats were massive, as if they had entire floral arrangements on their heads, and the fashionable silhouette looked precariously top-heavy, and bent forward to great extremes that could not have been healthy to maintain. To him, it resembled how an older lady might have hunched over without a cane for support. There must have been a method to it that he did not understand. Ladies' clothing was a mystery to him.

Alma did not fully embrace this radical wardrobe shift. She didn't feel that her apparel needed to be heavily updated, and he agreed, only because he did not know what she was talking about. He, himself, had been mistaken for being stylishly old-fashioned, but the truth was, he could not be bothered to update his clothing with the times, and he would wear his old clothes until they were worn to scraps.

Autumn, on the other hand, was eager to acquire the newest styles, and pestered her mother a great deal to make her dresses a certain way. She demanded rag curls almost twice a week, until she learned how to do them herself. Alma would not allow her to use heat on her hair.

But she gladly gathered up the dresses she'd grown out of and offered them to other little girls. Seeing her mother's active charity efforts inspired her, and she nearly gave away everything she owned, because like Michael, she did not play with many toys, and grew bored of them very quickly— once she turned eight years old, Michael just stopped buying them.

Another habit she picked up from Alma was gardening. In the back garden, they gave her a patch of daisies and pansies to tend to, and she liked to host little tea parties there.

In 1901, Grant Abernathy returned and brought the photographs he promised, as well as a lovely young lady named Sarah Rivers— at least, that was what she preferred to be called. She appeared to be a native, or at least the descendant of one. Regardless, Alma took a fast liking to her, and Grant Abernathy expressed his intentions to marry her very soon.

He presented Michael with heaps of manuscript needing to be sifted through, and he readily

admitted that he spent most of his time in the
English settlements, as the wild jungle was far
more formidable than he credited it with being.
He had a greater respect for nature, now. Still,
his recollections of nearly being killed (or
believing so) were entertaining enough.

Since Michael was never artistically gifted in
any capacity, he took great pleasure in seeing the
work of talented individuals. The only leisurely
skill he was even peripherally qualified to teach
was the piano, and the way he learned and
taught it did not seem to make sense to others.
Alma really disliked music lessons from him, so
he let her be. Her singing was more than enough
for him, anyway.

Autumn grew into such a pretty and
hard-working young lady, and at twelve, she
began taking up tasks around the garden
compound. She also began to gain the attention
of new young men working there, but none of
them dared to approach her. Michael's bad knee
did not make him any less frightening, because
they knew pain would not deter him from
pursuing them.

Ashley had Michael's stammer. When he started
school, his teachers urged them to seek the
means to correct it, but Michael remedied it
simply by having him sing, and read his writing
aloud— these activities lessened it considerably,

and made him realise his love for choir and talent as a boy soprano.

Alma was always leading them in bible studies, and making sure they prayed over their meals. Michael did not mind. These were good values that he just didn't keep up with.

Michael took them all outside as much as possible. He did not want them to grow up afraid of bugs, toads, and dirt. He took them on long camping trips way up north in Scotland, and far southwest, in Cornwall. He planned to one day take them to the continent, and to Asia— he wanted to see the whole world, and imagined the potential to further his work— Alma wanted it as well, and planned for that future with him.

His dogs at that time were Süß and Wolfgang. Süß was small and timid, and missing a corner of her ear; more specifically, she was Autumn's dog. Wolfgang was large, frisky, and loud. Sometimes, he brought Michael "presents" that were actually just his shoes, but with bite marks needing to be buffed out. This habit was hard to break. They were both foundlings, as it seemed some folks thought that because the garden was a sanctuary to animals, they were free to discard unwanted pets on his property.

Autumn said that the dogs were a gift from God, since Ashley needed dogs to grow up with, too, as Autumn had Jeannine.

It was hard to keep up with those dogs, now. Though not to the extent of Mr. Kelley, he had indeed aged horribly; he did not need a cane to walk, but he had slowed down quite a bit, and sometimes, while outside, he wore a long, unsightly brace on his right leg. His father-in-law told him that this was a consequence of ignoring his creaking joints.

He first started wearing it shortly after a bad fall he had in 1900. He had Ashley on his shoulders, walking in a secluded part of the garden, and he lost his footing on a steep pathway— or rather, his knee had simply gone out from under him, and he spilled face-first onto the ground.

Little Ashley was unharmed, but understandably terrified, and immediately began screaming.

"Chi-Chi, it's alright!" he peeled himself out of the moss and scrambled to grab his son. "Daddy had a great fall, didn't he? Sorry, little mouse. We'll just stand right back—"

His leg would not cooperate. The pain brought him back down. He could not easily hold himself upright and also carry Ashley, and it was steep and muddy, and he had just learned to walk. Ashley was still acutely distressed, but fortunately, he had sounded the alarm. His howling alerted a worker to come to their aid.

"Ho, there, Lindsay!" Michael called to him, and lifted up Ashley. "It seems I cannot get up. Here, take him to his mother, and—"

Ashley made it known that he would not be separated from Michael. He screamed and panted for all he was worth until his father took him back.

"Alright, that won't do," Michael chuckled. "Well, please be a dear boy and fetch me Lorelei, would you? I suppose I will be waiting here."

Lindsay was dispatched.

"There now, see," he pulled grass out of Ashley's hair. "You can ride the horse with me, and you can hold the reins!"

Michael got a well-deserved tongue-lashing from Alma for treating his joints as if they were disposable for ten years. He was distressed about having to stay off of that leg for over a month, and Alma scolded him, as wearing his bones down to meal was what had gotten him in this predicament.

That injury had forced him to ease up on his work. As they say, if you do not schedule a time for maintenance, your machines will do it for you. In the following years, he spent much more time confined to his study, but still getting up just as early as he always had. Alma was pleased to have him in the house more often, and if a ruined knee was what it would take to get him to stop working himself to death, then such is life.

In 1902, they attended Grant's wedding to Sarah Rivers in London. The Bennetts gifted them a sizeable trousseau, and named an aviary in their honour. Abernathy was already well-known in the sphere of journalism, but his acting dreams were realised shortly after, and his wife joined him.

Dr. Webb was not travelling anymore. He deemed himself too old to easily tolerate train rides, and that was the end of his wanderlust. As such, he did not come to visit, and they went to see him instead, and as his health was starting to decline, the visits were scheduled in advance.

One spring, Alma departed with the children, and Michael stayed at home to take care of some business, and would catch up to them in a day or two.

He woke early, as usual, and started water for Alma's coffee. She was up earlier than she normally was, and he knew it was because she was not terribly fond of train rides. She was always in a foreboding sort of way during transitions, and would not take breakfast. He entreated her to at least have a little milk in her coffee.

He went with them to the train station at nine o'clock. Autumn did not want to be lifted out of their carriage, as she believed herself to be "grown" at thirteen.

"Oh, you are much closer to the cradle than the grave," he asserted. "And since my knees can still handle it, I'd say you are certainly not too big!"

Ashley obliged, electing to be carried on his father's back.

Mr. Abernathy came and visited with him when he returned, which Michael appreciated, but he did not have enough self-restraint to stop talking to him and focus on his work, so Grant elected to wander the grounds for a time. The garden was not open to the public that day. Most of the workers were not present. Mary Jones was sent on holiday, as well.

At around noon, Michael finished up his papers, and then he went to the gallery and called out for Wolfgang, who'd been suspiciously quiet.

Sure enough, he was on the stairs, eating one of Michael's good shoes.

"Wolf!" he snapped, calling the dog to attention. "What is that in your mouth?"

Wolfgang sprang up and bolted down the steps, and Michael took off after him.

It happened in about three seconds.

Michael stepped hard on the edge of a step— in that moment, his knee failed, the dog crashed into him, and he went flying down the stairs.

His face hit the bottom step, and everything hurt— for only a moment. The force rattled every bone in his body. Immediately, he tasted blood. Wolfgang descended the stairs and nudged at him, whimpering as his master lay there.

"MICHAEL!" Grant Abernathy shrieked from the hall and was upon him in an instant, pushing the dog away. He lifted up Michael's face, and then rolled him onto his side. His neck made a disgusting sound. "Oh, what happened, what happened?"

But he could barely open his mouth, or even breathe well enough to form the words.

"Fell," he choked out a barely audible rattle as he spit blood.

"Did that damn dog trip you on the stairs?"

"No," was all he managed to say, as Wolfgang had found his way around Abernathy and was pawing at Michael, licking his hair. That was all he could feel.

"Come, old boy, we'll get help! We'll get you to a doctor!" he insisted and tried to gather him up.

"No!" Michael puffed again. He could not feel his arms and legs— or much of anything, really.

He could not summon the strength to lift a finger. Being paralyzed truly had to be the worst thing that could happen to him. It wasn't possible. It couldn't be real.

"What! Michael, up!" Grant Abernathy tried to pull him up on his feet, but his body would not have it. Wolfgang barked and paced. He only smiled.

"You bastard, get up! This isn't funny!"

But he was so tired, he couldn't even raise his head. Everything sounded as though he was submerged in water.

"Michael?" Abernathy tried once more, softly this time, tenderly stroking his hair.

XLV

Lord Michael Ashley Glasse Bennett, of Ashwood Hall in _______, England, passed away in his home at approximately half past noon, on Monday, April 10, 1905. Grant Abernathy witnessed his death, testifying that he had broken his neck on the stairs. Minutes after the incident, he'd fallen unconscious, and died within the hour. He was thirty-seven years old.

He is predeceased by his parents, Samuel and Mary (neé Glasse) Bennett; his sister, Berthe Bennett; his life-long servant, Abraham Reed; his uncle, Gabriel Bennett; his daughter, Lillian; his dogs, Jeannine and Ginger. He is survived by his wife, Alma (neé Webb) Bennett; his children, Autumn and Ashley; former employer and father-in-law Dr. Henry T. Webb; his dogs, Wolfgang and Süß; his horses, Bismarck and Lorelei: his aunt, Hannah (neé Bennett) Lavigne; twenty-three cousins.

Bennett was born into nobility on February 27, 1868: a damp and mild Thursday morning. He left home in 1887 and briefly lived as Dr. Henry Webb's hired man, before leaving and working for Mr. Adam Kelley, a nonconformist naturalist. On December 18, 1889, he married Miss Alma T. Webb: a nurse, reformer, and devout Christian woman. The pair dedicated themselves to

His belongings included over seventeen years
worth of diaries, which were acquired by
Abernathy with the permission of his widow,
who also went on to publish his previously
unseen research papers, which were not
appreciated in his life, but vindicated in his
death. His final dreams are a mystery.

Abernathy stated, jokingly, that it was fortunate
he had died as he did, because spending many

weeks bedridden by some wasting disease would have been intolerable to him. Still, it was unbelievable— almost absurd— that a single moment of carelessness had so quickly ended his life.

He is buried behind the Bennett family chapel, alongside numerous ancestors. At his prior request, he was not embalmed. Ten people attended his funeral. It was a beautiful, sunny and windy afternoon. A moth alighted on Alma Bennett's veil.